Who would be

A mermaid fair,

Singing alone,

Combing her hair

Under the sea,

In a golden curl

With a comb of pearl,

On a throne?

I would be a mermaid fair;

I would sing to myself the whole of the day;

With a comb of pearl I would comb my hair;

And still as I comb I would sing and say,

"Who is it loves me? who loves not me?"

-Tennyson

I sat upon a promontory,

And heard a mermaid, on a dolphin's back,

Uttering such dulcet and harmonious breath,

That the rude sea grew civil at her song;

And certain stars shot madly from their spheres,

To hear the sea-maid's music.

- Shakespeare

PADWOLF PUBLISHING BOOKS BY JOHN L. FRENCH

PAST SINS: The Matthew Grace Casebook

BAD COP... NO DONUT
    -edited by John L. French

MERMAIDS 13
    -edited by John L. French

BOOKS IN THE PADWOLF 13 SERIES

APOCALYPSE 13
    -edited by Diane Raetz

MERMAIDS 13
    -edited by John L. French

Coming 2014

FANTASTIC FUTURES 13
    -edited by Robert E Waters & James R Stratton

TALES FROM THE SEA
MERMAIDS 13

Edited by
John L. French

PADWOLF PUBLISHING

PADWOLF PUBLISHING INC.
WWW.PADWOLF.COM

MERMAIDS 13: Tales From The Sea

Edited by John L. French

Padwolf 13 Series: Managing Editor Patrick Thomas
Art Director Roy Mauritsen

Cover Art © Roy Mauritsen

ISBN 13 digit 978-1-890096-51-9; 10 digit 1-890096-51-2

First Printing

When I was a boy, I used to watch Diver Dan before going to school. It was on that show that I saw Miss Minerva, my first "real" mermaid. Much, much later, there was Splash – and Madison.

And so it is to my two favorite mermaids:
Suzanne Turner
and
Daryl Hannah
that this book is dedicated.

CONTENTS

INTRODUCTION

What do you think of when you hear the word "mermaid?" These days most people think of Disney, a young girl in a seashell bra and singing crabs.

Fortunately, the writers in this book are not "most people."

"Write me a mermaid story" was what I asked them after Patrick Thomas talked me into editing this anthology. They did, and none of them even came close to the now popular ideal of a mermaid.

Instead they gave us the Mer – some of whom are as familiar as we and others as alien as whatever might be found in space. They wrote of what it means to be human and in love and how it feels to be outcast and hunted. They told stories that might make you hungry or might forever kill your appetite for seafood.

Mermaid.

What did you just think of?

Read the stories, then say the word.

You won't ever again think of a children's movie.

SYRENKA
Roy Mauritsen

Author's note: This story takes place after the events in Hans Christian Andersen's "The Little Mermaid" and before the events in Roy Mauritsen's novel, "Shards of the Glass Slipper."

"**D**id they believe the story that I died and turned into sea foam? Will they stop looking for me now?"

"Yes. Your story will forever be that, in the end, you died," said River, Syrenka's sister. She twitched her silvery tail flukes in annoyance. "But I do not understand why. Why give up a life as a mermaid and a princess… for this?"

"Humans love stories of magic and monsters," replied Syrenka, breathing a sigh of relief as if the weight of the ocean had finally receded from her shoulders. "They would search for me," she continued, "a magical mermaid turned human. The merfolk would hate me, or gaze upon my form with pity or curiosity. I would never have any peace or the anonymity I desire unless the stories ended with my death. This way, I can finally be free to live as a human. I can explore this world and see beyond the sea. It is better that Father thinks I am dead then to have his youngest daughter yearn to walk amongst the humans."

"True," River yielded. "His anger would be great. He has no love for humans and wishes to start a war with them on the sea."

"He always speaks of this, River, but has yet to act," added Syrenka's sister, Ice, with a swish of her fin. "He's not serious. It is just talk when he gets upset."

Ice lazily floated in the water, her long bluish hair spreading out behind her as she enjoyed the sun's warmth on her face. Then, with a quick flick of her great blue tail, she turned and brought herself up to lean on the small pier where they had gathered. "I'm still not sure this is wise, Syrenka. You risk hurting your family for your own selfish interests."

"Please, don't think of it as selfishly running away, Ice. Think of me as an explorer of this world of dry land, an ambassador. The more I can learn up here, the more I can share with you." With a twinge of sadness, Syrenka added, "I know of no other merfolk more experienced than I in matters of men."

Syrenka had settled in a small, crudely-built house on a secluded section of beach that was hidden by large cliffs and rocky outcroppings. The house was protected from the ocean by a span of dunes, and the cliffs sheltered both the beach and the house from the worst effects of storms. Syrenka was far enough away from town, ensuring her privacy, but close enough to travel to the market from time to time and sell her wonderfully-carved driftwood trinkets and shell jewelry. And, for the mermaid that was still very much a part of her, Syrenka was close to the sea. A simple planked pathway and sturdy railing connected the house with the water's edge. It culminated in a small pier just wide enough for Syrenka to sit on the edge and dip her feet in the water.

Syrenka was the youngest of six mermaid sisters. River, Shy, and Ice would visit with their littlest sister and tell her of all that was happening under the sea.

Her oldest sister, Moon, could not visit with Syrenka, for she had married a prince from another merfolk clan that schooled in the warmer tropical waters. As a human, it was not possible for Syrenka to attend her eldest sister's wedding, an event that she had been deeply saddened to miss.

Syrenka's second-oldest sister, Swan, refused to visit Syrenka on the beach. As Ice had explained, "Swan made it very clear to us that she did not agree with what you were doing, Syrenka. She wanted no part of it, but as one of us, a sister, she stopped just short of telling Father."

"They are so ugly! Wiggle them again," Shy squealed in perverse delight and morbid fascination. She quickly ducked her head back under the water to watch Syrenka kick her feet and wiggle her toes. "They are like little sea cucumbers," she said as she broke the surface again, this time holding a wet, brown leather satchel. She hefted the satchel onto the pier next to Syrenka's feet. The heavy, muffled clinking of gold coins could be heard. "This is all we could find in the wrecks this month."

"It's more than plenty for what I need here," said Syrenka. "Thank you, Shy."

"Why do you need these shiny gold things?"

"They are coins, Shy, money. It's valuable to the humans. You can give some of these coins to someone and they will give you something of theirs. How much you have to give them depends on what it is they have. You can also give them coins and they will do things for you, like carry a message or fix something that has broken." Syrenka pulled back her long blonde hair as she regarded the most innocent of her older sisters. Money was not a concept with which the merfolk were familiar.

"The coins make people do things, but they are not magical?" wondered Shy. "So if River had kelp, I could throw a coin at her and command her to give me kelp, and she would have to obey? How odd."

"It's not quite like that," Syrenka laughed. "It only works if River wants to trade her kelp for a coin. I bought this dress at the market with coins." Syrenka typically wore a simple brown dress, and on colder days she wrapped herself in a warm, wool blanket.

"And I would not want to trade any of my kelp for something as stupid as a coin," River added irritably. "Kelp is far too valuable as food or decoration, or as a tool. Besides, I would not want to be burdened down with the weight of these coins; I would sink to the very bottom of the sea!"

Syrenka was about to continue the conversation, but was interrupted when Shy added, "And I still cannot understand the books you talk about. What is the point of them? In the ocean, the Great Current provides for all. Our stories would not last on that paper of yours. That is why we sing our stories! Books are silly and pointless." Shy paused for a moment before adding absently, "But even though you are the youngest of us, you do know so much more about this world, Syrenka."

Shy marveled as she looked upon the beach and the bluffs that rose up around it. "I don't know how you do it…It's all very confusing to me."

"Much of it is still confusing to me, too," sighed Syrenka. "But that is what is so exciting about being here, Shy."

Syrenka was no longer able to speak the names of her sisters in her native tongue because of the deal struck with the sea witch, so she created her own nicknames for them. These names were easier to translate in the other languages of the sea. She spoke a mixture of different ocean dialects, pieced together in a manner that didn't require any tongue-based vocalization, made difficult by the fact that most of the nuances were lost when not spoken underwater. As a former mermaid, Syrenka was adept at such languages, but at the water's surface, the languages became clumsy and awkward.

"Dolphin is a language full of nuance and inflection. The beauty of its voice is how it echoes out in the water. You butcher it, Syrenka," chided River. But as stilted as the language sounded to her sisters, it was altogether useless as a means of communication with humans. For that, Syrenka relied on other methods.

Even when she was very young, Syrenka and her sisters had explored the wrecked ships that had come to rest on the ocean's floor. In these wrecks, they had recovered all manner of intriguing objects. As a child, Syrenka had kept a large stone statue that sank and came to rest in Syrenka's own garden. But Syrenka was always fascinated by her grandmother's stories of the surface. She found more of these land stories in books. She had secretly recovered hundreds of them from various shipwrecks and studied them thoroughly until they became too deteriorated from exposure at the oceans depths. When Syrenka finally did spend time on land as a human, she realized she could recognize many languages from the books she found. Though she could not speak any of them, she could read several different languages of the land. She could also write in many of these land-based languages with a piece of chalk on the slate she kept with her at all times.

"You have disfigured yourself to try to be accepted by them," continued River. "You were the prettiest of us and had the loveliest voice. You threw it all away. Now you walk amongst them, but you cannot talk amongst them. You will never be accepted. You will never be a part of them. You scratch their symbols on your slate. Syrenka, you do not earn their respect, just their pity. You are lucky you can still communicate with us in Dolphin."

"We tried to find the sea witch again," Shy offered, trying to deflect the tension of River's frustrated remarks. "After she made us cut our hair off for a dagger with which you could change back, we went back to the cave. She was gone, and nothing remained there."

"That dagger was a waste of a haircut." Ice grumbled, remembering that whole terrible ordeal when Syrenka refused to killed the prince on his wedding day, throwing the magical dagger into the ocean instead.

"What is done is done," Syrenka replied stoically. "I do not regret the choice I have made, sisters. You do not have to keep looking for her."

"Maybe there is another way you can change back into a mermaid. Then you can find the witch... wouldn't that be a surprise!" Shy continued.

"Oh, Shy, always the optimist!" Syrenka laughed. "Maybe someday I will become a mermaid again, and if I do, the first thing I will do is see my sisters!"

"And your grandmother," River added, driving a more somber tone back into the conversation. "She is too frail these days. I wish you had the chance to see her again."

Syrenka's heart saddened. "I, too, wish I could see her again. She still has her twelve shells on her fins? Pride goes before pain, she always said."

"Yes, her health declines though," said Ice. "She would not even survive the journey to visit you here on the beach."

"If it would make her happy, tell her that I still live. But tell her ..."

"It's a secret. We know, Syrenka." Shy's face brightened. "It would make Grandmother very happy to know that you still live," she said excitedly.

Then Syrenka suddenly raised her hand and made a broad waving motion toward the sea. Her sisters turned and looked. Seeing a small boat off in the distance, they quickly jumped from the little dock and disappeared into the water.

The two men on the boat waved back to the shore as they continued on across the bay.

"Sisters!" Syrenka called for their return to the pier. "Do not worry; they are too far away to see you as mermaids. I see them every day in the morning and the evening as they pass by, and they wave to me, so I wave back. Someday I might invite them for tea."

The sisters swam gracefully around the dock, keeping a wary eye on the small boat as it passed beyond the distant rocks.

"They are not all bad," Syrenka offered, trying to ease her sisters' anxiety. She got to her feet, trying her best not to reveal the aching pain in her legs. "I have a surprise for you, my sisters," she said, smiling. Steadying herself, she stood and walked to a small, covered basket.

"It's going to get worse, Syrenka," River keenly observed. "Your legs – eventually they will fail you."

"Perhaps someday," Syrenka admitted with a smile. "But for now, the pain is bearable." Syrenka retrieved the basket and returned to the pier's edge to sit again, putting her feet back in the water and ignoring the pale cloud of blood that floated from them. The sisters gathered around with curiosity.

"What is that smell?" asked Shy.

"Bread," replied Syrenka proudly. "I finally have the means to make it myself."

"What is it, though?" asked the sisters. "It looks like a brown rock."

"This is something that merfolk have never experienced before," Syrenka replied, tearing off a chunk of it and popping it into her mouth. Speaking with a mouthful of bread, she added, "Still warm from the oven!"

Syrenka loved bread. She was fascinated by it – the crusted outside and soft billowy texture inside. A freshly-baked loaf of bread was a world of wonder for her. The delicious aroma wafted into the air. It was the most mouthwateringly delicious smell she had ever smelled. She was amazed that so many different flavors could be added to it, and that it could so easily be formed into different shapes and sizes. Part of her fascination with bread was how it was made... with fire. An amorphous wet lump could be turned into the softest, tastiest loaf of bread by the magic of fire alone. Fire could take dough and make something edible and delicious, or toast it into a crunchy brown treat. Sometimes, if Syrenka was not paying attention, fire could make it a charred, black square that was not very enjoyable at all. But fire was mostly helpful and always fascinating to her. It gave warmth and light, and had the ability to destroy and consume the very things that it had created – such as this wonderful, delicious bread!

Syrenka tore off more chunks and handed them to her sisters. At first, they were hesitant and unsure; the mermaids inspected it carefully and smelled it.

"Go on, taste it!" Syrenka joyfully encouraged them. Egged on by their youngest sister's enthusiasm, the three mermaids cautiously sampled the bread.

Instantly, Shy scrunched her face. She worked the bread back out of her mouth with her tongue and let it drop into the water. "I don't like it!" she announced unceremoniously.

Ice's reaction was similar. "Much too dry and too warm. I've eaten sponges that were more appetizing. Perhaps it would taste better in the water." She dunked the rest of her piece in the water. Instantly, the bread became soggy in her hand and then dissolved into a cloud of particles. "I'm sorry, Syrenka," she said.

River managed to finish her piece diplomatically. "It's not that bad, but I would not want any more. It seems you like it the most."

Syrenka dropped her shoulders, frustrated that her sisters did not understand or like what she loved. River saw the disappointment cross Syrenka's face. "Maybe we can try something else on our next visit," she offered. "We should probably be going before our absence is missed." The sisters said their goodbyes, and a few moments later they slipped quietly under the water, leaving Syrenka alone with her thoughts and her basket of bread.

Syrenka sat sad and lonely on the cold, wet planks of her little makeshift dock. Wrapped in a warm blanket from the chill of the evening sunset, she had waited for her sisters to visit as they had done at this time every month. But this time they did not show. She sipped a cup of hot tea as she watched the water for any sign of their approach. But the sea was calm and no shadows darted about beneath the surface. As the sun began to dip, her heart grew heavy; she had always looked forward to their reunions. She looked out to see the familiar boat in the distance, the two men giving her a friendly wave. Syrenka stood up, and a sharp familiar pain shot through her legs. She obliged the fishermen with a quick, halfhearted wave before turning and making her way back to her house.

"Her body may sink into the dark abyss, but the Great Current shall send her spirit to dance upon the waves of the sea. Now my mother rests, carried along by the Great Current." The sea king paused, letting the final words of his eulogy settle with the crowd of supporters. Then he added, "The Great Current touches everything in the ocean. It provides for all."

"We all swim with the Great Current. The sea is always in motion." The small gathering recited in ceremonial unison. With that, the sea king nodded for the release of his mother's body. He watched as two dolphins carried her under each outstretched arm, past the coral wall shimmering in the deep blue expanse, floating above the endless abyss. Her tail was still adorned with twelve seashells, more than anyone else in the colony. Her hair still waved and floated about her face, finally settling about her shoulders. The body had been decorated with colorful coral and adorned with shells and rocks, all tied with long strands of colorful kelp. The weight would help the body sink.

"May her body in death provide for those who live. Those who sink will one day rise."

"The Great Current touches everything in the ocean; it provides for all," the supporters replied.

Then the dolphins parted and the sea king and others watched solemnly as the beautiful, ancient mermaid's body descended, ghost-like, and was slowly swallowed up into the blackness of the all-consuming deep. After the king's mother was fully out of sight, the large procession of merfolk floated somberly by the drop-off in respect for their king's loss. Swimming closest to him were his four remaining daughters.

"My daughters are all that I have left," he murmured somberly as his strong, silvery tail swayed back and forth, burdened with sadness. "Your mother died shortly after the birth of our youngest, Syrenka, who also swims with the Great Current, and now my mother – your grandmother, has passed to the abyss. What has our great family done to deserve such tragedy?"

As they swam back to the colony, the sisters recalled their fondest memories of their grandmother and of Syrenka, trying to ease their father's grief. As they made their way along, the sea king suddenly paused. He spied a piece of netting that had snagged on a rocky coral outcrop, now rolling aimlessly along the sea floor. He swam to it with his daughters following dutifully. A brown-shelled female sea turtle struggled and strained, near death. Its flippers were entangled in the mess of old ropes and shred of the discarded fisherman's net.

"Curse the humans and their nets! I would drive every last one of them from the water's edge so that they would fear to step near the ocean ever again. Tomorrow, I shall rally an army and we will wage war on every sea vessel!" the sea king ranted, his seething anger amplified by the loss of his mother. He pulled a sharp shell dagger from his belt and began to cut the ropes. His daughters dutifully joined in, carefully pulling and removing the net delicately from the coral.

"Father, would a war truly solve such problems?" Swan asked.

"Violence is the only thing humans respond to," he replied.

Once they had freed the turtle, the family helped the exhausted creature to the surface, giving it a chance to breathe and regain its strength. They paused on the surface and watched it finally swim away.

"She was a pregnant female," the sea king observed, "undoubtedly on her way to lay eggs. Had we merfolk not been here, she would have died along with her unborn." The sea king breathed in the night air, pausing in thought. "Your grandmother told me something, right before she died. 'Our little mermaid lives,' she had said. Do you know what she meant by that? I think she was talking about Syrenka." His voice began to quiver with emotion.

His words were met with silence. Shy's face went as pale as the underbelly of a stingray. She wondered if she had been foolish to tell Grandmother about Syrenka, despite the good intentions behind her actions. She had hoped to give comfort to the dying woman.

Finally, River spoke up in an attempt to respect her sister's wishes. "Toward the end of life, Grandmother's memory and thoughts must have failed, I fear," she said lamely.

But Swan could no longer tolerate her sisters' string of lies. "It is time to put an end to this!" she announced into the uncomfortable silence. "Father, there is a secret my sisters are keeping from you, but I cannot participate in this treachery. It is time you were told the truth."

"No, Swan …," the others pleaded with her. But their faces betrayed them as Swan glowered beside their father.

"Syrenka still lives," Swan continued. "My sisters have been visiting her, and still visit her now."

"What?" gasped the sea king. Their father was stunned by the news. He looked at each of his daughters, but only Swan returned his gaze. His mother's words resonated in his ears as the realization of the news took hold. "Take me to her now," he ordered in a tone that was neither jubilant nor relieved, but stern and angry. "You will explain yourselves along the way."

Now that Swan had revealed their secret, there was little point in continuing the lie. Syrenka's sisters relived for their father the many visits they had taken, and they tried to explain why Syrenka wanted them to spread the rumor of her demise.

"I want to hear it from her," the sea king answered. Swan and the sea king swam quickly ahead. The others, concerned for their young sister and curious to see what would happen, followed along behind. No one noticed that Shy had broken away from the group.

Once out of sight, she raced ahead of the others, hoping to warn Syrenka before the rest of the group arrived. Shy felt guilty that it was her comment to her grandmother that undermined Syrenka's plan for peace and anonymity. And she was greatly concerned for Syrenka's safety. It was just before dawn when she finally arrived at the beach, well ahead of the others, but there would not be a lot of time.

"Syrenka!" Shy yelled from the pier. The windows were dark. "Syrenka!" she repeated, with a note of panic in her voice.

Then Shy looked at the railing of the pier and acted on instinct. With a powerful push of her tail, she propelled herself out of the water and up onto the small pier, grabbing the railing for support. Desperately, she began to shuffle down the plank path, dragging herself. Her strong tail flipped clumsily to help her move herself along, putting all of her weight on the creaking handrail. Shy was not used to being out of the water like this, and supporting the full weight of her torso, long tail, and flukes. But the upper body of a mermaid is strong, and struggling hand over hand with determined grunts, she pulled herself toward Syrenka.

Again, she called out to the darkened house. With labored breathing, her tail aching painfully with gross misuse, Shy dragged herself to the front door. In fiery pain from her efforts, she anxiously pounded on the small wooden door. Then, unable to hold her mermaid body up any longer, Shy collapsed upon the ramshackle wooden porch, utterly exhausted.

There was a creaking sound from inside, and a soft orange glow feathered out from the crack of Syrenka's door. Then, with a soft click from inside, the door swung open slowly, bathing Shy in a warm caress of candlelight.

"Shy! Is that you?" asked Syrenka, cautiously peeking through the crack of the doorway. She threw the door open and rushed to Shy's side, shocked at the sight of her sister so far from the ocean.

Shy looked up. "Father knows. He is coming!"

Syrenka did not acknowledge what her sister had said; her concern was for Shy's safety. "You should not be here like this. We have to get you back in the water," Syrenka said in an anguished torrent of Dolphin.

Syrenka placed the candle on a nearby table and bent down to help. With arms wrapped around each other's shoulders Syrenka began to drag her fallen sister back down the wooden walkway. For Syrenka, each step was an agonizing, white-hot flash of pain, and she could feel the warm wetness of blood oozing down her calves. Slowly, the two made their way back to the sea. It took considerable exertion from Syrenka to get Shy to the pier, and as soon as her mermaid sister was safely back in the water, she quickly grabbed the railing for support.

Shy rushed to explain to Syrenka what had transpired after their grandmother's funeral, but a deep voice suddenly boomed as a dim silhouette rose from the ocean in the brightening morning sky.

"Syrenka, explain yourself!" ordered the sea king.

Syrenka's stomach tightened at the sound of the voice that she knew all too well – a voice that did not appear at all to be in a gracious mood. She saw her sisters in the water nearby, their faces fretted with concern. They did not dare to interrupt the sea king. Syrenka's eyes locked with Swan's and she knew instantly that it was her sister who had betrayed her.

"Syrenka," repeated the sea king, this time in a calmer tone with a hint of something else. "Answer me, child."

Syrenka stood quietly on the pier's edge, looking down at her bloodied feet as she fought back the tears that threatened her in the face of her father.

"Why run away and hide?" he continued softly. "Worrying your family so? What was so terrible that you had to fake your own death?"

"She cannot speak, Father," Shy reminded the king. "Remember, the sea witch took her tongue."

"She can talk, but in broken dialects, Father …," corrected Ice.

"Her Dolphin is very bad," added River, who was then suddenly interrupted.

"When my anger has tempered, I will address my daughters who thought it best to hide this secret from me!" he boomed furiously in a sudden outburst. "Now is when it is smartest to be silent. Not all the while past to keep such news from me!" Then quickly regaining his composure, he spoke in softer tones. "The only voice I wish to hear right now if that of my youngest daughter. Why Syrenka?"

Syrenka suddenly had an idea. "I will return," she managed to say in her cobbled language before making her way back to her humble home. In a few moments, she emerged from her doorway and gingerly limped back down to the pier, carrying a small, covered basket.

"I cannot show you all the reasons why in any of the human books, Father… the words, their stories, the drawings. A book's significance would be lost since merfolk do not keep such things. To show you in their art would be a waste, since no painting as wondrous as it may be, no canvas survives in the ocean, and even statues grow defaced with coral. I cannot show you what I know because you have no basis for understanding what you see. Your perceptions of humans extend only as far as you can see from the sea, but there is so much more to them."

She pulled out a small slice of bread. "I made this." She offered a piece to her father. "Something I could never have done as a mermaid. It is a small thing, but for me it represents one of the best things I love about this place. People at the market like it, too. Someday, I hope to sell it. Taste it, Father."

The sea king took the piece of bread from Syrenka, puzzled at what appeared to be a small brown rock with chunks of fruit.

"It is bread," Syrenka explained. "It has raisins in it, and sweet spices, like cinnamon and sugar."

Tentatively, Syrenka's father took a bite. Instantly, he was met with wonderful soft textures and the most incredible flavors that he had ever tasted. His eyes widened at the deliciousness, and he marveled proudly at Syrenka, greatly impressed with her skill. Pride glowed on his face for a moment, but it was fleeting. He would not reward his youngest daughter with the satisfaction of a compliment as he stared at her disgusting human legs. "Imagine the things you could have made as a mermaid," he hissed, and he dropped the rest of the bread in the water. "Is this why you have run away, so you can make… bread? Did you think to impress me with food so I would forget everything else?"

Syrenka began to explain, jumbling her words awkwardly. "At first, I feared your wrath, Father, at my failure… my foolishness to love a prince of the land, at what I have become. I wanted to run away. But then there was this small glimmer of realization that I was given an opportunity to do something that no merfolk had ever done. It was an opportunity to be a human, and it was exciting to me. This bread… I gave it to you because I had hoped to show you something wonderful and different that you would like, so that you might see the human world as I see it… and you would like it because it was something made by me."

Her father stared down at Syrenka with squinted eyes. "And you've done that. Now it is time to return home."

"That's just it, Father," she whispered. "I am home."

"Syrenka!"

"I don't know if I can return to the home I knew," Syrenka stammered, near tears from the many nights of fearing this very moment. "I don't know if I will ever be able to change back. I don't know if I want to, Father. But what I do know is that I'm happy here, like this. It was not enough for me to rise to the surface to see the sunset, to sit upon an iceberg and observe, or to sing from the rocks. It is a deeper desire. I don't know that I can explain it correctly, or that you can understand."

Then Syrenka said something that thoroughly enraged her father. "I am happier to dance on two legs on the beach than I ever was swimming in the sea."

"Humans are an abomination, an unnatural blight upon the world. You are not a human. You are a mermaid. You are not one of them!" He spat the last word like venom, his anger palpable. Denial crept in upon the edges of her father's reasoning.

"Why are we so similar then?" Syrenka shot back, finding courage in her conviction. "Why do we have breasts like mammals, but tails and fins of fish? What of our hands and face? Do we not resemble humans? There must have been some purpose to this! There must be some connection; maybe we are wrong to despise them so …"

"How dare you question such a thing?" asked the sea king. "Both the shark and the dolphin have fins, but they are vastly different beasts – fish and mammal, predator and prey. We need arms like humans so that we can pull their filth from our world. Do you know how many miles of fishing lines, how many thousands of fishing nets our families have pulled from the bottom of the ocean, discarded by surface dwellers that care little for where they dump their waste? Would we take our garbage to the surface and throw it onto their land? No! Do we go into their homes and take their food? No! And their vessels that sink and litter the floor of our ocean, our home! How many fish and animals have died, how many merfolk have died, due to their carelessness, their inconsideration, and their slovenly ways?"

"Then maybe having one of us here to talk to them, on land, might be a good thing," Syrenka challenged. "Maybe from here, I can help them see the error of their ways."

But her naivety only served to further infuriate her father. "You cannot change them!" he bellowed. "They killed your mother, Syrenka!" His voice crackled with fury and echoed in the silence surrounding the pier.

Syrenka and her sisters were stunned. They had never heard the story before.

With great sorrow, their father continued. "When your mother was pregnant with you, we went to our birthing spot – a little coral reef cove, warm and shallow, and full of life. We had birthed all of your sisters there. Just as we had gotten settled, waiting to begin, a boat pulled in and blocked off the cove's entrance with nets and ropes. The humans had herded a small pod of dolphins into the shallow waters. Your mother, although she was about to give birth, swam to the dolphins in trouble and tried to help them escape from the nets and return to sea. We both tried to help them. But as the nets were pulled in by the humans, she became entangled as well. Being with child, she was not as agile as she normally would have been. Before I could get there, the nets were dragged up into the shallows and she was trapped with the dolphins. In the mass of netting, while the dolphins were being clubbed to death, your mother was unable to escape. In the confusion of the doomed dolphins, she was crushed, battered and beaten by the humans as well. Unlike the helpless dolphins, she was finally able to free herself, and managed to escape back into the little cove. Her wounds were grave and the trauma triggered labor. Your mother died shortly after you were born. You were so little, but even then you were beautiful."

He paused, looking at his youngest child, his memories and grief awash upon his face.

Her father then continued. "I swam holding you, and carrying your mother's broken body all the way back home. That was the longest swim of my life, and I will never forget it. But that night, when I returned to the cove, the boat and the humans were still there. They were celebrating and preparing their 'catch of the day.'

"I killed them all, Syrenka – every human there. And even to this day, they still do the worst of it. They don't do it for their own personal survival. They kill and sell the flesh for profit, for money. Oh, yes. I am old enough and worldly enough to understand their ways. I'm sorry, child. There is nothing you can say to convince me that humans are worth anything. You are the exact image of her, Syrenka. It saddens me to see you walk about on those accursed sticks of flesh. You shame your mother's memory."

He could no longer look at Syrenka and turned away. In the dawn of the morning waves, the sea king saw something out of the corner of his eye. His anger welled up even more at what had appeared. It was something at which he could direct his frustration and anger. A small, white boat with two fishermen moved silently in the distance. Syrenka saw it, too. It was the boat she exchanged waves with almost every day.

"No, Father! Please, don't. They are innocent," Syrenka shouted desperately. But it was too late, and she knew it. Her father had already summoned the means for his retribution.

"They are not innocent. They are men," he replied. "They shall be an example of the war I will bring to them."

Without thought or further delay, Syrenka pushed past her father, skillfully grabbing his shell dagger, and dove into the water.

"Father! Stop her," the sisters pleaded. "She'll drown!" But the sea king raised his hand and forbade his daughters to move.

"Let her learn this lesson," he said stonily.

Syrenka struggled, unaccustomed to swimming with her human legs. She lacked the power of the mermaid's tail she had grown up with. But it was only for a matter of moments, and then her natural swimming instincts took over to compensate. She tucked the shell dagger into the belt of her dress and swam toward the unsuspecting men in the boat. Even as a human, she could swim amazingly fast. She quickly refocused, and with powerful strokes of her arms, Syrenka hurried, closing the distance by using the waves and the momentum to dive under the water. She swam with all of her strength and made considerable distance from the shore, but was still too far away. She tried waving, but she knew she had to get closer. Her body ached from the exertion. Her feet and legs burned like knives that dug into her flesh. But Syrenka ignored it, determined to stop what her father had begun.

Every time she glided under the water, she could feel its presence coming closer. Syrenka knew what her father had done. He had summoned a shark. There was a certain stillness and a heightened energy in the water when a shark was near. Syrenka sensed it; she knew there was not a lot of time.

She was only about fifty yards from the small fishing boat, but with no voice, she could not scream to get their attention. The men's backs were turned to her as they worked to prepare their nets. She splashed frantically in the water, but to no avail. Then, as she drew a breath to dive again, she saw the shark attack.

In a silvery explosion of water, a huge great white shark erupted suddenly from the ocean in front of the men. Rising forcefully from the water, the enormous shark, easily eighteen feet long and well over a ton in size, seemed to hover for a brief moment in mid-air. Its dark coloring and stark white underbelly glistened in the early morning light, dwarfing the startled men and showering them in a rain of cold seawater.

The great white came down upon the hapless men and smashed their small, wooden boat. The screams of the men mixed with the cracking of splintering wood and a loud boom as the shark landed; its huge jaws gaped open as it slammed the shattered boat into the water. Everything happened in a matter of seconds. Syrenka floated in the water as she watched, stunned by the sight of it all. Two men bobbed to the surface, one floating listlessly, held above the water by a section of planking. The other one had barely cleared his face for a panicked breath when the water in front of him bulged with a large mouth of teeth. The shark rolled to its side in the water, its black eyes turning back to white as its deadly bite closed around the dazed man's chest. The doomed man screamed an ungodly scream, cut short by a gurgle of air and blood from his crushed lungs as the shark pulled the man underwater in a cloud of crimson.

Syrenka sprang into action, swimming desperately to save the other man. His eyes fluttered open weakly as she arrived.

"Are you a ... mermaid?" he whispered, only half awake and lapsing back into unconsciousness.

Syrenka pressed her finger to her lips, signaling the man to remain quiet. He seemed younger, perhaps the eldest son of the man, and luckily, he did not seem visibly injured. Syrenka reached out and grabbed some floating debris to help keep his legs afloat. These were the people that had waved to me every day, Syrenka thought. They do not deserve this.

She pulled the shell dagger from her belt and dove under the water. She had sensed the shark returning, and as she held her breath, she scanned below. In the blue haze, she saw the unmistakable silhouette of the approaching monster. Diving down, Syrenka swam defiantly toward the shark, challenging the deadly predator in his own territory. Only her experience as a mermaid made this otherwise foolish and dangerous act possible.

Syrenka held the dagger firmly in her outstretched arm. I won't let you take him, she thought to herself. The shark closed in, and Syrenka moved to keep herself between the man floating on the surface and the shark. Her lungs began to burn, demanding air. The shark eyed the challenger. Wary and curious, the fish seemed to hesitate, but then with a powerful push of its muscular tail, the great white darted past her and toward the man on the surface. Syrenka reached out with the shell dagger, feeling it strike the solid flesh of the fish, digging into its eye and slicing down its body. Syrenka felt the dagger break off within the shark's thick muscle. She had wounded it!

With a sharp turn, the shark broke off its attack, bolting into the darkness of the deep.

Syrenka could feel her lungs screaming for air now. It was not something she was accustomed to, and she quickly scrambled upward, taking a huge breath of air as she broke the surface. She paused only for a moment to recoup her strength, and then swam over to the young man. Then she grabbed the wood plank and pointed frantically toward the shore.

He stammered a bit, still in shock, as he looked around and saw only a few pieces of his boat floating on the surface. "Where is my father?" asked the dark-haired young man with a look of apprehension in his sharp, blue eyes.

Syrenka could only shake her head; she silently formed the word no with her lips.

The realization of what happened began to slowly show on the man's face. "The shark just came out of nowhere," he remarked in a daze.

They began to swim back toward land with the young man using a large plank of wood from the boat to help him. The man swam much more slowly than Syrenka could as a human. She tried her best to hurry him along, but they were making little progress and it quickly became frustrating for the former mermaid to swim with such little speed.

The man looked toward the shore. "It's too far," he gasped with exhausted, heaving breaths as they rested on the surface for a moment, treading water. "I recognize the beach though. Are you that woman we always wave to?"

She nodded with a smile, and then waved for him to continue as she resumed swimming toward the shore. She could see her father and her four sisters watching them from a distance.

"You've been injured!" the man said suddenly. "Your legs… there's blood!"

Syrenka rolled on her back, looking at her legs just under the surface. A faint cloud of red billowed about her in the water. Syrenka was used to pain, and her focus had been on rescuing the men. But her legs, with all of the kicking and swimming, were bleeding just as they did when she walked heavily on them. Blood in the water was not good. And it was her blood. That's when she saw a dark blur of movement and a flash of white just below them in the water. With a gasp, she met the gaze of the man, knowing it would be his last moments.

"I'm sorry," she whispered silently.

He tilted his head. "What?"

It was the young man's last uttered word, and it abruptly died in his throat with a grunt as the air was knocked from his lungs with the force of a battering ram. The water around him exploded, lifting his body completely out of the ocean as the massive great white struck from underneath. With a flash of deadly teeth, the jaws of the shark extended out and closed on the man's torso. A primal dying scream was cut short as the shark pulled the man under the water.

As quickly as it had happened, it was over. Syrenka treaded the water alone, trembling in fear and anger. Just like that, the man was gone, and the ocean waves continued as if nothing had happened. Then Syrenka let out a silent frustrated scream, nothing but a whisper of air escaped her mouth, but she did not care as her face contorted in a gut-wrenching sob. She punched at the water with her fists and yelled at the open ocean with her screams again. She tried to save them, she cried to herself, to save at least one, at least symbolically to defy her father's will and to prove him wrong. But she had failed.

With a roar of rushing water, the sea bulged and the dark grey head and onyx eye of the great white appeared on the surface. It moved toward her swiftly, its mouth opening to show its rows of deadly, serrated teeth. Instinctively, Syrenka swam backward, but she was resigned to her fate. Escape was impossible, and in a moment the shark would lunge for her as well. The shark turned on its side and rushed in, its deadly jaws shifting forward, opening wide for the kill. Syrenka looked away, raising her arms in futile defense. She hoped it would be over quickly, but she knew she was about to face a painful and agonizing death.

The attack never came. A shadow fell across her as a voice commanded, "That is enough!" The sea king was now between her and the huge great white. The shark stopped instantly at her father's command, and then it closed its mouth and turned away, disappearing beneath the bluish green waves.

Syrenka began to cry, torn between her conflicted emotions. She was relieved that her father had rescued her at last, realizing how close she had come to death. At the same time, she hated him at that moment for putting her through this and taking the lives of two innocent people.

Her father turned to her with sorrow etched deeply on his face. "I am truly sorry, Syrenka. It did not occur to me until the last moment that our sharks would no longer consider you a mermaid. Even they can no longer sense your true nature. We've a rapport with every living thing in the ocean that is natural to us. You know that. Please believe that I did not think you would be in danger with this, which is why I did not stop you from coming out here."

He paused, holding back tears until he was able to speak again. "It was because of my actions this time that you almost died, and I had only just learned that you were still alive. I could not save your mother when you were born, but I could not let my daughter die because of me. I'm sorry, my child." His voice cracked with emotion, and he offered his open arms to his only human daughter.

Syrenka sunk into her father's arms and sobbed, emotionally exhausted.

"Father, those were good people that died, innocent men, and though our interactions were from a distance, I looked forward to seeing them. They were friends. They did not have to die to prove your point," Syrenka whispered in her makeshift language.

She let her father carry her back to the pier.

"After the death of your mother at the hands of humans, after I thought you had died from your involvement with humans, I was ready to take my anger to them and every one of their human ships that embarked across our sea. The grief of losing your grandmother almost made that happen. If it was not for the revelation that you still lived, I would have made good on my desire for war. But beginning now, my little mermaid is no more. If you had been a mermaid, Syrenka, you could have swam gracefully and quickly to the boat and not floundered about in the waves. You could have directed the shark away or created a great wave to push the boat to safety. But as a human, you risked your life, and you have stopped me from considering a war. You have taught a foolish old sea king a lesson."

Once Syrenka was safely on the pier, her sisters gathered around her, happy to see their youngest sibling was still alive.

"What I see before me is not a human, nor is it a mermaid," said the sea king. "All that stands before me now is my daughter. I am happy beyond words to know that you are still alive, and as long as you live here on land, I will not call for war. I will not risk your safety. Instead, I will find another way. If you are happy and this is what you want, then I do not need to understand any more than that. Make your bread; explore this world, Syrenka. But do not fool yourself to think for one minute that you can change them. You are more likely to change back into a mermaid then they are to change their ways."

The sea king turned to his daughters. "Say your goodbyes to Syrenka now. You are forbidden, all merfolk shall be forbidden, to come here anymore. Let your sister lead her life as a human."

Ice and River hugged Syrenka tearfully as they parted, and even Swan, who told her, "I was doing what I thought was best for you. I hope one day that you will understand that."

Syrenka hugged her sister tightly. "I never would have had the chance to see you again," she said. "For that, I will be forever grateful."

Shy was the last to say good-bye. Visibly upset, she held Syrenka tightly. "I will still try to find the sea witch," she whispered in a wobbly voice, "should you ever want to be a mermaid again."

"It's a deal," Syrenka replied as tears streamed down her face.

When they were done, Syrenka stood on the pier on her human legs. "Thank you, Father," she said.

"I hope your skill with the human language is better than your Dolphin," he replied in a half-hearted attempt at humor. "Your sisters are right; Dolphin is horrible when spoken out of the sea."

He hugged her and placed a kiss on her cheek. Then he leaned in and whispered something that made Syrenka smile. With one final glance and a wave goodbye, her family slipped beneath the ocean waves and was gone.

Syrenka watched the shadows of her father and sisters returning to the ocean. As tears once again welled up in her eyes, she recalled what her father had whispered to her moments before.

"If it means anything to you," he had said, "the bread you made was delicious. I loved it."

It meant the world to her.

THE GOLDEN TICKET
KT Pinto

Welcome all of you to the caves of the Mer! What a fine looking group this is! I must congratulate you on outbidding everyone else on the auction site to get a spot on this very exclusive tour. I heard that a few of you waited until the very last seconds to outbid everyone else with impressively high amounts. It's obvious that you are shrewd people who understand the value of this opportunity. As you know, it's very rare for us to open our doors for outsiders to see what goes on in our lair. What was that, Sir? No, I didn't mean figuratively. This cave is not always accessible to the upper world. It only appears a few times a year in order for us to have access to the upperdwellers and serving as means of reminding them – that is, you – about the truths of our people, dispelling the odd rumors that continually float around … especially those that became abundant once Disney movies became popular.

Yes Ma'am, there are different color tickets, even though they were auctioned off at the same starting price. The meaning of those colors will be explained to you at the end of the tour; if you could wait until then to have your questions answered... thank you.

I know how excited you are to see where all the magic happens… excuse me, Sir? Oh, no! The caves on this tour are all dry. That is why my tail is split in leg form. No need for swimming skills. No no, there is no such thing as a dumb question, Sir! Feel free to ask whenever the mood hits you. Does anyone need to use the facilities before we start? No? Not even the little ones? OK, then let's begin!

Ma'am, please don't touch the glowing fungus. It's been known to adhere to human skin and then the skin had to be removed or the whole specimen died. It's OK, ma'am, you didn't know… and the bright blue is rather attractive to the eye. Just remember, make sure not to wander or touch things without permission. We can't be held responsible what might happen to you if you do…

As you know, the season of Christmas is truly insane! It really is a busy time of year for anyone of Christian faith, but it's especially so when you're Italian. I know I don't have to tell many of you that Italians spend most of the holiday season cooking and cooking and cooking, and for variety, more cooking. Christmas Day is a feast in itself, filled with macaroni, various cheeses, gravy… that's tomato sauce for those non-Italians among us. I can see from some of your faces that you were picturing some brown sauce on pasta and mozzarella… and various types of land-raised meat of course are part of the Christmas Day feast. But that is nothing compared to the food on Christmas Eve.

Italian women work tirelessly for weeks in preparation for the Eve meal… I see those lovely ladies back there nodding; they know I'm telling the truth. The dinner courses range in number anywhere from three to nine to fifteen, and each course alone could serve at least fifty guests. It is a feast that is a tradition for families all through Italy, but nowhere more than in Sicily whose inhabitants, like ourselves, spend most of their lives on the sea, risking the threat of us so-called bloodthirsty mermaids… oh don't look embarrassed, we are well aware of the stereotype… and the ravenous sea monsters in order to earn their keep. This was especially true during the holidays, when the sea was filled with all types of Italians preparing for the holidays, and we are no exception.

There's a reason why this time of year is called the Feast of the Fishes.

My grandmother has a huge book filled with recipes specifically for this season of the year… you will be able to view it in one of the anti-chambers later on in the tour. There is no other time like the holiday season to find the biggest variety of treats for our dinner table. Not only are they available en masse, but they are the most plump, most tender, most succulent delicacies Italians like us could ever wish for. This is also the time when trappings from foreign lands are readily available to add a little flavor to the holiday… and how could we, good Italians that we are, not enjoy exotic delectables when we are able?

We've been called cannibals for our holiday feasts… no, please don't deny it; we know it to be true. Although some beings may think us to be fish because of how we look while in water, it is not the case. We aren't fish, nor are we human…we are merfolk. The only way we'd be cannibals if we ate other mers. Besides, what else is really accessible for us to hunt and eat on a regular basis? Cows? Mountain goats? It's not like our options are limitless!

I apologize for my ramble, but sometimes statements not proven by fact just dry my scales!

Besides, why in the world would we want to stop hunting for food so wonderful that we can't resist cracking open a succulent catch and sucking out the sweet meat within… even if we look ridiculous in the big plastic bibs?

Don't worry, I do have a bib for each of you; a little gift to remember this fun adventure of ours! No Ma'am, we don't have child-sized ones; our young ones' mouths aren't formed well enough yet to eat such treats, so no bibs are made in their size. But of course you sweet little ones can each have a large bib; you are all guests, no matter what size, and will all be given the same perks and treated the same way on this tour. None of you will be left out.

We've divided our dining area into three different spaces, so you can get the full impact of how large and important this feast is. This first area is… what was that, Sir? Well, yes, I guess it would to you look like a giant aquarium, but as I'm sure many of your compatriots know, our youngest don't develop lungs until their second year, and have to stay immersed all the time. Normally that isn't a problem, since we mostly spend our time under the waves, but during the holidays we stay in the caves. So our little ones spend their time in the tank while we eat.

No, they don't just sit and watch us, Ma'am. Ah, here come two of our little ones now… see them swimming through that tube above? As you can see Ma'am, our youngest don't have the dexterity in their bodies to sit, as you have suggested. And it would be rather rude of us to have them swim around in circles while we eat some of the best food available. So they get their feast as well.

As the young lad has been screaming over and over, there is another tube connecting to the tank. From this tube we give our little ones food. I believe it's what you would call chum; is that the correct term? Look at them go… like little sharks, aren't they?

Oh, I apologize; I see some of you turning sickly colors. Is watching our offspring eat that offensive to you? I would think, after seeing your children spit mushed peas all over themselves, this wouldn't be that big a bother…

But no matter, let us keep moving.

What the… Ma'am, I can't understand what you're saying, please calm down. What did… well, of course they're going to charge at the glass if your son presses up against it. They are only babies, after all. They know nothing of subtlety. Ma'am, I did say in the beginning not to touch anything, didn't I? We cannot be…

No, Ma'am, I'm afraid I cannot have someone escort you and your child back. Not only do we not have the extra staff to do so but, as you can see, the security system has closed off that part of the cave for your own safety, so no one can go wandering away without our knowledge.

No Sir, you are not trapped here. Trapped would imply that there is no way out. There is of course an egress at the other end of the cave. As you have seen, there are alien things here that could be harmful to you. It would be careless of us to make it easy for you to get injured or die before your time while in our caves. Now is not your time to die; we are only in the first room and it's getting late... please follow me.

That sound you hear is out young ones despairing over not getting the yummy treats they had just seen up close. No, Ma'am, I am not making fun of the situation. I am simply stating that our offspring know no better even with an elder nearby, similar to how your young ones throw rocks at our kind when we come ashore while adult humans watch and sometimes encourage. Not that I would encourage our children in this situation by any means; things happen as the fates wish and not to be left in the fins of ones so young...

This is the dining area for our adolescents and adults. As you can see, we have put out examples of the types of delicacies we will be enjoying at the Feast of the Fishes. Some of you look confused... oh! You had expected the plates to hold the blatant creature: the full animal lying there with glazed eyes, various creatures on a half shell, the arms hanging limp on top of a salad or fried a golden brown... those are in the next room. Those not used to the regional favorites may find those plates rather disturbing.

Here we are showing you our soups, our stews, our rice and pasta dishes... some of our fried meals. Like here, we have cuscusu Trapanese, with different flavors mixed with the semolina grain and vegetables. It makes its own unique flavor that only those who created it know exactly what the stew portion of the dish is made of.

This here is pasta con le minuscolo, a dish made difficult because it uses the smallest of our favorite treats, and deboning something so small takes a skilled hand and a lot of training, then it gets made into a paste, which gets made into a sauce with pignoli nuts, fennel and white raisins... yes, I know Miss, my stomach is starting to growl too...

I don't know about your families, but in mine the elders sometimes have odd traditions, like eating those little things right out of the original packaging. They just roll back the cover and pop those hairy buggers right into their mouths. It's rather messy when they do that, which is why we have that separate table in the corner... they're almost as bad as the young ones sometimes!

But to continue... when we can get them away from the old timers, we also use those little treats in this, vermicelli alla Siciliana, made with peppers, vermicelli and, as you can see, eggplant.

One of my favorites is this soup, zuppa di pescatore Siracusana, another dish with various flavors, made with dry white wine and tomatoes. Next to that is pizza Calabrese… no Sir, it wouldn't look like what you get from the local pizzeria. These are old school recipes handed down from the generations. Yes, Ma'am, that is a salad… insalata de frutti di mare, the fruit of the sea! There is nothing better, is there?

In these shells we… I'm sorry, Ma'am? Scolapasta? No, Ma'am, I think you're confused… a scolapasta is used to drain macaroni. Do you mean scungilli? Yes, that's the name of the animal that lives in those shells. We clean out the shells, chop up the flesh and mix it with lemon and breadcrumb, fry it all in extra virgin olive oil until it's a golden brown and stuff the shells to their limit with the mixture. It makes a rather lovely plate, doesn't it?

Over here we have the various steak dishes… no, Sir, not steak like from a cow. Many dishes use the term "steak" to mean something other than beef. In this dish is scapece alla vastese, and in that one is capigliatura rossa sul focone. See from their shape and thickness how they can still be called steaks even though they aren't made from cows?

Yes, young Sir, those are like shish kabobs! These are our come parte dell'anguilla dishes. They are rather serpentine-like, so the best way to cook them is on a skewer. Here we have them in gratella… grilled… and marinata... yes, young Sir, marinated. Very good! You are a smart one!

Yes, Ma'am, those ringlets are very similar to calamaretti. That's pescatore le dita alla Siciliana. They're cut into the ringlets as you have mentioned and baked with breadcrumbs and nutmeg. The dishes next to them are very popular among our kind: muscolo. Here we have them for you fried, baked, with rice, as a soup, and boiled with spices and displayed on a pile of spaghetti in shiny black shells…

And over here on this side table are our holiday dishes, made out of giant scallop shells, and utensils and chalices made from bone. And look here… there are just enough settings for each of you! Oh no, I'm not joking! It is akin to sinful to make all this food and then have it go to waste! And what kind of Italians would we be to invite people over and not feed them?

No, no, please don't stay standing! Those chairs around the table are for you! I do hope you like it; our ingredients are a little different from yours, so the flavors may be unusual to you. What do you need, Ma'am? Oh pecorino romano? I have the grater right here. Let me know when… ok! Sir? You as well? How about you, Miss…

...Has everyone had their fill? Yes? Wonderful! Now we're going to continue the tour... oh yes, Sir, we do have facilities right down here, how silly of me not to offer... No, I'm sorry, Ma'am, we don't separate our facilities by gender. We tend not to be bothered by such things. I do apologize that your child will be uncomfortable... maybe you'd like to wait until everyone else is finished and then... no, I would feel rather bad making others wait when there's enough room for everyone to... feel free to ask them, Ma'am... I will wait for you by the far doorway...

Do we have everyone? Ma'am, please gather your child from the table so my colleagues can finish cleaning up the dirty dishes. I am happy to see that our food hadn't gone to waste; it's obvious that you enjoyed our fare, alien to you as it was. I hope that you will have memories of that feast for the rest of your lives, as you will never have food like that again, I promise!

We must continue with the tour; we have quite a way ahead of us. It will be a pleasant way to walk off a little of what you've eaten before we get to the next room and the next course.

Why of course there is more food! Remember I had mentioned it before? It may not be as appealing to some of you as this one was, which is why it's in a separate area, but it is available to those who want to indulge. Trust me, I won't be insulted if few of you volunteer...

There are also a few surprises ahead, so please follow me, and stay close! Also, don't hesitate to let me know if you need to rest for a moment, as there are stairs involved. Don't seem so surprised! We use stairs. Not often, but it happens...

Now please be careful, the coral on these rocks can be rather... yes, Ma'am. We do have means of taking care of your son's wound...

We normally don't have to worry about the tightness of the cave. Remember, this is just a mockup of where we usually celebrate. Under normal circumstances, our entire meal is in one big room off of the kitchen.

I am sorry, Ma'am... we don't have control over where the coral grows. Your little one may want to consider keeping his hands down at his sides...

Yes, Sir, this is a rather steep incline; even with the steps it is quite a trek. That is why we're going slowly, even with the inconvenience of the coral. But it is worth it, I promise... we're almost there. I know you can make it. Yes, Sir, that light is at the end of our tunnel, as the saying goes. Good one, Sir! He must keep you laughing all the time, Ma'am.

Yes, Miss, it isn't good that that young boy is running up and down the stairs; he could injure himself... or worse, others. Ma'am, I must insist if he's going to flirt with pain and injury, he must do it at the end of the line.

The wall to the dining hall has closed so he will eventually figure out how to find us…

No, Ma'am, I cannot slow down any more than I have in order for him to catch up. It's not fair to the others… We're almost to the top. Now remember, this may not be pleasurable for some of you to see. In fact, it might be rather gruesome… ah, I thought that would bring the little Sir back to us! Now if you would all come this way…

Yes, it is very much like an elevator… I assure you it is very stable. It is a much easier way to get where we're going, unless you would like to walk up a few more stories of stairs…

I know, it's a little rickety… yes, and it is dark. You don't realize how much light the coral gives off until you're away from it…

Ah, we are here! Now give me a moment to slip out and get us some light in here… I'm sorry, young Sir, but you really do need to stand still in the dark or your hands will get caught again! Please don't try to push me out of the way, it is not the best idea… Oh my young Sir, you must be careful! It's easy to trip and fall in the dark! Is everyone away from the door? I don't want anyone else's hands to get injured…

There we go! Now everyone can see what our favorite part of the meal is… oh, before I forget… will everyone take out their colored tickets? Very good, very good… now in this envelope I'm holding is the winning… yes, Ma'am, I see that your son has a sapphire ticket…

Sadly for him, the winners are holding the golden tickets! Who has… oh, there you are! Come to the front, please, so we can see you! Good, good… I'm going to unlock the door so you can exit… no Ma'am, it wouldn't be a good idea to try to sneak your son in with the winners. We may be Mer, but we're not stupid. Step back so I can relock the door until I return. As usual, we don't want any of you to wander and fall into something… messy…

Would you lucky winners please follow me? Come right this way…

Welcome to our dessert and caffé room! Feel free to enjoy your fill of crispelle, cassata alla Siciliana, two different types of cannoli, and amaretti d'Oristano. You also have various choices of caffé, including your choice of liquors if you're inclined to have caffè corretto. There are also non-caffeinated choices for those of you who don't want the full Italian experience. But, there's one more surprise! Before you dive in, please enjoy a candied lotus leaf to cleanse your palette…

I will be back as soon as I take care of the others. Again, enjoy!

My apologies for the wait… we just wanted everything to be perfect. No ma'am, we will not take extra money so you and your son can have the prize as well. Please come this way…

This is what we call our "old school" course. Where the meals don't look much different from when they were alive…

Ah yes, I see from you faces that your brains are processing what you are actually looking at. Yes, those are legs: di gamba umana al forno… roasted leg of human…

You seem surprised! All the food that you've been seeing… and eating… what did you think it was? I'm sorry… fish? Why in the world would you think we were eating fish? Oh, "Feast of the Fishes"? Well, we are more fish than not, aren't we? And it is our feast. I had before mentioned about how humans see us as blood thirsty and cannibals, yes? Rumors and stereotypes exist for a reason, don't they?

Yes, those are skulls… at least, the top half of them. Have you never heard of cervello alla Tarantina? Brains on a half shell? Ah, you have not lived until you've tried that delicacy. Of course, you will not live so we can enjoy that delicacy this holiday season…

Please do not fight them, Ma'am. Your son is a fine specimen and will be perfect for our centerpiece dish: capretto alla paesana… roast kid country style. Excuse my salivating, but you have just enough fat on you, little boy, to make your meat so nice and tender…

Yes, you can try to run, but as you can see, my colleagues have weapons made out of that so-called annoying coral you passed in the hallway. As the little brat can tell you, they are sharp and painful. If you play nicely, I can promise that our chefs will knock you unconscious before preparing you for our meal…

Some of you will be salted, some of you boiled, some of you stuffed, some of you fried. I was saddened to see that none of you brought a little baby with you… usually there is one stupid human who thinks this is a place where a baby should be brought. But no matter… we've harvested enough of them to satisfy our cravings… we even put a special one aside for the elders to rip apart…

Now, now… crying won't help you. In reality the salt just makes your flesh that much tastier.

What was that, Sir? Ah, the others? The winners with the golden tickets? They won't remember that there was anyone else on the tour but the five of them. They will remember that they walked through our caves and ate a huge seafood dinner – and that is true, most of the food we eat is taken from the sea, usually by the boatload – prepared with love by us Mer, and then they enjoyed coffee and authentic Italian desserts, and were given cheap lobster bibs to remember their adventure. Or at least to remember what we want them to remember...

The guards will be taking you to the holding pen. I suggest you don't struggle; it will only cause you injury and that will damage the flavor of your meat...

I bet you all don't feel as shrewd now, outbidding all those other potential dinners at the last second before the auction ended... bet you now wish someone had outbid you...

Arrivederci a presto, la mia cena! I am craving our next encounter, truly...

...I am back! Thank you so much for your patience! Have you all had your fill of caffé and pasticceria? Of course you may take a cannoli with you... or any other sweets you like. Here, I even have little plastic boxes for you to carry them home in. Don't forget to take a couple of pieces of marzapane on the way out.

One last thing... a little present for being such wonderful guests! Here's a t-shirt for each of you. Just a little joke on our part, really. It says I Feasted with the Fishes and Made it out Alive! along with today's date. Wear it with pride; it will be a good conversation starter so you can tell all your friends how much fun you had today!

The bus here will take you to the boat back to the mainland. Addio, uomo deliziosa! Get home safely, and we look forward to you hopefully being a part of next year's feast!

THE SIX MILLION DOLLAR MERMAID

Hildy Silverman

It t took two or three strokes for pain to begin. It took almost five strokes for realization to sink in.

Raw instinct drove her to seek the depths after the spinning blades came within inches of shearing off her head. Shock must have insulated her from the agony. What alerted her that she hadn't made a clean escape was her sudden inability to maneuver with the grace natural to her kind.

Something screamed in the back of her mind, warning that her body was wrong. She was missing something so integral, so expected, that its lack simply would not register.

She had to look to believe it.

She turned her head, the current sweeping her long, sea foam-green hair out of her eyes to reveal the impossible truth.

My tail!. Where is my tail?

Dark blood pulsed from the shredded ruin where her tailfins should have been, formed puffy black clouds in the deep water and slowly wafted away to attract predators. As if the sonar bursts that had surrounded her since a whirling death interrupted her swim home weren't already summoning them.

She realized then that she was the source of the sonar. She must have been emitting it since impact, along with high-pitched whistles and clicks of suffering. Pleas for help from other mer, along with a signal to guide them to her location.

They came, of course. Her people would never ignore the agonies of one of their own. But as she reached for them, she saw them assess her mangled form, read the inevitable conclusion on their faces.

Unsalvageable.

They bowed their heads in sad acknowledgement of her end. Then they turned and swam away.

She bit her lower lip, refusing to weep, though the pain was unceasing. They were right, of course. What was a mer without her tail? Nothing they could do but alert her family and leave her remains to the ocean predators.

The warm, enveloping waters, their embrace familiar as her mother's arms, relaxed and chilled.

Silent now, she drifted and waited to end. Instinct screamed that she should evade, plunge into the cave only ten strokes below her and to the left or duck under the coral reef edge a mere five strokes behind, but her body – what was left of it – refused to respond.

What does it matter with so little of me left?

Her agony faded as she drifted into shallow waters, easing from overwhelming to distant, along what she expected to be her final thoughts.

May as well fill a hungry shark's belly, she mused. At least then, I will have fulfilled some purpose in having been spawned.

She closed her eyes.

At first, she couldn't move, couldn't think beyond realizing that she was waking up, yet didn't remember falling asleep.

Then the realization struck that she shouldn't be waking up at all.

How am I not dead? I was dying. Then…what?

She tried to turn her head and moaned as a wave of nausea struck. Not moving was better. She decided to do that some more.

"Doctor?" A woman's voice, close, and yet somehow coming from very far away. "She's starting to come around."

"Excellent. Let him know." A male voice, deep in tone and filled with relief. "Now we can figure out if it took."

She felt a hand brush her forehead, her cheek. The warmth told her that it was human and she instinctively turned her face away, bringing a fresh wave of nausea to her belly, another whimper from her lips. She felt shame that these surface-dwellers should see her so weak, so helpless. Frustrated tears filled her eyes.

One or two must have escaped her lashes, because the hand that cupped the side of her face gently brushed each of her cheeks. "Shh, don't cry. You're okay. You're going to be fine. You're in Bayside Hospital and we're taking care of you."

Memory struck her like a fist. She gasped and opened her eyes, but immediately regretted it. Bright artificial lights stung her eyes and she became sick, retching and coughing weakly.

A woman dressed in loose pink clothes quickly shoved a small plastic bowl under her mouth. It caught the mixture of seawater and bile she spewed. The woman stroked her hair and held it back so she didn't foul it. She felt some gratitude.

Finally, the convulsions passed and she sank limply against the bed, what humans laid their crippled, tailless bodies in each night to sleep. How sad for them, she thought, never knowing the peace of drifting into oblivion in the ocean's womb.

The male, called Doctor, apparently noted her discomfort and thoughtfully dimmed the false light. Relieved, she blinked and found herself able to keep her eyes open.

"Hi, there," he said, smiling as he pressed his fingertips against the inside of her wrist. She wondered if it was some sort of attempt at comfort. "I'm Doctor Goldman and this is Nurse Jaime. Can you tell us your name?"

She cleared her throat a couple of times, reached into her still-fuzzy memories for their language, which she understood much better than she spoke. Words felt so strange in her mouth, the sounds guttural and hard to form, but she knew they were necessary in order to communicate with the humans.

Her people deigned to learn multiple surface languages over the ages in order to communicate. Unavoidable, especially since humans couldn't be bothered to learn the language of ocean-dwellers, not even with all the time they spent studying dolphins and other sibling races. The phrase she needed was basic, learned when she was a child hundreds of swims ago. "My name is Thessalonike."

"Thessalonike?" Doctor Goldman looked at her and she offered a small nod to indicate his correct understanding. "That's quite a mouthful." Nurse Jaime punched him lightly on the shoulder and he quickly added, "Very pretty, though. Thessalonike. Um, is it okay if I call you Thessa?"

Like it mattered. It wasn't even close to her actual appellation, either way, just something she'd been called by a Greek fisher with whom she once toyed. "Yes. That is okay."

He looked pleased. "All righty then, Thessa. Can you tell me if you are in any pain?"

She considered before answering. It felt as if pain were out there, lying in wait to pounce and overwhelm her again, but something held it at bay. "No. I am not in pain."

"Very good." He glanced at Nurse Jaime, who nodded. "Guess the meds do work cross-species."

Thessa studied them as best she could with vision that was still blurred and wavering. They seemed pleasant enough, but humans were so hard to assess for attractiveness. They could be pretty on top, but then went so horribly wrong from the waist down, ruining the entire effect.

His expression turned serious. "Thessa, can you remember how you came to be so badly injured?"

Horribly wrong from the waist down.

Terror struck her anew and she bit down on a scream. "My tail," she whispered. Her voice rasped in her own ears. "Oh, Lord Poseidon, my tail! It is gone, gone, and I am…."

She didn't have the language for what she was now. Her own tones for it were too bereft, too profound, to express in human tongue. Why hadn't she died? At least then, she wouldn't be trapped and maimed, but safe in the Void beyond all such cares.

Nurse Jaime held her hand and patted it, making soothing noises that accomplished nothing. Thessa closed her eyes and whispered, "How did I come to this place?"

"You washed up on the beach, not far from here," said Dr. Goldman. "A couple of tourists pulled you out and called the authorities. When they realized you were still alive, they rushed you here."

"Why would they do this to me?"

The doctor hesitated, seemed confused by her question. "Well, um, I guess they knew about the research we've done with other sea cre...beings and thought we could apply that to your situation."

She nearly choked on a sob, unable to control her grief. "They should have allowed the sea to take care of its own!" She cried, too weak to control her sorrow, shame only making her sob harder. The nurse petted her hair and looked to Dr. Goldman for some kind of response.

"Thessa, it's going to be all right," he said, crouching so that he could look into her face. "We fixed you."

It took some time for the doctor's words to register, but when they did, her breath caught mid-sob. "Wh…what? What by this is your meaning?" She was too stunned to remember the correct grammar.

"Your tail. We, well, we couldn't fix the tail itself. So, we replaced it." He smiled as if he'd merely told her where a nice batch of krill could be found for lunch.

"I…do not understand. My tail, it was gone. Ripped away by your boat." Anger joined her deep, aching grief. The boat, running at full speed and in mer waters. It had come upon her so fast that there was no escaping as it passed over her. She was fortunate, some would say, that she'd felt the disruption in the water behind her, glanced up to spy what appeared to be a giant red eye glaring down at her. She'd had a split-stroke to dive before the great propeller could behead her, except her rapid dive must have thrust her tail right into its path.

"How am I to live without half of me?" she demanded, yanking her hand away from the nurse. Her face warmed with rage. "How should I swim? How will I survive at all?"

"Thessa, please calm down," Dr. Goldman said, his eyebrows pinching closer together. "You're still weak from your ordeal. If you would just let me explain."

"I heard your words. I understood them!" she spat. She struggled to sit up, but only managed to slide back a bit against the pillows behind her. "They make no sense. I know what happened." The memory of seeing ribbons of meat, where her tailfins should have been, brought a fresh rush of bile into her throat. She forced it back down. "I saw!"

"Yes, yes, that's true." The doctor nodded slightly at Nurse Jaime, who backed out of Thessa's line of sight. "Your tail, the one you were born with, I'm afraid we couldn't save it. There was too much damage. The fins were sheared off, and we actually had to amputate more, to avoid infection setting in."

They cut off more of me?

Thessa couldn't catch her breath. Her fury burned white-hot, gave her the strength to force herself upward. She grabbed for the blanket covering where her lower half should be, but before she could pull it aside, the doctor grasped her wrists, stopping her.

"I'm sorry, I know this is overwhelming," he said, maneuvering his face so she had to meet his eyes. She saw compassion there but it did little to ease her fury. "Before you look, you need to understand that this was the best way to help you. The only way, really. It's a miracle, truly cutting edge science."

"What is?" She peered down at the blanket. It lay over a shape, not nothingness.

A tail shape.

Dr. Goldman offered a gentle smile and nodded. "Now, I should warn you, it may look a little odd right now, but with cosmetic work, I think we could get it to look similar to your original tail. We may be able to add artificial scales tinted to match the stump."

The stump.

So it wasn't her tail, magically reformed and reattached. Then what was it?

She tore the blanket away. Stared. Squeezed her eyes shut and looked again. Struggled to understand what she was seeing.

I'm a thing. They made me a thing!

She screamed. Again and again, even as Dr. Goldman and Nurse Jaime clutched their ears and staggered about, agonized by bursts pitched higher than humans could endure. She didn't care. They had taken her already maimed body and attached a mockery to it. Now she wasn't just crippled, she was false, a mechanism, a melding of human technology and mer that was monstrous, horrific…!

Something pierced her shoulder, a sharp and sudden sting, like a ray's barb. Even as she snapped her head around, Nurse Jaime stumbled back from her, one hand clutching a needle, the other still pressed against her left ear. A trickle of blood ran down from her unprotected right ear.

Thessa thrashed; an instinctive response to attack. The abomination that the humans had forged into a tail obeyed, rose up and smashed down on the bed, collapsing it beneath her.

She didn't feel the jolt of hitting the floor before blackness closed in and she mercifully floated away from her nightmare.

Thessa learned much more about her detestable appendage in the days – or was it weeks? – that followed. She found it difficult to translate her measurements of time and distance (by strokes, swims, and spawns) into human terms with much accuracy.

At least Dr. Goldman had the decency to move her out of the miserably uncomfortable bed and into a tank at the local prison (aquarium, Dr. Goldman insisted on calling it) to get proper rest. The tank was in a solitary area where other sea beings were taken to recover from illness and injury. Visitors were restricted other than the medical personnel who checked her condition and fed her, so at least she retained the dignity of privacy.

That was short-lived. One day, just after feeding time, she was introduced to "The Team."

The Team consisted of two marine biologists and four scientists who proclaimed a company called EvoSolutions employed them. They all took turns babbling about the great achievement her new tail was. She understood little of what they said and cared even less.

One white-coated female waved her hands excitedly while talking about the benefit of "Winter's Gel," which kept the tail affixed to the "sock" over her stump, even underwater. Another male explained in sonorous tones how the technology was based on EvoSolutions' research into improved automated underwater vehicles constructed with similar bionics that mimicked designs found in nature, including the movements of manta rays and the mer.

From all their prattle, Thessa realized the following: They have been studying us for a while, for their own profit. No wonder they were so prepared to 'fix' me after my little misfortune. How long have they waited to experiment on a mer 'volunteer?'

Was she even the first? Thessa considered asking, but the fury, which had flared the first day she opened her eyes in the hospital, had grown to a conflagration that reduced ugly human words to ashes while still in her throat. Couldn't they feel her loathing? Such hatred must radiate, had to be sensed. Yet no one who spoke to her showed the slightest hesitation in the face of her rage. Not one feared to touch her during treatments nor trembled in her presence.

Their ignorance of her kind's capabilities was astounding.

One male stood with The Team but didn't speak to her. He came on subsequent occasions they visited to observe and yammer about her, examining the progress of the monstrosity in which they took such obvious pride. He was tall, tanned, and solid beneath suits spun from worm excrement. He stared at her with grey eyes that revealed neither curiosity nor care.

Normally, such attention would have made her uncomfortable coming from any male. But when contrasted against the eager gazes of the scientists, the pitying expressions of the marine biologists, and the wondering doe-eyes of the medical personnel? She found herself welcoming his cold, unreadable observation.

One day, he came alone.

He strode into her room without knocking, came over to the elevated tank in which she languished, and spoke without preamble. "So, darlin'. Betcha you'd like to get on back home, am I right?"

She surfaced and rested her elbows on the rim of the tank, which put her face-to-face with the grey-eyed male. She realized, not for the first time, that she made the necessary turn and strokes with the tail as if it were truly her own. The Team had been right; it was designed well, mimicking the movements a natural tail made and – to her disgust – she was becoming accustomed to it, to the degree that its alien presence no longer intruded on her every thought.

She regarded the man as a small smile played at the corners of his full lips. It was the most expression she'd ever seen on his face. Speech came to her with greater ease than usual. "I cannot return home."

"Really?" He raised one eyebrow. "And why's that?"

She jerked her chin toward the attachment treading water beneath her. "I am dead to the mer."

"Exceptin' you're not dead."

She snorted. "I am nothing my people would accept now. I am hideous. Better I remain a fond memory than a pneuma." He looked confused and she sighed, searched for the English equivalent, "A ghost. A monster, returned."

He inhaled deeply then said, "That's not exactly the word that comes to my mind lookin' at you. Mm-hm, no, ma'am."

Disgusted, she rolled her eyes up to the ceiling. "They are mammary glands. I know they fascinate your kind." She flipped her hair to hang down her back and thrust her chest forward to give him a good view. "Enjoy. My people, they are not so easily distracted by these things."

He chuckled. She looked back and found to her surprise that he immediately met her eyes, not her chest. Suddenly embarrassed, she brushed her hair forward again until the long strands formed a curtain over her breasts.

"Darlin', I'm sorry. I truly am." His expression shifted, all traces of humor vanishing. "But if your folks are gonna go and blame you for gettin' put back together after bein' tore up in an accident, well, then maybe you're better off not goin' back there."

She considered his words. "Then where am I to go? Shall I remain in your prison – forgive me, aquarium – to perform three times a day?"

He studied her calmly. "That could be arranged. Would you like that?" She made a sound of disgust deep in her throat and he chuckled. "That's what I thought. How's about I offer you a better alternative to balancin' a ball on your nose?"

"What do you propose?"

"Well, you may not realize it yet, darlin', but my team gave you quite a gift there." He nodded at the abomination. "I don't think you understand all you can do with that there bionic tail."

"You mean besides swim as far as possible from my family's waters to live out my days in isolation as the stuff of nightmares?" She rested her chin in her hands and awaited his response.

"You could do that. You could swim more miles away than any mer ever did in the mornin' – and make it back home again before the lunch bell rings."

"Indeed?"

He nodded. "That there tail you despise so much comes with active wing propulsion and level glidin' – quiet, fast, and efficient, not to mention extraordinarily maneuverable. It's energy-efficient, enables long-distance travel at incredible speeds." He sounded as if he were reciting a liturgy from memory, up until a mischievous gleam lit his eyes. "Not to mention the sheer strength of the thing. Why, a shark comes sneakin' up on you, you smash its got-damned skull in before it has time to open wide and say, 'Ah!'"

Curiosity piqued despite her misery. At the same time, her suspicion, already high, increased a few pings. "So, this thing is...enhanced?"

"It's state-of-the-art underwater bionics, m'dear. A combo of humanitarian efforts on behalf of poor, injured fishies and corporate efforts to create better, stronger, and faster AUVs to explore the briny depths."

"Our depths." She struggled to keep a snarl out of her voice.

He fell silent. Assessed her. Only after she grew discomfited did he speak again. "What if I told you that fine piece of equipment you're hatin' on so hard could be exactly what you need to keep 'em that way?" She raised an eyebrow in query and he nodded. "Keep your depths – yours."

Her interest well and truly captured, she leaned closer to him over the edge of the tank. "Is that a," she searched for the right word, "propulsion I am hearing?"

He smirked. "I believe the word you're lookin' for is proposition. And yes, you heard right. Tell me, darlin', why d'you think I been droppin' by to see you along with the eggheads?"

She hesitated, considering the image of The Team having heads containing actual chicken ovum, dismissed it as a human colloquialism. "I assumed...I don't know." She studied him closely, mined her hundred-odd swims of life and interactions with humanity over that time for possibilities. "You do not seem to be a biologist or scientist." He shook his head. "You certainly lack the core empathy of a doctor." He arched both eyebrows at this, but didn't disagree. "Considering what I know of those involved in this experiment upon me, then, you must be the money man."

He grinned and nodded his approval, but then held up his forefinger. "Well reasoned, darlin', but you're only partway there. I paid for your repairs, but not just outta the goodness of my own heart. I did it so you could help us out."

"And you are...?"

"EvoSolutions." He paused, leaned in so close she could smell his breath, a heady mixture of stale smoke and peppermints, both nearly overwhelmed by a musky-sweet cologne slapped on his cheeks. "My company."

She coughed and dipped down to draw water through the gill slits between her ribs. He smiled, likely mistaking her preference for fresh breath for an exclamation indicating he'd impressed her.

"That's right, that's right," he said, rocking on his heels. "I'm the CEO and majority shareholder in the very company that produced your miraculous recovery."

"Why?" she asked, switching to air breathing again. "Why would your company use its many monies to pay for the repair of a stray mer?"

He stopped rocking, stood stiff and still. The self-confident grin on his face faltered and for the first time, he wouldn't meet her gaze directly, instead glanced off to the right.

Whatever he says next will be a lie, experience and instinct told her. She had yet to meet the human who could lie and evade better than any of her kind could. For spawning after spawning, her people had made it their business to entice, lure, and otherwise manipulate humans to their deaths or into perverse interludes – often both. In modern swims, however, they'd shifted to using their natural charms and craftiness for more noble purposes, such as securing treaties with surface-dweller governments in order to protect sovereign waters and driving off any that dared encroach on those hard-won 'aquatories.'

Humans had little chance of deceiving a seasoned deceiver such as herself. This one wasn't even impressive in his attempt although she had no doubt he thought himself a master of the liar's craft.

"Because, darlin'," he went on, "EvoSolutions is one of the few human businesses that gives a care whether the oceans—and their inhabitants—thrive or go extinct." He slid his eyes back to lock onto hers again, but she could see strain form crinkles at their corners.

"I can hardly respond to such...kindness as your business has shown me," she replied. Her eyes roamed over his clothing, seeking details. A gleam from an overhead light ignited a small gold lapel pin shaped like a fisheye with a ruby gleaming at its center, a diamond ring on his pinky, gold-and-diamond links attaching his shirt cuffs. He possesses the monies he claims, she thought, mentally filing his details for future knowledge.

"You can, though." He continued in a more composed tone, "You can pay this caring company back for its investment in your future."

"Ah. But I have no monies," she said, feigning innocence while twining a strand of pale green hair around her forefinger. "Despite the mer reputation, I possess no chests of lost pirate booty."

He smirked. "Not a problem. Y'see, what I told you stands. You can help me by helpin' your own. Use your new abilities to protect the waters from those that would foul 'em with human waste, human greed."

She stopped twirling her hair and wondered, where is he going with this?

"My business has nothin' to do with the rape of your ocean, quite the opposite! We respect it and only wish to explore it, to increase knowledge and foster understanding between our peoples." He tapped his chest and pointed to her. "And," he held up his hand as if to keep her from interrupting, though she did not attempt to do so. "I don't just mean the aquatories reserved for you in the Treaty of Triton. All the waters of the Earth should be safe for you and yours."

She couldn't resist the bait. "How?" she demanded. "The oil companies drill, chemical companies void, the rest of your kind dump or steal. Aquatories are artificial divides in the sea. Do you really think nothing you do in surface-dweller governed waters affects our waters? It is all one! Yes, it should all be ours!"

Anger made her thrash – a mistake. The tail snapped back and forward, smashing a hole through the front of the glass tank beneath the rail on which her elbows had rested. Water rushed out over the floor and she flailed her arms to keep from falling as the water level abruptly dropped.

She didn't fall, though.

The tail snapped straight down and the fins rotated and flattened against the floor of the tank, holding her upright. She watched in amazement as the center of the tail split from the fins – now feet – up, smoothly folding into tight curves above the feet and ball joints popped into place. Continuing up, gently rounded slopes led to an arch just under her fortunately still-internal genitalia.

She was standing. On legs.

Mechanical legs, to be sure, the same metallic grey-green as the tail, but there was no denying their form. She made to shuffle forward a tiny, experimental step and found they responded as if she'd practiced with them her entire life. The step was smooth, as sure as any lifelong surface-dweller would take.

All she could do was stare down at herself standing in a puddle of water and sparkling glass, mouth hanging open like a guppy drowning in air.

A baritone guffaw tore her attention away from the shocking vision. "What can I say?" the grey-eyed man said with a shrug. He'd sprinted out of the way of the flood with remarkable ease for a human, and now observed her from atop a low cabinet onto which he'd perched. "I just lo-o-oved me some Transformers when I was a kid!"

He said his name was Austin Stevenson. She didn't trust him. But she worked for him anyway.

As long as his desires align with mine, why not? she reasoned whenever she questioned her mission. Whatever EvoSolutions' true motives were for remaking her in this monstrous image, so long as its directives caused no harm to her or other mer? She would cooperate.

And train.

At least she had a purpose now, and even her early missions did indeed seem designed to drive the worst of humanity out of mer aquatories. Besides, they were fun.

After a few introductory forays (to warm her up, Austin explained) he sent her after a pair of illegal trawlers. He identified them as part of a much larger fleet from a land that regularly turned a blind eye to acts of environmental piracy. They recklessly netted anything – dolphins and even the occasional mer taken unawares – causing great suffering and death to the superior races of the sea.

EvoSolutions sent her from the shores of the surface-dweller land of California with a schedule to pick her up on the *Evo II* once her mission was complete. According to Austin, what authorities would look for a mer aboard a company yacht?

It was no hardship to her, swimming from California to the violated aquatory. The speed with which she reached the waters the fishers regularly invaded was truly impressive; faster than the swiftest sea denizen of any kind had ever traveled.

She entered the region mapped out for her in the mission brief, identified the two rogue trawlers by the symbols painted on their hulls. Following the blueprints she'd memorized during rigorous drills, she dove under the first vessel and aimed for the most vulnerable segment of its underbelly, the room that contained sensitive navigation and other equipment.

She hesitated. So far, she'd only broken a bed, the side of a glass tank, and stationary targets during training drills – actions she might possibly have accomplished with her fleshly tail and enough fury.

Doubt is pointless. It's time to find out just what this thing can do. Thessa drew water through her gills deeply, focused all her hatred for these thieves and murderers into the bionic extension, and then slammed it against the hull.

The jolt shook her to the top of her skull, but the tail did its job. The hull caved in deeply and a fault line revealed machinery within. Encouraged, she smashed it again, this time rewarded by a gaping hole. She swam inside and quickly adjusted her position so that her torso was upright, shifting the tail as she'd been taught to convert it into legs.

Once stabilized, she grabbed the first of the tools inserted into the wide belt fastened around her waist and went about destroying the most vital equipment for function – navigation, propulsion. She counted to herself as she worked, knowing she had until a slow count to 100 to accomplish her task before moving on to the next target.

The fisher-pirates came – the wailing alarms and flashing lights having alerted them to sudden danger. She had tools in her belt for dealing with them, as well. But no need to resort to those when her natural defenses would do.

As the first three howled and rushed her, she smiled sweetly, swept her hair back, and began to sing. They froze in place within three strides of her first note, expressions transforming from murderous anger to confusion before going entirely blank. She returned to her work, singing steadily, her song one that took hold of a human's nervous system, each note a lure twitching at the end of a line, hook embedded within.

More of the fisher-pirates scampered down after their compatriots, only to join them in captivated attendance to her siren's dirge. She couldn't help but grin and pat the butt of the clunky armament provided in her tool belt, the one Austin personally insisted she bring. How cute he thought such a thing necessary for my safety.

Her mental countdown soon exceeded the amount of time she had been allotted per sabotage. Too slow, she scolded herself. She'd have to go faster on the next tub if she were to rendezvous with the *Evo II* on schedule.

Before she departed the sinking vessel, she shifted her melody to a lullaby. The ship's would-be defenders sank to a floor already knee-deep in water and slid into dreams of a life spent eternally in her arms.

At least they will die happy, she thought. More than they deserve for their crimes.

By the time she breeched the second vessel, the first was nearly vertical in the water. Not surprisingly, the alarm had been raised before she even smashed her way in. Unfortunately, several of these defenders had the foresight to stuff wax in their ears. She was obviously not the first disgruntled mer they'd ever encountered.

She quickly sang the first half-dozen to sleep before the next, the ones with their ears blocked, swarmed into the engine room. Their guns barked, but before the flashes from the muzzles subsided, she'd already back-flipped from the exposed center of the room to shelter behind a large boiler.

She withdrew her gun, took aim, and squeezed the trigger, just as Austin's weapons instructor had taught her. Her bullet pinged off a steel wall and ricocheted, causing her enemies to shout and dodge, but did no other harm. She muttered a curse. This sort of weaponry was too foreign, the hand-eye coordination required strange and uncomfortable.

Fortunately, she'd learned many ways to fight.

She launched herself at the first raging fisher-pirate, who didn't have time to adjust his aim before her mechanical foot caved in his chest wall. He fell spluttering to the floor and she righted herself, pivoted, and kicked another, who flew into a control panel with an explosion of electrical arcs and flying parts.

One less item for me to dismantle, she thought, congratulating herself for multitasking.

One of the trawler's defenders shouted and his still-standing companions dropped. She had only a moment to see him raise a large weapon before it belched forth a wide spray of bullets.

She dove through the gaping hole in the hull. Though the water slowed the projectiles, they still carried enough force to follow her into the water. She ducked and maneuvered out of their trajectory, cursing even the scant moments it took for her tail to reconstitute from legs. It slowed her enough that two of the bullets grazed her, one along the right arm, the other dangerously close to her left gill slits.

Then the divers arrived.

Through the hole in their vessel, wetsuit-clad, armed with spear guns. Five of them. At first, she thought to simply out-swim them, knowing they would be left in her wake within a few strokes. But then the sharp pain of the bullet grazes reminded her of the far greater agony of having her tail sheared away, probably by a vessel owned by other such pirates. Whoever had severed her given tail and left her floating like so much chum in the sea had gotten away with their crime.

This scum would not.

She flipped over their heads with a single stroke, came up behind them. They struggled against their forward momentum to turn and face her, but couldn't hope to maneuver with her ease. As they fumbled to bring their spear guns to bear, she caught the first by his ear, tore away his facemask, and ripped the breathing device from his mouth with such force that she broke several teeth. He convulsed, mouth gaping in a silent scream, blood clouding the water in front of his face. She yanked the spear gun from his nerveless hands, twisted, and smacked him with her tail.

The force was such that the ocean current barely slowed his trajectory. His limp body slammed into two of his fellows like a cannonball, driving them back at least fifteen strokes, limbs flailing like jellyfish tendrils.

She barely had time to enjoy the sight before the sound of a trigger pull alerted her to immediate danger. She twisted to the right and dove, the bionic tail giving her the boost of speed and maneuverability needed to avoid the spear fired at the top of her head from close-range. She shot back up before her attacker could hope to reload. His eyes widened at her approach and he raised the spear gun to jab into her gut.

She curled into a backward somersault as her upward momentum carried her to him, cocking her tail to the left as she traveled. Before he could hope to dodge, she swept her tail to the right. The edges of her artificial tailfins sliced through his neck as if through a bubble. His head and body parted ways.

Alone once more, completely satisfied, she swam away, finding herself oddly anticipating seeing Austin again. She couldn't wait to relay the tale of her triumph to him.

He isn't one of your own, she condemned herself, yet couldn't summon indignation to go with the thought. She realized that she'd come to think of him and the EvoSolutions team as hers. All those times during training they'd stressed she was an integral member of their organization, made her feel valued and trusted—though she'd resisted the notions intellectually, along the way she'd accepted them emotionally. They felt like kin.

Because they are an actual part of you now, aren't they? She glanced back at her tail, which had performed so amazingly, now effortlessly propelling her back to them. She couldn't summon disdain for it any longer. It was truly a remarkable gift, engineered or not, and EvoSolutions had given it to her. Austin had given it to her. How could she feel anything but gratitude for the blow on behalf of her people it enabled her to strike?

She glided through the ocean, whizzing past predators and sibling dwellers so fast that she was gone before they could exhibit a reaction. She found herself laughing, almost giddy with adrenaline and triumph. She couldn't feel the stings from the bullet grazes any longer.

A few hundred strokes later, she surfaced, briefly, and spotted the *Evo II* exactly where Austin had told her it would be. The vessel, a good-sized yacht that Austin said he raced each year, was meant to whisk her away to the Gulf of Mexico, well away from the incident she'd just created and on to her next mission knocking down an oil platform being erected by an unscrupulous company that had already polluted the region once through its negligence. The massive cost and negative publicity should discourage any further attempts at construction.

She approached the *Evo II* from the front-left, slowed down to a crawl stroke, reluctant as ever to leave the sweet comfort of the sea. She saw a lookout on deck, dressed casually as if he were just a regular deckhand going about his duties for a wealthy boss on a leisure cruise. She surfaced and started to raise her hand to signal him, when her eye was drawn to the stylized *Evo II* lettering along the lower left bow.

At first, she wasn't sure why it drew her attention, other than the fact that it was bright red. Then she focused on the illustration in the word, where the O should be. Her hand dropped without conscious guidance.

A three-dimensional fish eye replaced the letter. The pupil seemed to gaze back into her own, challenging her to remember where she'd seen it before.

Remember…

She clutched her gut as though some invisible force had punched it. Gasping for air, for water, she couldn't catch her breath either way. Her vision narrowed to a tunnel and all she could see was that red, protruding eye…

…the same one she'd glimpsed, oh-so-briefly, right before realizing the whirling prop was spinning toward her head. Right before it tore her tail away.

"Father Poseidon," she murmured and numbly genuflected the symbol of His triton. "Forgive this fool."

It had been an EvoSolutions boat that penetrated mer waters, recklessly maimed her, continued blithely along its way. Perhaps it had been this same vessel, or another in their fleet – it hardly mattered. The point was that they had violated sovereign territory without a care or thought, maimed her and probably slain others. They'd done what Austin accused others of, vowed he and his would never do.

He'd lied. And she'd believed.

Loathing filled her. She clutched her waist, where the sock affixed the tail to her stump, and strained as though she had hope of ripping it off. Idiocy. They were a part of her now until death.

Her hands drifted over the belt around her waist. Tools of destruction, of revenge. And this tail is just another, she reasoned. They had given it to her, true enough, to force her into their service, but it was hers now, to do with as she pleased. To use against her enemies.

All of them.

She ducked down, hands lightly brushing along the bow and midsection as she determined where best to strike. Something nagged at her, though, made her pause and think. A question.

Why?

Why would a company, one apparently operating in blatant disregard to treaties and mer sovereignty, go through so much effort only to send her to attack other, equally heinous violators? She had to know.

Besides, Austin and his team had made this personal. She intended to look each one of them in the eye before meting out their punishment.

She prayed Austin's grey eyes would be last.

Setting her jaw, she treaded water and waved to signal the lookout. He spotted her almost immediately and called to someone over his shoulder.

She heard the engine, which had been idling, rev to life and the terror of the sound nearly paralyzed her. It was all coming back to her now, every instant of the boat sweeping up on her where no vessels were permitted, traveling at speeds completely banned anywhere near mer populations, so fast that she barely had time to react. And even then…and then…!

She fought down the scream that bubbled up from deep inside, along with the drowning nausea of panic. It's a mission, she disciplined herself, drawing on her training, her preparation. Focus on the goal, map out the path to it. Take each step necessary, keep emotion out of it.

Thessa made herself suck in a final rush of ocean water through her gills until the thrum of her pulse in her ears ebbed and the pins-and-needles sensations running down her arms into her fingertips subsided. Under control once more, she swam to the ladder hung over the edge of the deck into the water.

She eyed it contemptuously, folded forward in the water, and sprang. She cleared the railing easily and briefly met the wide-open eyes of the lookout. Encouraged by his awe, she stretched mid-air and converted.

She landed on two legs with an impact that shook the vessel. Splinters flew and the teak deck bowed beneath her mechanical feet. A quick assessment informed her that had she not pulled back at all, she'd have gone straight through the lower decks.

Duly noted, she thought.

The lookout continued to gape at her. She tapped him under the chin with her fingertip to close his mouth. "It isn't polite to stare," she whispered, booping him on the nose. Then she turned and headed down the stairs to the forward cabin where Austin and his people waited.

"Welcome back, darlin'," said Austin as she entered the sizable room.

He sat at the head of a long, stainless steel table, a sheaf of papers scattered between him, four other men, and two women. The others appeared to represent different surface-dweller lands, two fair-haired, three dark-haired, one wearing some sort of headdress. Each looked her over then averted his or her eyes as soon as she evenly returned each gaze. Only one of the dark-haired males offered a curt nod of acknowledgement.

"Did you enjoy that little foray?" Austin asked, leaning back in his chair, fingertips steepled beneath his chin. "Your first gen-u-ine mission and a complete success. Color me impressed, Thess." He chuckled at his weak rhyme.

The others followed suit, which told her all she needed to know about the dynamic in the room. These people recognized Austin as their superior. Yet their dress and poise told her they were used to being leaders themselves, in whatever businesses or governments they represented.

She forced a smile and said, "Yes, it went as planned."

One of the dark men stood and walked to Austin's side. He reached into a pocket in the breast of his jacket and removed a thick envelope, then held it out with both hands and bowed deeply.

"Nice doin' business with you, Hoshi-san," said Austin. He accepted the envelope, indicated the upper deck with his chin. "Go on up to the wheelhouse, Cap'll show you on the monitor."

The one called Hoshi-san headed for the stairs. Thessa quickly considered her options, decided to target the one with obvious knowledge and separated from the crowd. "Austin, I am weary. May I go to the berth and lie down?"

"No worries, darlin'," said Austin, his attention already shifting back to the papers – which she could now see were maps – on the table. "Now, Madame Governor, about that pipeline problem of yours…."

Thessa bit her lower lip, resisting the urge to finish with him immediately. Instead, she made her way upstairs, straight for the wheelhouse of the *Evo II*.

Hoshi started when she came in the room and she caught the fear in his eyes. He was the one who'd acknowledged her below. His people likely had a longer memory of the mer of old. Good, she thought, respect born of terror. She could use that.

"Hoshi-san," she addressed him as Austin had, "I wish to have words with you."

He blinked rapidly. "We have nothing to discuss, ningyo."

"You know my kind well, don't you," she said, trying to catch his eye, but he refused to meet her gaze. "You bear no love for the mer."

He cleared his throat. "I have much respect for ..."

"Respect? Yes. That I do not doubt." She sauntered closer to him, until her breasts nearly touched his chest. He shrank back but the wall at his back halted his retreat. Perspiration beaded on his forehead. The captain cleared his throat loudly but she ignored him. "Respect does not equal affection. Even I know enough words to separate the two."

He met her gaze briefly and she saw a flare of defiance in his dark eyes. "You belong to Austin Stevenson," he said. "This makes you acceptable."

"I believe you mean useful." He tried to sidestep her, so she thrust her arm out and slammed her palm against the wall. He attempted to duck around the other side, but she blocked him there, too.

"Miss Thessa," the captain said, warning in his tone.

"Tell me, Hoshi-san," she whispered into his ear, "how was I useful to you?"

"I...I do not...?"

"Yes, you do," she continued, smoothly. "Those fishers on the pirate vessels I sank, I saw them. They looked much like you." She ran a finger lightly through his short black hair, tapped his temple by his right eye. "Now tell me, why would you want a being you so clearly despise to attack and destroy your own kind?"

Hoshi's eyes darted wildly, seeking escape. The captain stepped away from the controls and said, "Mr. Stevenson wouldn't want you harassing his guests like this, Miss Thessa."

She glanced over her shoulder at him, saw his hand rested on the butt of a large gun holstered at his side. The holster was unclipped.

She estimated the distance between them and smiled. Then she kicked back and up while keeping Hoshi-san trapped between her and the wall.

Her heel caught the captain squarely under his jaw. His feet left the floor and he landed a few moments later with an echoing thud.

Hoshi's eyes rolled in his head and he tried to shove past her. With both her feet once again planted firmly on the floor, he may as well have tried to shove the entire yacht. A cry caught in his throat as she slapped him hard across the face, irritated by his hysterics.

"I'm not finished," she said, forcing him to look into her eyes. He blinked rapidly, eyes glazed with tears.

"Wh...what is it you want of me?" he stammered.

"I only want the truth. And you had better give it to me, because ningyo can see into your soul. Your soul cannot lie, so if your mouth does, I will know it and I will be – upset."

He shook his head so hard she heard his vertebrae creak. "Tell me what you wish to know!"

She suppressed a grin. She'd made up the soul-sight thing, knowing at this point she could have told him she had the power to transform into a bird and fly and he'd believe. "All I want to know is why are you paying Austin to sink your people's vessels?"

"They were not my people," he said. She raised an eyebrow and he quickly added, "I mean, yes, they were from my country, but they serve a rival enterprise. By dealing this blow, they will think twice before fishing those waters again."

That gave her pause. Perhaps it wasn't all a lie, then. Maybe Austin was really trying to stop those who would damage the oceans. Does he know one of his fleet injured me? she wondered. Is this his way of making amends? She was surprised to experience a rush of hope, realizing that some part of her still wanted Austin to turn out to be her hero.

The terrified Hoshi dashed her last vestige of goodwill. "Once word gets out that ningyo are attacking surface-dweller interests, taking human lives, the Treaty of Triton will be voided. We who dwell on land will seize full control of all waters."

Thessa pulled Hoshi close and then slammed him back against the wall. He yelped. "How would the surface-dwelling authorities know that a mer caused those ships to sink?" she shouted, only half-addressing him. Her mind raced to its own conclusion, putting together the last pieces of the puzzle.

Her arms felt heavy all of a sudden. She released Hoshi and stared into nothingness as he scampered away. "Austin was going to take me to the authorities," she said, raking her fingers through her pale-green hair. "He was going to send me out to sabotage targets in exchange for payment from different businesses, different lands, and then turn me in as a mer terrorist. Deny that he had anything to do with me."

She reconsidered and shook her head. "But no, how could he escape suspicion with this thing attached to me?"

"Well, I'll tell ya how, darlin'."

She whirled around and found Austin standing in the doorway, leaning almost casually against the doorframe. She was about to lunge for him when he quickly stepped into the room, revealing the armed men behind him. He pulled a large spear gun of his own out from behind his back, held it pointed to the floor but made it obvious he could bring it to bear within an instant.

She relaxed back and opened her hands at her sides, palms out. "Why would you use me like this?" she asked, glaring into his steel-colored eyes.

"Well, you just about worked it out already, darlin'," Austin replied. "You're just missin' one little piece."

"Which is?"

He chuckled and gestured to her tail. "You're on candid camera." When she stared blankly in response, he sighed. "Your tail, there, has recording capabilities. Your little escapades have been recorded and transmitted right here for my viewing pleasure – and for any authority I decide to give it to."

He strolled closer. She tensed but the guards brought their weapons up so she could only watch as Austin crossed to the captain's console. He stepped over the captain's body and fiddled with some controls.

A monitor flared to life, displayed mostly blurs of motion. She was able to recognize images from one of her early missions, smashing a chemical plant's drainage pipe. Although most of the images were jumbled, at least one or two glimpses of her upper body were shown, distinctive seafoam-green hair swirling. Austin pressed a button and her reflection in the water froze on the screen.

"Ain't exactly high-def, but enough to damn you and yours, don't you think," he said, nodding as if to agree with himself.

"But when your authorities came after me, they would have seen the truth of what you made me," said Thessa, slapping the sides of her attachment.

"Oh, darlin'." Austin rolled his eyes with an expression of false pity. "They'd've never find you, or what was gonna be left of you when we finished. The most they'll ever see are carefully-edited images that 'someone'," he waggled his fingers, "captured on their I-this-or-that, of some mer destroyin' surface-dweller property, takin' human lives." He shrugged. "Who's to say only one mer was behind all this destruction? After all, it doesn't seem likely one little fish-girl could accomplish all this, all over the place, now does it? More like a widespread conspiracy among the mer to attack human interests."

"Putting us in clear violation of the Treaty of Triton," Thessa murmured, an icy chill suffusing her body. She had vastly underestimated her enemy and the scope of his plans. She cursed her gullibility, clenching her fists until her nails dug deep into her palms.

"The Treaty'll be a thing of the past," Austin said. "The phony-baloney boundaries of your aquatories will be erased. The oceans will be ours again, finally, without havin' to pussyfoot around you lot to get our oil, take our fish, do whatever the hell we want to do. The way it should be!"

His grey eyes flared with rage and she shrank back. "Do you know how got-damned sick and tired I am of workin' around you freaks? How much it's cost me in business because I couldn't drill here, send divers there? You have no idea how many companies answer to me, the bath I've been takin' because of the limits of that fuckin' treaty!"

Spittle flecked his lips and he marched across to stand over her, his face hovering just above hers. "Well, party's over for the mer! And it's all thanks. To. You!"

His first mistake was misjudging her deliberately affected, cowering stance for defeat. His second was getting too close with only a long-range weapon in hand.

She gazed into his eyes. Smiled sweetly. And kneed him in his poorly designed external genitalia.

She barely put effort behind it; knew she didn't have to. Still, the impact was enough to hoist him off the floor by a sizable measure. He landed, clutching himself, in a contorted heap a short distance away. A piercing keen emanated from his gaping maw and his eyes bulged far out of their sockets. Wetness darkened the legs of his trousers and a nauseating combination of blood and piss filled the cabin with its stench.

She didn't have time to enjoy her handiwork. Guns barked and bullets flew within moments of Austin's fall. She leapt, cartwheeled through the air, and kicked in the heads of two of Austin's guards. They fell away, but she heard shouting and the clamor of more of Austin's men as they stampeded for the upper deck.

She needed the advantage of the water.

She ran forward, paused only long enough to wrap her arms around Austin as he staggered to his feet. He stared at her with wide, rolling eyes.

She grinned. "Take a deep breath."

The remaining guards pounded across the deck shouting impotently, unable to fire their waving guns due to her having their boss in her embrace. She crouched and sprang, launching her and Austin in a long, arching dive over the railing.

Moments after they hit the water, her tail reconstituted. She slammed it into the ship without hesitation, smashing through the double hull, leaving gaping holes in her wake. Fueled by the fury of Austin's betrayal and her own self-loathing, she screamed in clicks and whistles, cursing Evo-Solutions and herself, but especially Austin, right into his purpling face. It wasn't until she'd smashed the blades of the large propeller into crumpled junk that her rage cooled enough to surface and survey the result of her handiwork while Austin hung limp and wheezing in her arms.

The yacht took water and sank with a satisfying rapidity. Twin splashes as two rubber life rafts hit the ocean's surface. Amused, she grasped Austin by the shirt collar and dragged him along as she sliced through the rubber of each raft with the edge of her tail. Screams of despair filled her ears as the only means of escape popped and deflated beneath the survivors of the *Evo II*.

Only after watching the last of them tread water, weaken, and sink did she return her attention to Austin, hauling him along until they reached an outcropping of rocks. Then she released her grip.

Sometimes, the best ways were the old ways.

She lithely hopped out of the water and rested atop them. He floundered, grabbed onto one of the rocks, but hesitated to climb up.

"I have a proposition for you," she said, sweeping her seafoam-colored hair back from her breasts and arching her back.

"Wh…whatever it is, I'll t…take it," he stammered through chattering teeth. "Remember, all in all, I did s…save you. I made you b…better than you w…were."

"And stronger. And faster." She smiled and inclined her head as though thanking him. "Hence my offer." She pointed to a beach in the distance. "A strong, healthy male like you should be able to swim that distance, even in your current condition." He glanced toward land. Hope relaxed his pained, oxygen-starved face. "Exactly. You have a chance – if you choose to leave my side."

He tilted his head to look up at her, confusion warring with contempt. Then he let go the rock and began to swim as fast as he could primarily using his arms.

She gave him a few strokes, just enough to allow confidence to take hold of his heart.

Then she began to sing.

He shook his head back and forth, ducked underwater to muffle the sound. But his fate was as inevitable as it had been for generations of other fools unfortunate enough to violate mer waters.

Slowly, mechanically, he turned and swam back to the outcropping on which she rested. His face, at first contorted with resistance, relaxed as the hypnotic tones wiped away all thoughts of escape and replaced them with a desperate hunger to be with her.

She smiled and held her arms out in welcome as he dragged himself up onto the rocks, crawled toward her with longing and despair battling behind his grey eyes. He pulled himself hand over hand and came to rest embracing her waist, his head resting on her mechanical lap.

"Th-essa," he said, words stilted as though struggling to stop his mouth from forming them. "I l-ove you. P-please say we can be together. N-never. Leave. M-me."

She cupped his chin in her hands so she could look into his eyes one last time. "Of course," she cooed, bending down until her lips brushed his as she spoke. "Darlin'."

His eyes widened as her speech broke the spell. But as in the times when her people still regularly lured sailors to their ends, by the time he realized what was happening it was far too late.

She embraced him once more and dove forward, plunging them down deep into the oblivion of the ocean floor. Only the echo of his final, ragged scream marked their passage from surface to sea.

FISHTALE
Michael A. Black

It's all in how you kick, Sharon thought as she moved her legs in unison, flipping the fishtail to propel herself forward while holding the bubbling oxygen line discreetly out of sight in her left hand. She looked through the water at the casino on the other side of the glass. It was starting to fill up. Two idiot guys had left the slots and moved up to the expansive window to watch her swim by. The window extended the length of the massive room and the pool was decorated with artificial coral, the replica of a wrecked pirate ship replete with open treasure chests, a huge assortment of live fish – and her. What would a treasure trove be without a real, live mermaid? Every man's fantasy. The two idiots pressed their faces against the thick glass.

What a couple of horny creeps. But it was her job to give them a show. It was what the cheap-ass Indians who owned the place paid her for.

Sharon turned on her side, giving them a good view of her front as she flipped past, her right hand reaching up to make sure her top was still covering the girls. She thought about the first time she'd seen Mickey looking at her from the other side of the glass wall, standing there with his wavy black hair and handsome face. When he'd asked her out for a drink later, they'd ended up in bed in his cheap motel room. Ordinarily, it would have been a turn-off, but she'd had a long night and the cuddling was nice. Besides, she needed to sober up anyway. But after they'd started talking, and he told her his lofty scheme, something lit up inside her head. It had been what they call an epiphany.

One of the losers waved at her from the other side stirring her from her reverie. The guy's tongue was practically hanging out of his mouth, hoping for a little bit more.

Mickey's right, she thought. One little slip so my top comes off and it'll send these hormone-driven losers crowding around the window like they'd just gotten tickets to a free peep show. She parted her lips slightly to flash them an alluring mermaid's smile before rotating the other way to take a breath from the hose, figuring they'd enjoy seeing her ass – fish-scales and all.

Just wait, losers, she thought as she felt the oxygen filling her lungs. Two more days and you'll be thrilled beyond your wildest dreams.

She rotated back, giving them a full frontal view again and saw Mr. Bernson, the casino general manager standing there next to the two jerks, pointing and grinning.

Yeah, Bernson, you prick, go ahead and smile, she thought, thinking about the time she'd spent on her back and knees earning this job. She saw him wink at her through the glass, a wide grin plastered over his face.

So the big boss is down checking out my boobs with the rest of the losers, huh? She thought. Well, let's give them something to talk about.

Sharon purposely brought the oxygen line close to her boobs to let the trickle of air bubbles caress her top a bit almost exposing the areola portion of her nipple. Her right hand moved quickly to readjust her top.

One of the horny jerks slapped the other one on the shoulder with a shit-eating grin on his face.

Sharon smiled again, tantalizing them while inside her head her voice shouted back, "Just wait, you losers, just wait!"

Two more days and it would be all over but the crying.

🧜

On the other side of the glass wall Al Zuckerburger watched Mr. Bernson talking to the two guys who were watching Sharon swim past. Yeah, she was a looker, all right. Outstanding set of tits, tight midriff, great hips.... He bet her legs were first class too, except he couldn't see them because of the fishtail. What he wouldn't give to get some of that. But Mickey would never allow anybody to tap into his private stock. Once this thing was done, though, Al knew he'd be able to get all the good looking broads he wanted. After all, he'd be rich.

The casino boss turned around and cast a glance at him, raising an eyebrow as a bit of an acknowledgment. Bernson turned back to the two jerks and patted them on their backs, urging them to enjoy themselves. He looked one more time at Al as he walked away.

At least he knows I'm on the job here, Al thought. Not that he appreciates me much.

Al bit his lower lip and felt himself start to sweat, the wetness under his arms seeping through the armpits of the light blue security guard shirt.

I got to calm down, he told himself. The job ain't going down till Monday.

One of the gawkers turned with a simper on his face and did a double take. Then the idiot smirked and slapped his buddy on the shoulder.

"Look at that," gawker number one said. "The casino's rent-a-cop copping a peep."

Gawker number two's head swiveled around. He was grinning too. "Watching us check out the chick, pops?"

Drunks, Al thought as he straightened up so he'd appear a bit taller, not that it would add much to his five foot nine frame and squared his narrow, sloping shoulders. For further emphasis, he locked both thumbs behind his pistol belt and pulled it away from his paunch. The belt was fine, black leather, crosshatched and his stainless steel, Smith & Wesson Model Sixty-Six .357 gleamed in its holster.

Gawker number one giggled. "Hey, look, Kenny, he's carrying an old wheel-gun."

"Just like a cowboy," number two said. "What's the matter, pops? Can't afford an automatic?"

Al pursed his lips. He felt like telling them the proper term was "semi-automatic." No respect. Drunken punks. They shouldn't allow them in here. They didn't know he got the Security Guard of the Year Award back in '89.

He gave the pair a stern look and they shuffled off toward the blackjack tables still laughing.

Just a couple of jerks, he thought. Can't let them get to me. Can't let anything get to me. Not till the job's done, anyway.

Al turned and walked away, eyeing the heavy metal door that led to the vault room and glanced at his watch.

Two more days, he thought. Two more and I'll be home free.

He felt more sweat dribble down his sides and caught a whiff of himself. He stank. God, he needed a drink.

It was almost midnight and Mickey Nelson took particular pride in the clarity and detail of the casino diagram he'd drawn on the dry-erase board. It was, like everything he did, brilliant. He knew it, and so did they.

They – Sharon, Al, Hutch, and Street – all sat in the dingy little motel room and stared at the board. Mickey knew he had their attention and figured it was the appropriate time to remind everybody again of the importance of going over the synchronization. He uncapped the red marker and drew two circles on the board outside the box that represented the side entrance.

"As we all know," Mickey said, "the pick-up of the weekend receipts, which is generally the heaviest amount, occurs every Monday morning at nine." He paused and studied the group. All their eyes were on him.

Good, he thought. That's the way it should be. "And it's also what?"

"The time of heaviest security," Sharon said.

Mickey frowned, cocking his head to the side as he cupped his hand behind his ear. "All together now, people."

"The time of heaviest security," the group repeated in mismatched unison.

Mickey nodded his approval. This was the way he liked it. Everyone working as a team, just like his days as senior man at the frat house.

"However," he flashed them a quick grin to show he could be a benevolent leader, "in anticipation of the impending holiday weekend, they're delaying the pick-up until seven PM on Monday night so they can get all the weekend tally's done. And, as Al has told us, they have it all pre-sorted so as not to attract undue attention."

Al beamed at the acknowledgment.

"How many fucking times we going over this?" Street asked.

A threat to my leadership? Mickey wondered. He let his frown deepen. Street and Hutch. Mickey didn't like these two toadies and wished he didn't have to involve them, but it was unavoidable. Two big ex-cons working at the auto rebuilders . . . Two more players he needed to pull the heist off . . . And, after all, it was the score of a lifetime.

"We'll go over it as many times as necessary," Mickey said. "Or have you forgotten who's running this show?"

Street looked about ready to say something but Mickey transferred the red marker to his left hand so he could keep his right close to the Beretta 92F he had tucked inside his belt. But the two ex-cons looked so burly he wondered if they felt even the least bit intimidated. If they did, neither one showed it.

Hutch reached forward and slapped the back of Street's shaved head. "Shut up and let the man talk. If it wasn't for him and Al we wouldn't even have a shot getting in on this."

Street rubbed his head, looked down, and nodded.

Mickey took this as an affirmation of the quality of his leadership and the brilliance of his plan. They were his again.

"Okay," he said, placing the marker back in his right hand. He drew a rectangle next to the side entrance. "This is where the armored car normally pulls up." He tapped the marker on the board. So when our truck pulls up at six-thirty, a half an hour early, nobody will be the wiser. We get out, go inside, and make the pickup. In and out in ten minutes tops, and that takes into account securing the vault guard and the two flunkies inside the room with our plastic cuffs." He held up the long flex-cuff. "We'll take Al with us when we leave as hostage to make it look good. By the time the real truck arrives, we'll be long gone. Sound like a plan?"

"It sounds good," Hutch said, "but there's a couple of loose ends."

Mickey didn't like criticism of his plan, but he cocked his head. A good leader will listen, then act. "What loose ends?"

"I mean," Hutch continued, "what if someone gets loose in the vault after we're gone and tips the cops?"

"Don't you see?" Mickey flashed his most ingratiating grin to placate the moron. "That's the beauty of it. Even if someone does get loose in the vault, and that's not likely." He paused to pull on the flex-cuff to show its sturdiness, "They'll point the finger at some guys dressed as armored truck guards and the cops will be zeroing in on the real truck that'll be on the road, not us." He stepped over and tapped the marker on the drawing of the highway. "We'll be zooming in the opposite direction with the armored car logos removed from our van." He lifted his eyebrows. "Speaking of which, they are done and in a safe place, correct?"

Street and Hutch exchanged smirks.

"They been done," Street said. "We finished painting them a couple days ago."

"Just like you told us," Hutch added.

"Yeah, Mick," Al said, "I got them stored in my garage with a sheet over them."

"Anything else?" Mickey asked.

"Yeah," Street said. "What if someone notices us in the masks? We got to walk what – ten or fifteen feet through the casino from the outside corridor door to the one leading to the vault-room."

"It's actually twelve-and-a-half feet," Mickey said, "and everybody will be too fixated on our beautiful, topless mermaid here to notice us." He held his palm out toward Sharon who puffed her chest and held a hand next to each of her tits.

Mickey let his eyes linger over each of their faces, silently reasserting his leadership role. The plan was practically foolproof. He'd thought of everything. They'd pull up in their van which would look like the armored truck on the video cameras, they'd mask-up and Al would let them in the side door for the Monday night pick-up. The brief time they'd be seen going through the casino, Sharon's strip-tease would be diverting everyone's attention so their masks wouldn't be noticed. Al would say they pulled a gun on him and forced him to take them to the vault. He'd escort them down the corridor to the vault room and tell them to open up, at which time they'd tie up the three vault room personnel, the inside security guard making it look good. Then they'd load up the bags and leave. Once they'd exited the casino road and gotten on the highway, they'd fold-up the sides of the fiberglass box with the armored truck logo on them, and be home free once they reached the auto-body shop. The weak link was Al, who would let them in the side door and escort them to the vault room.

It all depended on the proper interaction, but despite a few intangibles he knew the plan was solid. Perception is reality and people, witnesses, would see what he wanted them to see. Plus, with Sharon's diversion, nobody would be watching them too closely.

"Looks like we're set then," Mickey said, glancing at his watch. "We've got sixty-seven hours and ten minutes left before execution."

Hutch and Street looked at each other, two stupid, muscle-bound ex-cons used to waiting and doing time. Al licked his lips – a washed up drunk who's forgotten more than he ever learned. And Sharon, his current squeeze and current, pleasant diversion, stared up at him, all adoring adulation.

Jesus, what a motley crew, Mickey thought. It's a good thing I'm so brilliant.

❧

Sharon and Mickey lay entwined together under the sheet. Thank God this is the last weekend she would have to spend in this dingy little motel room. She'd offered to let Mickey stay with her, but he'd said no.

"Too risky," he told her. "We can't have anyone seeing us together, remember?"

She did, but had only made the offer in keeping with the "dumb broad" image he had of her. It was obviously what had attracted him to her in the first place. When he'd asked her out for a drink that first night she'd seen him watching her through the glass window, she wondered if he was only attracted to her body, or if it was only his ticket into the inner-workings of the casino. He was full of questions about the place. How long had she worked there? What times did she do her swim-show? Did she know anybody in security? She figured he wanted her to try and get him a job, or something.

But that wasn't it.

Little by little, after that first night when he got her drunk and took her back to the crappy little motel, he sold her on the plan, sketching it out in "what ifs" until ripping off the casino seemed not only possible, but justifiable too.

"What are they doing except stealing money out of people's pockets?"

he asked. "They keep people's judgment skewered by offering free drinks, and having a beautiful, semi-nude girl dressed as a mermaid swimming along in an expansive fish tank."

She loved the way he used words. His vocabulary was so large. Almost as large as his ego.

"What you thinking about, babe?" Mickey asked as he rolled on his side and pressed his face against hers.

"Nothing."

"Come on," he said. "Tell me."

"I'm just wondering how everything will work out, is all. It seems like there are so many pieces . . . so many things that could go wrong."

"And each part will fit together perfectly," he said. Mickey brought his hands up and cupped her breasts. "You just remember your part and bring these beauties out at the right time."

She felt an increased anxiety. "But what about Al?"

"What about him?"

Sharon frowned, then said, "He smelled like booze earlier when I picked him up from the restaurant parking lot, but he kept popping breath mints. I think he was sneaking a drink."

Mickey looked irritated for a moment.

"I mean," she continued, "even after they find him unconscious, what if they smell it too? And if they grill him, will he be able to stick to the . . . the fishtale?"

"Fishtale," he said. "I like that."

"Well, will he?"

Mickey squeezed her boobs and smiled. "I told you, I've got all the angles covered. Trust me."

"You make it sound so easy," she said.

"It will be easy. And foolproof. After all, I planned it, didn't I?"

The dilapidated old house that Al rented was in the poorer section of town, and Mickey hated parking on the next block and walking through the neighborhood to get there. With so many people out of work it increased the chances that someone might see him. Or maybe even accost him. But after all, he did have the Beretta, with the new attachment he'd picked up today, so he wasn't too concerned about that. Still, it wouldn't fit his plan if he had to use the gun now. The ballistics would leave a trail, and he was all about eliminating trails.

No one paid him any attention as he cut down the alley and came to Al's yard, a piecemeal carpet of crabgrass, weeds, and patches of bare dirt. Sort of like the man himself, Mickey thought and he went to the side door of the garage. He was careful to slip on his tight, black, leather driving gloves before he twisted the knob. He could hear the whirring sound of the electric screw-gun. The boys were busy.

He opened the door and stepped inside. They'd set up a portable electric lamp on the floor. Hutch was holding one of the fiberglass sections in place against the side of the van while Street used the gun to fasten the screws. The tattoos on his muscular arms glistened with sweat. His head swiveled toward the door.

"I told you to keep this locked," Mickey said and he closed the door behind him.

Hutch's face twisted into a frown. "We had it locked. Al must've left it open when he went to work."

Street fitted another screw into the fiberglass and pressed the bit into it. The gun whirled, twirling the screw into place.

Mickey assessed their work. The fiberglass shell fit the van like a glove, displaying the company logo of Armor Tech Security in the customary green and red letters against the olive drab background. If he wasn't up close and personal, he'd almost swear it looked like the real thing. And, as Mickey reminded himself, perception was reality.

"You guys do good work," he said.

"Yeah, we know," Hutch said. "Where the hell you been? I thought you were gonna help us?"

Mickey smiled. "I had a few last minute things to take care of. Besides, you guys seem like you have it well in hand."

"Now that all the heavy lifting's done," Street added as he sunk another screw through the fiberglass frame and into the side of the van.

Mickey ignored the comment and walked around the van. The fiberglass shell was almost fully secured.

"Make sure that those screw-guns are fully charged," Mickey said. "We'll be on a strict time-table once we leave and I don't want to waste a lot of time on disassembly."

"With three of us working," Street said as he sank the last screw, "it shouldn't take no more than five minutes."

Mickey mentally rehearsed the disassembly. Stow the money in the back of the van and depart the casino. Once they reached the side-road turn-off they'd stop, don their coveralls, use the electric-guns to remove the screws, fold the side sections onto the top, and secure them with the bungee cords. Then they'd proceed to the body shop in an inconspicuous fashion. Once inside, the only thing left would be to remove the roof section of the fiberglass framework and place everything into the compactor to crush it. Well, that was almost the only thing. Mickey didn't want them to know about the last part of his plan. That could wait until the proper time.

Timing is everything, he thought with a smile. Along with the proper interaction.

Street stepped back and wiped the sweat off his forehead with the back of his hand.

"You know," he said, "if I didn't know better I'd swear it really was one of them armored trucks."

"Perception is reality," Mickey said with a grin, slapping him on the back. "Come on, let's change into our uniforms."

Al felt the cell phone vibrate in his pocket. That meant that Mickey, Street, and Hutch were on the way. He knew they'd keep the tarp over the shell until they got to the turn-off, then stop and slip it off. When they were a hundred yards from the casino entrance they'd buzz him again, and he'd flash Sharon the high sign that it was time to begin her strip tease. That Mickey thought of everything. The only thing Al regretted was that he wouldn't be able to see her with her top completely off.

Yeah, Mickey thought of everything, all right.

He felt a tightening in his gut, his whole body craving for one little sip of booze. Just one tiny shot to tide him over . . . to make him sharper. Al glanced at his watch. They were still at least ten minutes away. Shit, why not? He had time. And it would make the little tap on the head that Mickey was gonna give him more bearable.

Looking over the moderate crowd, he rotated his neck and glanced at the long glass window of the aquarium. Sharon swam past in her fishtail, her white body looking like a fantasy spread in some men's magazine and Al felt a slight stirring in his groin – like someone had touched him on the prostate.

Soon, Al thought, I'll have all the broads like that I can handle. Soon I'll be rich and outta here.

He glanced around and pushed open the door to the men's washroom. Two guys were pissing in the urinals. Al nodded at them and headed for one of the stalls – the handicapped one which allowed him a larger space to take off his pistol belt. It was also used less often so the smell of the alcohol would be less noticeable. His left hand snaked down into his back pocket for the hip flask as soon as he'd closed the door.

Just one little drink to tide him over . . . to see him through this. Then everything would go as smooth as clockwork.

"How come you got an automatic and me and Hutch just got revolvers?" Street asked as they drove down the freeway toward the casino exit. Mickey arranged the blue coveralls in the back of the van so they could change into them with the minimum of confusion once they'd completed the heist.

"What does it matter?" Mickey said. "The plan is to get it done without firing a shot." He smiled to himself adding, Well, almost.

Street grunted. "I just don't like being at a tactical disadvantage is all."

"Aw, shut your mouth," Hutch said. "Like the man says, we ain't planning on storming Fort Knox, or anything. This operation calls for what they call firnesse and timing."

Mickey smiled at Hutch's mispronunciation, but didn't correct him. Finesse and timing were the keys, all right. And once they got back to the body shop he'd show them just how it all came together. In the meantime, they had to stay on schedule. He glanced at his watch. They were almost at the exit. Two more minutes to get to the side-road and remove the tarp to display the armored car logos, then five more to reach the casino. Buzz Al to let him know to signal Sharon and then meet them at the side exit. It was all going down like clockwork. Mickey felt a slight twinge of nervousness thinking about the upcoming interaction. But that was what it was all about . . . interaction. And he'd planned for every contingency.

Al glanced around one more time before slipping back into the men's room for the third time. He hoped that tap on the head that was supposed to render him "unconscious" wouldn't hurt too bad. Mickey had promised him it wouldn't, but still, another little sip would make it hurt a lot less. Al strode to the handicapped toilet stall again, but this time it was occupied. So were the other three regular stalls.

What the hell was going on here? A fucking laxative convention?

His own wit made him crack a smile and he glanced at himself in the mirror. The image of the late-middle-aged man in the baggy security guard's uniform starring back at him with a simper stretched across his face both startled and pleased him. It pleased him because, hell, he didn't look half-bad in his uniform . . . Startled him because he realized he'd imbibed a little too much from the damn hip flask before and was feeling the slight but cloudy buzz of the alcohol. He put his hand on top of the Smith & Wesson and struck what he thought was an intimidating pose. The reflection pleased him some more.

One of the toilets flushed and the door slammed opened. A drunken patron stumbled out, looked at Al, and nodded.

"Evening, Officer," the drunk said as he walked past on unsteady legs.

Another loser heading back to lose his paycheck, Al thought. He was debating the wisdom of going in the stall to sneak just one more sip.

Somebody in one of the other stalls made a loud deposit. The accompanying odor was suddenly overwhelming.

Another toilet flushed.

Al started to move toward it when he felt the vibration of the cell phone in his pants pocket. He took out the cell phone and looked at the text.

Three mikes, it said.

Dammit, he thought. They're only three minutes away. I have to signal Sharon to start now.

Al hit the reply button and sent an OK. It took him four tries to get the letters right.

He heard an extended bit of flatulence emanate from one of the stalls.

Yeah, fuck you too, he thought. Time to get on with the show.

He patted the hip flask one more time, mentally uttered a silent lament, and discreetly slipped it into the trash can along with the disposable cell phone. Mickey had been explicit: Don't have anything suspicious on you in case they search you later.

Al grinned one more time at his reflection in the mirror over the sinks.

That Mickey's something, he thought. He thinks of everything.

"Al's going to signal her now," Mickey said, slipping the phone back into his pocket. It would go into the compressor later. Even if they recovered the SIM card, the calls would only be traced back to the other disposable cell phones. So far, so good.

Now if only the sight of Sharon's boobs creates a big enough diversion . . .

He hoped Al wouldn't be waiting around to check them out instead of meeting them at the side door. Street twisted the wheel and the disguised van began to roll down the long drive towards the casino.

"Get ready to put on your mask and gloves," Mickey said to Hutch. He began screwing the long sound suppressor on the barrel of his Beretta.

"When you get that thing?" Hutch asked, his face obscured by the plastic, translucent Halloween mask of George W. Bush.

"It'll look better on the videos," Mickey said, and slipped down his Obama mask. "Let's go straighten out the economy for ourselves."

Sharon swam to the designated spot and pressed herself against the glass, making it look like an accident. She held the oxygen hose down to her side, the bubbles rising around her left arm. Through the glass she saw Al's herky-jerky walk as he approached the tank.

Oh no, was he drunk?

She hoped to God not. She hoped it was just the distortion of the water and glass that made his walk look funny. He popped something into his mouth. Probably a load of those breath mints.

It had been a busy night so far. There were already about three horn-dogs on the other side staring at her. If Al gave her the signal it should be easy to attract more. He moved to the window, pointed at her, said something to one of the patrons. The man grinned and nodded. Al put his left hand up against the window. A few inches thick glass separated them now. Al curled his forefinger and thumb into an O-shape and then walked away.

That was it. That was the signal. She pressed the stem closed on the tiny, water-resistant watch she'd fastened around the air hose. Both of the hands were set on the 12. A couple more minutes, then she'd start.

Al flashed his fob over the electric eye meter at the side entrance door. The lock popped open and Mickey and Hutch were standing on the side. At least he assumed that's who they were. With the hats and masks on, Al thought they looked amazingly like Bush and Obama. He couldn't help but grin. What the hell, the surveillance camera on the ceiling wouldn't pick up his face, only the top of his head.

"Want me to whistle 'Hail to the Chief'?" he whispered.

"Just look scared and keep moving," Obama said, flashing a long-barreled pistol. It had a silencer on it. God, it looked wicked.

Al grinned and started to raise his hands. "Christ, where'd you get that?"

"Never mind. Get your fucking arms down and get moving. We're on our time-table." Obama slipped Al's Smith & Wesson from its holster and put the weapon in his jacket pocket.

Al lowered his arms, trying to make things look good for the video cameras, turned and began walking. In thirty seconds they'd have their three-and-a-half second walk from the exterior door to the vault room corridor. He hoped Sharon was on cue.

Ten more minutes, he thought, and it'll all be over.

Sharon brought the hose up slowly, looking at the hands on the watch. Time to start. She let the bubbling air lift and tug at the side of her bikini top. She'd tied the string in back with a very loose knot. The force of the air-stream lifted the bikini cup and she felt it snag as she brought the hose up to take a breath. The bikini top floated lazily away from her breasts as she filled her lungs. She acted as if she hadn't noticed. But from the expression on the faces of the three horn-dogs, they had. Sharon let out her breath, letting the bubbles escape with a demure smile, and brought the hose to her mouth again, totally cognizant that both of the girls were now fully exposed.

One of the horn-dogs yelled out something. She could only surmise what it was, but several more guys ran over to the window. She caught a quick glimpse of Al being escorted by the masked Mickey and Hutch. One, two, three . . . then they were through. At this point Sharon brought the air hose away from her mouth and then did a quick feel of her breasts. She feigned what she hoped looked like a genuine shocked expression and brought her right hand up to cover her left nipple. She reached out with her left, which held the air hose, and intentionally let the air jet blow the drifting bikini top away from her grasp. Flipping her fishtail, she removed her right hand from her boob and extended it to swim up and away from the window, pretending to try to snare the errant top. But the air hose blew it away from her fingers.

Sharon watched as the top rotated through the water, propelled by the force of the air jet, away from the window. She swam with frantic strokes now, and purposely let the air hose slip from her fingers. It rotated lazily away from her, like a dancing snake. Sharon had previously inhaled a deep breath of the O2 so it was easy now to fake some ineffectual strokes as she sought to regain the lost hose. She rotated on to her side and flipped past the window her arms outstretched.

Great, she thought as she glanced at the window and saw a growing crowd of horny bastards on the other side thinking they were witnessing one of her most embarrassing moments.

Actually, you suckers, she thought as she took her time grabbing the hose and working her way toward the bubbling nozzle, you ain't got a clue to what's really happening.

Mickey checked his watch. One minute, thirty-five seconds to gain entry, another ninety seconds to disarm and tie up the vault room personnel . . . Three minutes, forty-seven seconds to load the money, which had been conveniently pre-bundled for them. He'd have to thank them later, he thought with a grin as he looked at the interior vault. The guard and the two money handlers were passively trussed up and lying on the floor with cloth sacks over their heads. Seven minutes, thirty-seven seconds. They were right on schedule. Hopefully his little mermaid was still chasing her top.

Hutch hefted both of his bags and stepped toward the door. Al stood there sweating and stinking. Sharon was right, the idiot had been sneaking the booze. Mickey motioned for him to pick up the other two bags and grabbed the straps of one of the stuffed money bags with his left hand. The Beretta remained in his right. He'd already used it once to shoot out the PTZ camera lens on the ceiling as they entered the room. The phone hadn't rung yet. He figured by the time the guy watching the cameras got around to noticing it was out, he'd call down to the vault to see if there was a problem. When no one answered he'd try to reach Al, or the other roving guard, on the radio by that time they'd be out the door.

"Move it now," Mickey said.

Al licked his lips and glanced around, as if he wanted to say something.

"No talking, Security man," Mickey said, motioning for Al to follow Hutch out of the room. "You're coming with us. Try anything and you're dead."

Al nodded and grinned and Mickey thought about slapping the idiot. Once you were in a role, you stayed in it till the job was through.

As they filed down the hallway, the two men in front of him carrying two bags each, Mickey glanced at his watch again. Twelve minutes. Sharon should still be chasing her top. They came to the end of the hallway and had to walk through the casino to get to the exit corridor. It had taken them three seconds before, but this time they were laden with money bags. Plus, they couldn't look rushed. Mickey opened the door. The crowd was still gathered around the fish tank. Sharon was just starting to hammock her boobs into the bikini-cups.

Good, Mickey thought and muttered for them to keep moving. We'll be the last things they'll be looking at.

Mickey flicked Al's fob in front of the electronic lock and the door popped open. They moved down the second corridor at a quick trot to the exit door where Street, the wheel-man, was waiting in the idling van. The back door of the van was open underneath the decoy fiberglass siding, so all they had to do was pull open the make-shift door, toss in the bags, and jump in themselves. Then it was a four-and-a-half minute drive to the turn-off road.

So far, so good, Mickey thought as one-by-one they got inside. He slammed the door shut and settled back as he felt the van begin to move forward. An incipient feeling of relief started to seep up from his shoes, but he knew there was still unpleasant tasks ahead of him. He could smell the booze wafting off Al like a hooker's cheap perfume.

Mickey, Hutch, and Al all sat in the back of the van with ear-to-ear grins as Street drove away from the casino.

"Shit," Al said. "We did it."

"Let's not lose our focus." Mickey picked up the bag containing the overalls, opened it, and tossed one pair to Hutch. "Slip this on so we can take down the sides. How much longer till the turn-off?"

"Coming up on it," Street said.

Al sat back and watched them. All he had to do was sit tight for the time being and act like the robbers had really abducted him. Once they got to the auto body shop where Hutch and Street worked Al knew they'd have to tie him up, blindfold him, and give him a bump on the head to make it look good. He hoped it wouldn't hurt too bad. He also hoped they'd dump him someplace where he'd be found right away. And when the cops asked him what happened, he'd stick to the plan: "I don't remember nothing."

Mickey was brilliant, all right. Everything was covered, nice and neat. He'd make sure his cut was safely stashed under the floor in his garage before they dumped him. It should be safe enough there.

I'll have to see what Mickey says, he thought.

Get moving," Mickey shouted once Hutch had lowered the overhead door to the auto rebuilder shop. "We've got to get the fiberglass sides off and into the compactor."

"Aww, keep your pants on," Street said as he slipped out of the van. "We're right on schedule, ain't we?"

Mickey glanced at his watch. He went to the trunk of his car which was parked in the adjacent stall, opened it, and took out a plastic garbage bag.

"Take off your armored-car uniforms and put them in here." He tossed the bag onto the floor between Street and Hutch.

"You know," Street said, "for a young punk you give a lot of orders."

"True," Mickey said, "but let's not forget whose show this is."

"What can I do, Mick?" Al asked.

"Just sit tight," he said. Mickey turned and saw that both Street and Hutch had dropped their pistol belts and were in the process of disrobing. "Oh, one more thing . . ." Mickey pulled Al's Smith & Wesson .357 out of the pocket of his overalls, brought it up, and shot both Street and Hutch in their chests. Both men stumbled backward, wounded but still alive. Mickey aimed the Smith carefully at Street, then shot him in the side of the head. As he dropped, Mickey turned, aimed again, and shot Hutch in the forehead.

Al looked on in stunned disbelief.

"Mick, what's going on?" he asked. His ears were ringing from the sound of the shots. A fierce smell of burnt gunpowder hung in the air.

Mickey walked over and picked up Street's handgun, hefting it in his hand. It was a big, mean-looking revolver of some sort. Al continued to watch as Mickey's arm rose with Street's weapon. The sound and the puff of smoke accompanied the terrific blow to Al's chest. That's what it felt like: a punch, a body blow . . . no pain . . . then all of a sudden the pain was there, ricocheting up to his brain like a delayed burst of lightning. Through the hazy air Al could see Mickey standing there, the big revolver still in his outstretched hand. The son-of-a-bitch was smiling.

Al's hands automatically went to his chest. He felt his shirt. Wet. He looked down at his hands – they were covered with blood.

The word sounded choked, his voice cracked as he sunk down to his knees and managed to say, "Why?"

"Loose ends, Al," Mickey said. He stooped down and rubbed the back of his gloved hand over Street's hand, then he placed the revolver in the dead man's fingers. "You see, the genius of my plan is there was a little shootout that started when you guys got back here to split up the dough. Then, a little fire started . . . I'll leave enough of the money scattered around to make them think the rest of it burned up or was taken by some unidentified third party."

Al was lying on his side now, each breath hurting worse than the last one. "But what about me?"

"You'll look like a hero, buddy," Mickey said. "Taking out two of the bad guys but getting shot in the process."

"Help me," Al said. He wasn't sure the words were audible. The ringing in his ears had gradually lessened to a constant, low humming sound, but he still heard the door open.

Mickey's head darted up, then he did a double take.

"What the hell are you doing here?" he asked.

"They sent me home after the boob thing," Sharon said. "Besides, I figured you might need some help cleaning up."

"Christ, and you came here?" Mickey looked like he was about to backhand her. "What if someone saw you?"

"I was careful," she said, surveying the scene. "Looks like it's all set the way you planned it, honey-bunny."

"Of course," Mickey said.

Sharon's smile looked mysterious. "Where's the money at, baby?"

"It's in the van. We need to load it into my car and get out of here. But first . . ."

He walked over to Al and flexed his gloved fingers. "Let me finish setting up the scene." Mickey fished another pair of the latex gloves out of his pocket and handed them to her. "I still have to make sure Al has some GSR on his hands before we leave."

"Ooh, is that a real gun?" Sharon asked. "Is it loaded?"

"It's Al's gun," Mickey said. "And it is loaded. Two rounds left. Think you can handle it?"

"Absolutely," she said, slipping on the latex gloves. "I grew up in Montana, remember?" She held out her hand. "Give it here."

Mickey handed her the Smith and stooped down, grabbing Al's right hand. "You're about to become a hero, buddy."

Al kept his eyes half closed and wondered how much longer he'd be alive. Maybe if he could somehow summon enough strength to jump upward he could twist the Smith from her hands. Maybe he still had a chance.

The sound the Smith going off jarred him once more.

It startled Mickey too. Al could see that. Mickey jerked up and held his side, his head swiveling toward Sharon who was holding the now smoking gun. He grunted and tried to go for the Beretta but she shot him again, this time in the left temple. He dropped all the way to the floor, his dead eyes staring at Al from a few feet away.

Curiously, Al noticed that the hole in Mickey's head was neat and round, with only a little bit of tearing around one side. Hardly any blood came out of the hole. A trickle dribbled from his mouth and nose, though. Sharon walked over to his body and picked up the Berretta with the sound suppressor.

Al heard the overhead door start to open again. It went about a quarter of the way up, then stopped. Al twisted his head to look. Big Ed Bernson walked in, surveyed the situation, and looked at Sharon. He held up a remote and pressed the button. The overhead door descended.

Al couldn't believe it. Maybe Bernson was armed. Maybe he'd be able to get the drop on Sharon and call the cops and an ambulance.

Al summoned all his strength for one Herculean effort. He raised his head. "Mr. Bernson. Be careful, she's got a gun. She's one of the robbers."

Bernson looked down at him and smirked. "I know what she is, you idiot." He looked over at Sharon and smiled, opening his arms wide. "Come here, beautiful."

Still holding the Smith, she walked over and let him embrace her.

"Mr. Bernson," Al managed to say, looking up at the casino manager. "I did my best for you, sir. I was …"

Big Ed still had his arm around Sharon's waist. "Yeah, I know, Zuckerburger. You were Security Guard of the Year once upon a time." He nodded at Sharon who was stooping over Mickey. "He dead?"

"As a doornail, lover," she said.

Al blinked twice. Lover? What the hell? "Please," he managed to say, feeling that burning pain in his chest. "Call me an ambulance."

Big Ed looked down at him, squinted, then shook his head. "Take it from me, Al baby. You're done for. The blood's dark. Bullet must have hit your liver. An ambulance ain't gonna help. Besides," he strode past Al and picked up the first money bag, "we're on our own time-table."

Al felt the pain lessen. Was that a good sign?

Big Ed began lifting the money bags out of the van and placing them into the trunk of Mickey's car. It took him three trips, then he slammed the lid shut. "I'll meet you back at your place. I'm sure they'll be calling me in there shortly once the cops arrive." He pulled her close and they kissed.

Well, what do you know? Al thought. Another double cross. He tried to speak but all that came out was a grunting sound.

Big Ed looked down at him, his arm still around Sharon's full hips. "I'll make sure you get a hero's funeral, Zuckerburer," he said. "And maybe another Security Guard of the Year Award. Posthumously. I should thank you, too. I've been trying to figure how to skim some dough from that fucking place, but it was always too much of a risk. But you guys had a good plan and executed it flawlessly."

Al felt himself slipping away, the asshole's voice sounding farther and farther away. He strained his ears to catch the words. Sharon stooped down and set the Smith in front of Al's outstretched hand.

"Careful, he's still alive," Big Ed said.

Al had a fleeting thought if he could summon enough strength to grab the Smith . . .

"Relax, it's empty," Sharon said. "Six shots." She wiped her own gloved hand over Al's. He couldn't feel her touch.

"What are you doing that for?" Big Ed asked.

"Gunshot residue," she said. "Got to leave some."

"Damn, baby, you think of everything," Big Ed said. "Where you want to go first? Aruba?"

"Where ever there's a nude beach," Sharon said. "But first there's one more thing I've got to do."

Big Ed's head swiveled toward her and a look of shock spread across his face. "What the hell?"

Sharon aimed Mickey's Beretta at his chest and pulled the trigger twice. Big Ed's mouth twisted into a grimace and he took two stutter-steps and collapsed, his knees striking the hard concrete floor. He put a handout to steady himself and Sharon aimed the pistol. It made a subdued but piercing sound and Big Ed's head jerked back.

"Much, much better," she said. "Nice action and not so noisy."

Al watched as she went over and placed the Beretta in Mickey's outstretched hand. Al couldn't see much anymore . . . Things were starting to go black, but in his mind's eye he could still picture her face, smiling with that alluring, mermaid's smile.

A KING REBORN
Darren W. Pearce and Neal Levin

It was a bitter cold night in the Kingdom of Ryalla. As the stars hung in the sky above the Royal Palace of King Romas, an altercation in a candlelit room beneath the West Wing threatened to wake the servants from their slumbers elsewhere in the sandstone building. The room belonged to a simple man, called Irdan, and he was backed up against the far wall, just short of a wooden side table and a single jug of water near his right hand.

"How dare he!"

Prince Aman's sword stopped an inch from the man's throat and as the prince narrowed his dark blue eyes, he brought his harsh face closer to the scribe and tilted the curved blade slightly so it pressed on the man's Adam's apple. He twitched his thin lips and searched the scribe's eyes for some hint of falsehood. He found nothing and reluctantly let the scared man go.

"Count yourself lucky," he said to the scribe, "that I am in a good mood, or you might be troubled breathing."

"Master, I am telling you the truth. Your father is furious with your campaign in Karta-Yava," Irdan bowed his head. "I overheard him talking about giving your inheritance to the people, because they deserve it. He accused you of squandering your fortune and gifts in unwanted wars and needless bloodshed."

"The people of Karta-Yava are SAVAGES!" Aman raged, his face contorted with anger and he swung his sword wide so a candle was neatly chopped in two. "They need to be taught the ways of our Empire. They need to be brought into line. They understand only war."

"Yes master," Irdan's brown eyes looked away to the window. He was thinking about jumping, ending his life before Aman lost his temper again and did it for him. "I only relay to you what I have heard. Would you rather I kept it from you?"

"I would have been very angry if you did," Aman softened a little; he swished his sword and laid it back into his scabbard. "You did the right thing to bring this to me though. Now I can make my plans."

Irdan winced as the prince spoke to him. "Master, what would you have me do?"

Aman thought about this for a while and shook his head. "Continue to listen to my father rant, bring all the gossip and lore to me. I, on the other hand, will do what I do best, continue my campaign against the savages of Karta-Yava ... and go to see an old friend elsewhere this night."

Irdan breathed a sigh of relief, took a glass, filled it with water and drank the whole lot in one go. He watched the prince leave and slid down the wall with a long sigh.

Prince Aman left his scribe and stalked the halls of the palace. He was furious and it was fortunate that there were no servants awake at this hour. Three in the morning was a good time for skullduggery and he knew where to go – to Sapphire's room. His path took him through marble corridors, past crystal statues etched with gold and through a vast courtyard that was home to a massive fountain. Made of gray marble, it had four horses cast from bronze in the centre and water flowed in torrents into the air from their mouths as they stood with their hooves beating towards the sky.

Finally he arrived at Sapphire's room and shoved the door open; he found her alone and sprawled across a massive circular bed. The dark haired woman was dressed in layers of blue and green chiffon, her pleasing figure mostly hidden from view. Her room was bedecked with tapestries, covered in expensive wall hangings and smelled of several kinds of incense.

"Prince Aman," she raised a thin brow and narrowed her amber eyes. "You really should knock, or are you here for wanton desire? Do you plan to storm the gates of my castle and ravage me?"

"I have no time for you tonight, woman, not like that."

"Unlucky me," Sapphire rolled to her feet and shook out her long hair. "Not as though I would have let you. A Seer cannot be sullied by even your royal blood. A Seer must remain pure and chaste or her power is lost."

Aman laughed at this and shook his head. "I am here to seek your wisdom, woman, not your body."

"It must be a terrible burden to be gifted with all these princely manners, to be so like your father and so loved," Sapphire scoffed and sat down on the edge of the bed. "So beloved by the people."

Aman's eyes lit up again and as he crossed the room his hand rose to strike the woman for her insolence. Sapphire, however, was not in the mood for the prince's antics, so she rolled to the side. Now behind him, her short knife was quickly at his throat and she hissed into his ear;

"Prince or not, if you do that again, I'll geld you."

"Let go of me woman or I'll..."

"Do what, cry to your guards? You'll be breathing through another hole before you could utter a single whimper." Sapphire tugged on his hair. "Do you forget who I am, who I work for, what we can do?"

Aman coughed a little and bit his tongue, forcing himself to relax. His hand came up and settled onto Sapphire's wrist to lower the knife, but didn't continue that particular course of action.

"Fine, I apologize...I have been under a lot of stress lately and I did not mean to cause you offense."

"You tried to hit me."

"I know..."

"Never again, prince, or I will seriously limit your ability to father children or even enjoy a woman's company."

"I understand," Aman bristled. "Sapphire, I came here for help. I want to hire the Shadow Guild."

Sapphire laughed a little and let him go. He tumbled onto the bed and she hid the knife again. "You want to WHAT?"

"You heard me."

"You know that the Shadow Guild will not touch people like King Romas. Your father is a good man and the guild only targets those who have done terrible wrongs." Sapphire moved away from the prince and shook her head. "Get out, you are an idiot."

"I can pay, half of the kingdom's treasury if you kill him, you could be my queen," Aman gambled as he sensed the deal getting away from him.

Sapphire continued to shake her head, "You're deranged!"

"Do not try my patience, Sapphire," Aman warned. "I will be king one day!"

"Only if you can change your karma. You may be the only son of the king but you're destined always to be second in this kingdom. You have a lot to learn about being a man and a prince." Sapphire waved her hand to the door. "Get out."

Aman took himself and his wounded pride out of Sapphire's room and slammed the door. Moving to a nearby balcony he ground his hands against the smooth stone, locking his fingernails into his soft skin until it bled. So focused was he on his anger and loss of face that he didn't detect the smooth steps of another figure until a nasal voice snapped him out of it.

He whirled around to see one of the servants out late, a thin and malnourished man that no one took any notice of. He was called Rhatt.

"My Prince looks angry and troubled."

"Go away, Rhatt." Aman shoved at him but the nimble servant dodged it.

"I overheard it all, I can help." Something behind Rhatt's reddened eyes caught the prince's attention and stopped him from kicking out. "I can even point you in the right direction to change your karma."

Prince Aman usually dismissed these kinds of ravings out of hand but that one word, used twice in the same night stopped him cold.

"You have one minute. Go on."

Rhatt gave a slight bow and a furtive look to each side. "The Karma Stone, my prince, lost in the City of Mursas thousands of years ago. Thought destroyed with every Merfolk that ever lived beneath the Sargassa Sea."

"You talk legends," Aman sighed. "Go away."

"Every legend has a basis in fact; every story has a grain of truth." Rhatt countered with a wan smile.

Aman was about to shove him away again and once more he stopped. "Say that I believe you, how do I find it?"

"You would need a merman, good prince. But as you said," Rhatt winked a little, "they are but legends."

"What do you know?"

"I know I can find you one who could lead you to the stone."

"How would I get to it? It's under leagues of ocean."

"Leave that with me."

Prince Aman gave the little man a curious look and then, perhaps against his better judgment decided that he would entertain Rhatt's fantasy. "I leave it to you then, but you best not fail me."

"I never would," Rhatt smiled softly. "I have too much faith in myself for that."

"Do what you must then."

"I always do."

"When can I expect news?"

"Tomorrow afternoon, we will meet at the fountain in the palace as the sun rides exactly mid-way across the sky." Rhatt walked off with a soft step.

"Tomorrow it is then."

Prince Aman made his way back to the palace interior feeling much happier. He even stopped to smell the blooming night flowers on the way.

It was exactly midday when Aman returned to the palace courtyard. He was dressed in his daily formal attire, a set of flowing robes adorned with gems and golden thread. Red and gold suited him and he'd taken the liberty to cut his hair shorter after his run-in with Sapphire. The sun beat down across the courtyard as the various servants, palace attendees and his father's guests busied themselves with their daily routines. Aman moved to the fountain, cupped his hands and took a drink from the cool clear water.

"My prince is on time. Perfect." Rhatt's nasal tones wheedled in from the side and the man appeared as if by magic. "I stand in awe of your Highness' punctuality."

Aman shrugged. "I hope this is not a waste of my time."

Rhatt chuckled and cocked his head to the side. "A waste of time? A single journey must begin with the most simple of steps." The man dabbled his fingers in the water. "So, are you ready?"

"I am. This has been long overdue."

"I am glad."

"Get to the point before we're disturbed," Aman grew impatient, "or my father's people overhear."

"Oh, I have ensured that only people loyal to the ideals of Aman the Excellent are present this afternoon."

"Aman the what?"

"Excellent. Do you not like it?"

"I don't."

"No matter." Rhatt put his back to the fountain. "I have arranged for you to meet a man called Sahreed. He is ruthless and willing to help you find the Karma Stone. He can get you to the depths of the sea to recover it."

"What about payment?" Aman ignored all the other details for the moment.

"We both wish to be given our dues in your New World Order." Rhatt gave a sly smile. "My King Aman to be."

Aman thought about this and he nodded. "Yes, you have my word," he said with a turn of his head. "So how will I know this Sahreed?"

"I will take you to him, but we must leave soon. He will not be able to wait in these waters for long; they are a little too dangerous for a merman."

"He's a Mer?"

"Yes my prince, a legend come to life for you to meet!"

Aman blinked and rubbed his eyes as whisper of sand blew across the palace courtyard. "How did a lowly like you come to meet a Mer, Rhatt?"

"We all come from somewhere my prince, even one such as I." Rhatt's smile did not reach his eyes. "It is my hope that in the New World Order you will remember this."

"I will."

"We will go to the shore then, my prince. Get your finest stallion and meet me on the Old Purna Road in an hour." Rhatt quirked a brow and made to look at something across the courtyard, where he thought he saw a glimpse of chiffon vanish around a corner. "One hour."

Aman followed his gaze and pursed his lips. When he saw nothing he turned back to Rhatt but the man had vanished. It was though he had never been there in the first place. A shiver ran down Aman's spine but he ignored it, focusing instead upon leaving the courtyard and making his way to the Royal Stables where his own personal steed awaited him.

He had his horse, named Sultan for the regal bearing of the beast, brushed and saddled then told the stable hands that he was taking the mount for a quick ride around the local roads. They did not question him. It was unwise to do so and Aman had built his reputation on cruelty to those who displeased him.

Aman turned Sultan away from the palace and out through the main gate of his father's city, striking a North West trail to the Old Purna Road, a trade route that ran West to East across the Great Dust, a massive desert that covered most of the Kingdom of Ryalla and was only stopped by the shores of the Azuren Sea, which eventually fed into the Sargassa.

One hour later and the stallion brought Prince Aman to the Old Purna Road. The ruins of the desert-blown city stood a few miles in the distance. The once proud walls that had held the treasures of an ancient kingdom now looked like broken teeth against the glowing horizon. It remained as a testament to the dangers of sorcery and pacts with otherworldly creatures such as the Djinn.

Rhatt stepped out of a hidden cleft in a nearby rock and gave Aman a bow. "Once again the prince is on time, this proves the strength of his conviction and perhaps the trust he places in Rhatt?"

"We have a mutual direction for now. So where is this Mer?" Aman smoothed down the mane on Sultan. The beast was a magnificent black stallion and it stood proudly defiant on the road.

"Follow me." Rhatt waved a hand and began to walk a small path that lead down to a glistening beach. "It is here that you will meet the legend."

Aman followed with Sultan and kept a slow pace behind Rhatt. Eventually they made their way down onto the beach and after a few yards the thin man came to a halt. He raised his right hand and waved his fingers.

"Here we are."

"What now?"

"We wait a little." Rhatt took out a silver whistle from his pocket and blew into it, making no sound at all that the prince could detect. "But not too long."

"Your toy is broken," Aman laughed. "You need a new one."

"Oh, my prince, just because you cannot hear a thing does not mean a thing is not making a sound." Rhatt watched the surface of the water and put the whistle away. "See?"

True enough, the surface of the sea began to bubble and churn, then from a small whirlpool appeared a humanoid looking head with small flaps of flesh on each side of its neck. Almond shaped eyes peered out from under a mane of seaweed-like-hair and the dappled blue/green skin of the creature glimmered in droplets of reflected sunlight.

"Prince Aman, meet Prince Sahreed. One of those Merfolk that came from Mursas." Rhatt bowed low and swept his hand to the creature. "Prince Sahreed, Prince Aman, a noble soul from the lands of sand and mud."

Prince Sahreed flicked his eyes towards Prince Aman and nodded just the once before he finally spoke.

"I see a boy that is not yet a man, but ambition isn't confined to the old." He smiled with shark-like teeth and looked back to Rhatt. "I will take your bargain."

"What bargain?" Aman blinked at being ignored.

"A little gift in return for Prince Sahreed's services ... just a formality, nothing more." Rhatt gave a cough and spat on the back of his hand. "Peasant's customs, Highness."

Prince Aman ignored the little man and concentrated on the merman, looking Prince Sahreed over and into the creature's green eyes. "Can you help me find the Karma Stone?"

"I can," Sahreed replied. "I only ask that you remember me in your karma wish."

"In what way?"

"You will have the power to change your karma, to alter history, to erase your spiteful father, Prince Aman." Sahreed flicked a tail out of the water with a great whoosh of liquid. "You will also have the power to change destiny of those loyal to you. You could raise Mursas again, I could be king... and you would gain a powerful ally."

Aman licked his lips at this, the idea of so much power went right to his head and he folded his arms as he sat astride the horse. "Very well, I agree to this. Help me gain the Karma Stone and you will be rewarded for your services, both of you."

"Your Highness is very kind." Rhatt's eyes twinkled. "Very kind indeed."

Sahreed smiled once more and dipped his head into the ocean for a moment. "I will meet you out at sea. Fly the black raven flag of the Eastern Corsairs and I will approach your boat. This water does not sit well with me." With that the Merman was gone back under the waves and out of sight as a flock of seagulls circled overhead.

Rhatt clapped his hands together and looked at Prince Aman, "My cousin is an Eastern Corsair. I can have his ship here in a day if you want?"

"Convenient," Aman noted dryly. "Do it."

"Your wish is my command!" Rhatt bowed and made his way back to the road.

Prince Aman spurred his horse along the beach, setting Sultan into a full run. He knew the sands well and the beast relished being given his head. They both needed to race for a while through the shoreline water and kick up spray behind them. Aman had a smile upon his face that was as bright as the sun itself, full of fire and scheming the likes of which the Old Djinn would have been proud. He was followed by the flock of gulls that traced his route for a while before they broke off.

His father would not rule for long...

Aman's race brought him back to the city and back to the palace of his father, King Romas. He left Sultan with the stable hands and hurried to his room. In a flurry of activity he began to pack all the things he would require on this journey, with at least two changes of attire and a pair of curved short swords just in case he was called upon to test his mettle. He put on his best chainmail armor and adjusted his robe over the top of it. He caught his reflection in the mirror and pulled a stern look.

"That is perfect," he said and turned to leave. "Father, count the hours."

As he moved swiftly through the palace and left through the back garden, he passed back towards the stables and took a different horse, his father's very own white mare called Moon. He knew that if he set off now he would soon arrive in Port Lorka to meet with Rhatt and this corsair cousin of his. As Moon raced out of the palace back gate and around the curved road that led to the port Aman left the palace behind just in time.

Two Palace guards burst into his room and found it empty. Behind them stood the towering mass of Kulani, the king's mighty warrior from the dark lands of Karta-Yava. The black skinned mountain of a man wore cured leather armor and carried a huge two-handed sword across his back. He was unhappy, and an expression of deep loathing etched itself against his ebony skin. His one milky white right eye twitched a little as he visually ransacked the room, finding nothing out of place.

"Go get the girl," he commanded of the nearest guard. "Bring her here."

"At once!" the guard said and departed leaving Kulani's side immediately.

Kulani waited and sniffed the air, smelling weak scents and girlish vapors. They made him feel sick. A prince's room should not smell like a young woman's boudoir.

"You called for me, Kulani?"

Sapphire swept into the room in a full length blue dress, her hair pulled back and loaded with precious gemstones. The dress' cut was modest and Kulani approved. He also spotted the concealed knife at her right hip. As his eyes roved over her Sapphire felt his gaze.

"The prince has gone. Do you know where?" Kulani folded his arms.

"I was about to ask you the same question. You interrupted me bringing news to the king," Sapphire grumbled. "Perhaps we should go see him together?"

"An excellent idea," Kulani nodded to this and gestured for the woman to leave. "You can explain to him why the prince was talking to you the other night."

"I intend to, because King Romas is going to want to hear all of this."

"I suspect treachery."

"You don't know the half of it, dear Kulani." Sapphire stormed on towards the king's throne room. "I object to being lumped in with that halfwit. You should know that if I planned King Romas, you or anyone in this palace harm, you wouldn't see it coming."

The servants, the guard, the people all moved out of the pair's way as they made a direct path to the king's throne room. It was only after they reached the grand iron double doors that both of them stopped, adjusted their attire and Kulani pushed open the doors with a large meaty hand.

"Thank you," Sapphire said and passed within. "Manners cost nothing."

"I do not lack them." The man answered.

The throne room of King Romas was part Eastern aesthetic with Western design. It was a meeting of both worlds and echoed the union of the elder man with his wife from foreign shores. It hung with tapestries and chiffon curtains, mixed with heavy wooden chairs and a massive iron and silver throne on which the Old King Romas sat, his crown perched on a brow heavy with a flock of troubles. He brightened when he saw Sapphire however and a rare smile crested his cracked lips.

Sapphire stopped and gave a tiny bow, Kulani on the other hand stood there for a moment and then bowed deeply.

"Sapphire, Kulani," Romas said with a soft voice. "I am pleased to see you, but when I read your faces...I am not so pleased. Tell me then; what troubles do you bring me?"

Sapphire looked to Kulani and then back to the king, pondering the correct way to approach the matter. Finally,

"Prince Aman is missing, he has taken his weapons, his fine armor and his room is empty. I fear he may be plotting against you. He visited me last night in anger, angry at your lack of support for his campaign against Kulani's people. He tried to hire the Shadow Guild."

Kulani's brow furrowed. "What?"

"Yes, he came to me and tried to get me to take out a contract on his own father."

King Romas' eyes grew dark as he listened and his shoulders shook with a slight anger, "Kulani, go to the stables, see if the prince's horse is gone."

"Yes, my king." Kulani was gone the moment he was ordered.

Sapphire watched him leave and frowned herself, "King Romas," she said. "I wish I did not have to tell you this, but your son was spotted on the beach talking to Rhatt. I followed him earlier and he left the city not more than an hour and a half ago. He met Rhatt at the crossroads and they shared a conversation with a merman."

King Romas knew that the Merfolk were not gone. He always held the highest regard for the legends of their people and the stories that followed. He knew that most of his kingdom's advanced technology had come from Mursas in the past. It did not shock him as much as Sapphire thought it would.

"Sapphire," he replied, his face grew stern. "My son is a fool but what can he do with a schemer, a Merman and no support from inside my court?"

"He has more support than you realize. Rhatt has been gathering those who think your son is right in his campaigns." Sapphire grumbled and wrinkled her nose. "I saw them by the fountain, I heard them plotting. King Romas, you have to believe me ... and there's more ... they mentioned the Karma Stone upon the beach."

"How do you know what they said on the beach?"

"I am a Seer, my king, I can see through the eyes of beasts and birds."

"So you spied on them?"

"With a flock of gulls, yes," Sapphire admitted.

King Romas's face grew into a thoughtful expression and he clenched his throne a little tighter. "I was told," he said, "stories of the Karma Stone and what it could do. If Aman can truly find this ancient thing, he could spin it, change his karma and destiny. He could do anything that he wanted."

"Even remove you, my king?" Sapphire sighed.

"Yes."

Kulani returned and he looked angry. "The prince's horse is still here, but he has taken Moon, my king."

King Romas' eyes widened. "Not only does he want my throne, but he takes my prize horse as well?"

"It is indication of his treachery, your Majesty. What do you want me to do?" Kulani was ready to chase the whelp down.

King Romas put his hands on his lap and thought for a while. He wasn't sure of the best course of action to deal with his idiot son. Aman had always been hot-headed, but this had gone beyond his usual brashness. He had to be stopped...

"My son has gone too far," he announced sullenly. "Sapphire, you will stop him. Kulani, I need you here to ferret out his conspirators whilst she is away."

Sapphire blinked and nodded her head, "If my king wishes me to track his son, I will do so. If Prince Aman does not wish to return, if gods forbid that he is to spin the Karma Stone ... what do you wish me to do?"

King Romas' face drew into a dark mood as he said, "Whatever it takes."

Sapphire gave him a bow and looked to Kulani; the dark skinned warrior had a bitter and angry expression. It was as though he wanted to go with her to put a sword in the prince's skull, but his loyalty to King Romas bound him to the Royal Court.

"I will go at once. You can trust me, your Majesty."

Sapphire turned on her heel and fled the king's throne room as quickly as she could go. She had a couple of ideas how to catch Aman and she needed to go see an old friend. Unfortunately, that meant going to the worst place in the kingdom – Blackwater.

The port city of Blackwater lurked like a naughty child in the dark recesses of the kingdom, in a crescent of shoreline that was affectionately dubbed Misfortune Bay. The black sails of the Corsair fleets fluttered prominently from ships large and small, great galleons and slaver vessels sat at the docks and bobbed up and down with the roll of the tide. Even the desert seemed to fear getting too close to this place and it had every right to stay away: Blackwater was trouble with a sharp edge and a bloody history.

No one man or woman ruled the port city. The ruler changed almost weekly and open conflict was a common place occurrence across the streets, violence spilling out from tavern and boarding house, escalating to involve the various factions, all save the Corsairs of Blackwater. They were the one constant that every infighting faction leader wanted to leave well alone. They had a mean streak as wide as the bay itself and one man kept them in check.

Corsair Captain Sebastian Crowcroft. He had been in the bay for around a week, had no idea that Sapphire, one of his oldest companions from back in the day, was coming to see him on a matter that might well see him dead. Sebastian didn't even know that she was only an hour's ride away from Blackwater, a day behind Prince Aman and his comrades in treachery.

Crowcroft was watching a small, fat man being turned upside down and shaken until every coin was dropped from his person. A gang of three men were doing the shaking and they were close to his ship – a dark, grey colored war galleon, with black raven embroidered sails. Its name was the *Silverfish*, a fast vessel, able to run the bay quicker than most racing sloops, and much more of a ship than she seemed.

Sebastian watched the swarthiest thief drop his victim into the water. The fat man landed with a great splash and began to flounder. As the three men laughed and began to collect their loot, the swarthy fellow looked up at the Corsair Captain and stuck his middle finger up at the man.

"If you continue to look at me, pig, I will put your eyes out," he said and spat. "Dog."

"A pig and a dog, Mister Markham?" Sebastian said to a short bald gentleman to his right. "Make a note that I am both a pig and a dog."

Markham winced; he knew instinctively where this was going.

"Did you hear me pig, dog, pig dog? Oink bark oink?" the thief smiled upwards with a gap-toothed grin.

Sebastian leaned over the rail and raised a brow. "I take no offence at those names you call me. Do you know why?" The lean corsair grinned fox-like from beneath a mane of shaggy brown hair.

"You're a coward!" the man said as his comrades laughed.

"Now that I do take offence at."

Quick as a flash Sebastian drew his pistol, opened up on the man with a single shot. A blossoming rose of blood appeared at the thief's forehead and he dropped into the water with a sudden splash. "There we go, problem solved."

The two remaining men dropped their loot and ran, their laughter cut short, replaced by swearing and the sound of receding footfalls. Markham leaned over as well and watched them leave.

"Seriously, Captain, did they not know who you were?" he chuckled.

"Blind, stupid and insolent. Those are the qualities that I like in a man," Sebastian replied and reloaded his gun, "that I am about to kill."

"I was just about to say..."

"So, Mister Markham, how long do we have to wait before we're ready to set sail again?"

"Two more hours, Captain, and we're as free as a bird," Markham replied.

"I like that, Mister Markham." Sebastian put both hands on the rail and took a deep breath. "I have a feeling that there's going to be a change in the air soon."

"I'll keep a watchful eye on the sky then, Captain," Markham answered and took a look over the port. "There's a bit more to do. I'll attend to it now and come see you a little later."

Sapphire rode hard towards the city. She watched every mile pass as she got closer and closer. Just as she crested the north side of the city road she caught sight of Sebastian's ship and dug her heels in further. The beast gave a harsh snort and complied. Gusts of sea wind pulled the sand from the edges of the nearby cliffs and tossed it across the ocean as she finally made it to Blackwater.

The guards watched her, since she was now attired in a travelling cloak and hood. She kept her face veiled and walked proudly by the men as she left her horse tied to a post outside the city at the stable. Passing a stable girl, she passed her a few coins and whispered,

"Keep the horse."

The girl looked at her hands and then at the animal, a wide grin appeared on her lips and she rushed over to it.

Meanwhile Sapphire had gone, making her way quickly through the streets and down to the pier where she headed directly towards the *Silverfish*. A couple of sailors stopped her to enquire her price as a working girl; one of them landed in the water, the other landed on his backside amongst a freshly caught box of snapping crabs. He didn't seem to appreciate that at all.

"Captain Sebastian Crowcroft!" she yelled at the top of her lungs. "Permission to come aboard?"

Sebastian was at the back of the ship and he stopped examining the wheel for a moment, he cocked his head and grinned. "That sounds like a voice I know too well." He raced to the front, mounted the rail and stood there with one hand on a guide rope. "I knew it, blow me for a Kraken! Sapphire!"

"Permission to come aboard?" she tapped her foot and repeated the question.

"Hell yes, lass, come on!" Sebastian kicked the gangplank down for her. "What brings you to my ship?"

As Sapphire mounted the plank she crested the rail and alighted on the deck, she looked to Sebastian's right and back again. "Where's Maria?" she asked.

"Swimming where no one can see her."

"Oh right," Sapphire nodded companionably. "Hiding away from mortal eyes as always."

"Well, the last thing she wants as a mermaid is to be put on someone's plate as a delicacy." Sebastian made a sour face. "You know what she's like with seafood."

Sebastian put his arm around the woman's shoulder and steered her away from the edge of the vessel. "You caught us just at the right time. We were about to set sail and do some corsair work," he grinned a little. "I don't suppose you'd like to join us would you, we could do with your talents and well, you know how much I love to catch up with old friends."

"It's business, not pleasure, my friend," Sapphire frowned. "Orders from the king and I can pay you handsomely."

"Handsomely eh, now that does beg the question. How handsomely, or are we talking a king's gratitude here?"

"Very handsomely." Sapphire tapped Sebastian's fingers on her shoulder. "You remember Prince Aman?"

"Oh do I ever," Sebastian frowned deeply and rolled his eyes. "What I wouldn't give to put a bullet right where the sun never shines on that man."

Sapphire measured her next reply carefully, regarding her friend with a searching gaze. "You may well get that chance."

"What has he done now?"

"Nothing yet, it's what we think he's about to do that concerns us."

"Ok, I'm hooked." Sebastian took his arm from around Sapphire's shoulder and tapped his finger on his chin. "Did he start a war?" He wanted to add an "again" in there somewhere.

"No. He plans to find the Karma Stone and use it." She watched Sebastian's reaction at this little tidbit of information. "To depose the king and make himself the ruler of the kingdom."

Sebastian sat down on a nearby barrel and just shook his head. "If I didn't know what I know already, thanks to Maria, I would say you're mad." He stood up. "I know you're not though and the stone is as real as I am."

"So I can count on you?"

"Always." Sebastian gave a florid bow. "If it means I get to shoot Aman in the arse, so much the better."

A soft voice came from behind the man and the silver haired Maria appeared on deck, she walked stiffly as though she didn't quite know how to move her human-like legs. Her lithe figure was captured in a white ruffled shirt, black breeches, small corsair's boots and she wore a red sash around her waist. Her neck had tiny white lines on either side and her eyes were deep sea green. She was five foot two and slightly muscled.

"Maria!" Sapphire ran past Sebastian and caught the Mermaid in her arms. "It's good to see you."

"Hello, Saph," Maria said and hugged back. It was a strange looking gesture, as though the First Mate of the *Silverfish* wasn't quite comfortable with it. "I am happy to see you again."

"Maria," Sebastian said with a smile. "Sapphire is here to make us lots of money, but you need to take us to Mursas. Prince Aman, the Royal Idiot is going to try and spin the Karma Stone to change his karma. The last thing we want is that brat being king!"

"Aman can't be allowed to get to the stone; it is sacred to what's left of my people." Maria looked utterly shocked.

"I know, but more than that my dear, it's a bloody dangerous artifact and he needs to be kept away from it." Sebastian turned away and began to shout orders to his crew. "Mister Markham, see the good Lady Sapphire is given a grand cabin. The rest of you scallywags and corsairs, let's get this vessel under way. Hop to it now!"

"Thank you, Captain." Sapphire followed Markham as he led her away below decks. "I won't forget this."

"I know you won't." Sebastian mounted the steps that led to the ship's wheel and stood behind it. "Alright you lot, come on, faster now. This ship won't sail itself!"

The crew went into action like a well oiled machine and the ship was soon underway, it cleaved through the waters of the bay and was soon out into the open sea heading towards the Pass of Midnight, which was a pair of black rock outcroppings that formed a natural entry into the bay and the

Craven Reef then finally out into deeper waters and the Sargassa Sea.

For seven days they sailed aboard The *Silverfish* across the Sargassa Sea, guided in part by Maria who spent her time flitting between the deck and the water. In her mer-form she was a beautiful fish-tailed silver-skinned woman that moved like light under the water. Just at the crack of dawn on the seventh day the galleon reached the location where Mursas once floated proudly on the surface of the ocean. Now it was an empty horizon and red tinged clouds floated on by.

Sebastian looked over the side at Maria and nodded to the mermaid. "Okay, my dear, time to go and see what you can see. Just a quick dip and back in a flash."

Maria answered with a quick slap of her tail before she vanished beneath the ocean. Down she dived, cutting the water like a knife, her eyes quickly picking out the various features of the deeper reefs. When she was leagues beneath the sea she stopped and peered out at the ruin of Mursas. It was a circular city, covered in seaweed and the once bright lights that burned there remained steadfastly dark against the murky depths. The once proud green marble towers had fallen to the sea bed and arches of stone lay cracked on the floor. Her heart sank though when she saw a massive iron ship that resembled a giant octopus just curled over one of the ruined domes. She didn't linger though; she retraced her steps and burst upwards at the port side of the *Silverfish*.

Sapphire looked over the side with the captain and waved, "Well?"

"Aman is there. The Iron Kraken sits over my father's observation dome, lurking and just waiting for them to return to it."

"The Iron Kraken," Sebastian stroked his chin. "That would be one heck of a fight."

"How about we sneak in?" Sapphire said helpfully and smiled. "Just for a change?"

"Oh," Sebastian shrugged. "Alright, we'll sneak in."

"Thank you," Sapphire gave him a kiss on the cheek. "So how do we get down there?"

"Old Djinn trick," Sebastian gave a wicked chuckle and walked to the wheel. "Okay, crew, prepare to dive."

Several sharp bells sounded in the depths of the ship and the sails began to pull closed, with a whisper and click of cogs, gears and pulleys they were drawn tight and the masts folded down along the deck. Sapphire marveled at the transformation, as in a few minutes the *Silverfish* changed from a galleon into something else. A large wooden construction ratcheted over the main deck and enclosed them in a protective shell. Lastly a few portholes slid open along the walls and behind the ship a circular notched engine locked into place.

"How?" Sapphire said as the interior lit up.

"The *Silverfish*," Sebastian said with a proud grin. "Is one of the Seven Ancient Devices of Mursas."

"How did you get it?"

"Maria brought it with her, it's how she escaped the demise of her people. Time enough for stories later, for now, we dive!"

With that the *Silverfish* dipped into the water and curled beneath the surface churning white foam as it did so. The ancient device from the Age of Mer had no problem navigating the reefs, the coral tunnels and the deeper water that would allow it to approach the city undetected. The quiet vessel made good time and soon arrived at the outer edge of Mursas; it approached stealthily from the Iron Kraken's blind side and slipped into an opening in one of the ruined walls. Maria followed closely to the side of the ship, guiding it as she swam here and there.

Finally the *Silverfish* made it to an internal docking hub, where it settled into a berth that hadn't been used for centuries. It still fit the mechanism like a glove and even Maria was amazed that the city still had enough power to operate the docking site.

Sebastian and Sapphire convened outside of the ship wearing collars of polished bronze and gold. These collars were gifts from the ancient Djinn and protected the wearer from the pressure of the ocean below, as well as allowed them to breathe under the depths. Maria didn't need that kind of protection of course, she was a mermaid and to her the crushing pressure was nothing.

Maria gave a swish of her tail to indicate they should follow and swam off towards one of the exits. Mursas was a beautiful place with curves and spheres, with no crude angles dominating its architecture.

Sebastian and Sapphire swam after her and the three of them flitted through Mursas' dead corridors as they searched for the chamber that held the Karma Stone. It didn't take them long to find it; Prince Aman's meddling had left a trail that even a child could follow and finally that trail led to a long forgotten chamber deep beneath the city.

Aman had had the foresight to bring with him a sorcerer. The robed woman held back the water with her magic, her hands outstretched and a low lamenting chant echoing from her lips.

The prince, Rhatt and Sahreed all stood at the centre of the domed room. Before them a giant wheel of green stone etched with the ancient tongue of the Mer dominated the chamber and stood over ten feet in height.

"The Karma Stone, my prince," Rhatt said and gave a little bow. "All you need to do is spin the wheel and be reborn as the true king."

"That's it?" Aman didn't sound convinced.

"Yes, just that."

"It sounds a little anti-climactic. I expected something grander."

Aman reached out his hand, just as Sebastian made a rash and possibly unwise decision. He drew a pistol crossbow from under his coat, aimed it and let the bolt loose at the sorcerer. It flew straight and true, quietly impaling the woman in the throat. She lost the words and the ocean came crashing back in just as the prince had spun the wheel. The water slammed in past the failing barrier of magic and Rhatt was swept off his feet and out into a nearby corridor, knocked cold by the force of the blast.

Sahreed flitted through the water and fought the onrush. He went for the corsair and Maria intercepted him with a snarl. Sapphire clung onto the nearest surface and kicked against the water as the whole area flooded and stabilized, the look she gave Sebastian enough to wither a tree.

Once the churning ocean onrush had died down Sebastian looked around and saw Maria grappling with Sahreed. She bit hard into the other Mer's shoulder and her sharp teeth drew a horrible wound. Sapphire was swimming towards Aman as the prince floated before the wheel. Aman gave the wheel a spin as the weight of water overwhelmed him, not quite turning it as far as he could however. His body lit with a bright glare, the water around him bubbled and vaporized as he simply vanished. The stone had done its job...

"No!" mouthed Sapphire and kicked at the wheel, it moved a notch but nothing else happened. "No, no, no!"

Maria finally managed to damage Sahreed's gills and he kicked away from her leaking blood into the water, as the whole room shuddered and a low sonar groan rumbled by. Out of the corner of her eye Maria saw a dark shape edge closer. This was no Iron Kraken, it was the real thing. She swam over to Sapphire and tugged her arm, the wild look in the mermaid's eyes told the other woman all she needed to know.

They rejoined Sebastian and left via the same corridor as Rhatt. Suspiciously the little man had vanished as well. They didn't have time to look for him as the first tentacle of the Kraken's massive form slammed into the room behind them. They swam quickly back towards the *Silverfish* and whilst Maria continued on and up towards the surface, Sapphire and Sebastian rejoined the crew aboard the ship.

The *Silverfish* wasted no time at all in getting out of the docking chamber; it broke free from the mechanism and flowed upwards. A single tentacle reached out and narrowly missed the sleek ship as it sped past. The Kraken turned its attention to the Iron Kraken that sat nearby and lurched towards it, both crashed together as the ship tore through the water and out of danger.

"Damn, Sebastian," Sapphire nearly hit the captain. "You could have warned us, you probably let him complete his task by shooting that sorcerer."

"Sorry," the captain held onto the wheel. "Shout at me later, avoiding large and hungry water beast right now."

"Later I might just kill you."

"Good, kill me later."

Meanwhile Sahreed was badly injured and swimming at half speed, he couldn't breathe properly and didn't notice the giant white shark close in until its jaws clamped shut with a final snap.

Once the *Silverfish* broke the surface of the water and Maria was safely back on the vessel, Sebastian frowned a little and ordered his crew to set course back to Blackwater. He looked at both women, they wore similar expressions.

"Ok, perhaps I was rash. You're alive; I'm alive and think about it ... Aman didn't get to spin the wheel the whole way."

"So?"

"Well, you only get your karmic wish if you spin the wheel properly."

"I hope you're right," Sapphire said and stalked off to her cabin. "I really hope you're right."

"Trust me!"

Maria gave him a look and followed the other woman, leaving Sebastian Crowcroft to stand on the deck of the *Silverfish*. He looked out at the sea and turned his attention to the view from the porthole as the ocean waves sped past.

After a few hours the vessel passed a small island and as Aman watched it from the shoreline, he looked out at the giant ocean beyond him and then at a very big bird that landed close by. He snorted and moved sideways to get away from the seagull.

"Away, vermin," he demanded.

"Squawk," said the bird.

"Away, don't you know who I am?"

The seagull looked down at Aman and ruffled its wings, then took off with a shrill cry. It had been disturbed by the figure of Rhatt who stood in the sand not far from Aman. The thin man laughed loudly.

"Oh my prince, my new king." He knelt down and picked Aman from the shore. "You wear that crown so well."

"What do you want, imbecile?" Aman asked.

Rhatt ignored him and sniffed the air. "Do you think you'd go well with butter?"

Aman looked at his hand, only it wasn't a hand, it was a claw. He clicked it near Rhatt's face in response.

"Ooh, be careful, you almost had me there." Rhatt held Aman an arm's length away as he walked across the beach. "Like any gift of the Djinn, little prince, you must beware of the price."

"I am king!" Aman said.

Rhatt couldn't hear him. "Spin the wheel, be a king reborn? Did you not ask yourself why the Mer never spun the wheel for themselves? Even with a proper spin, destiny's change is seldom for the better – as you now know, Aman, King of the Crabs."

He grabbed the prince by the claw and walked towards where he'd set his camp fire. At least tonight Aman would actually be of some use.

As the *Silverfish* receded across the ocean's horizon Aman let out a scream and fell silent. Rhatt dined well enough and lay back to watch the stars pop out, drifting off to a full and lazy sleep.

THE STORM DRAIN
C. Ellett Logan

Lolly slid her feet around on her bubblegum pink sheets to find a cool, unused spot – then aimlessly walked two fingers down a row of chenille sprouts on her coverlet. Elementary school was over. Middle school was three months away. All of her girlfriends were either at camp or on vacation with their families.

"I'm stuck in this dump," she cried, "with nothing to do."

Without enthusiasm she got up, pulled on shorts and a t-shirt and plodded to the bathroom to plaster her cowlicky bangs to her forehead with water. A white plastic headband smoothed her flyaway blonde wisps, its tiny teeth separating her hair like the tufts on her bedspread.

Downstairs Lolly found her two brothers – Trouble and Trouble's Shadow – in the kitchen scarfing cereal at opposite ends of the table. She ate her Captain Crunch standing at the counter, watching half in disgust and half in admiration as her younger brother James crammed his mouth so full, milk seeped through his tightly pressed lips. When her brothers finished eating, they bolted out the front door instead of taking their dishes to the sink.

"Hey! Get back here and clean up!" she yelled, knowing it wouldn't do any good. As usual, it fell to her to clear away the mess.

Trying in vain to think of something to do with her day, Lolly opened the back door to a warm June breeze that sucked through the kitchen, causing a door upstairs to slam shut.

"Guys?" she called as she walked down the steps of the side porch. Following the raised voices coming from the backyard, she found her brothers sharpening Popsicle sticks against the bricks of the garage.

"Give me one," she said.

She and her brothers dug for earthworms in the crushed-Oreo soil of their mother's newly-turned flowerbed. But as soon as Lolly snagged one of the fleshy things, Whit and James jumped up and headed to the next street and the yard with the German Shepherd puppies.

Lolly put her head down, kept her tears in, and hung back a few minutes. She wouldn't cry, wouldn't give them the satisfaction of hearing her beg them to wait for her. Until her girlfriends got back to town, she'd have to shadow her brothers around the neighborhood and play their sorry version of tag. It sucked, but not as much as being alone.

As soon as Lolly reached her brothers at the yard with the puppies, the kid who lived there walked straight up to her, jerked the plastic headband from her head, and sailed it over the fence.

"Hey!" Lolly's hand flew up, but not in time.

She forced her way through the gate and into yipping balls of brown fur to retrieve the headband, then the kids spent all afternoon goofing around in the shade of the carport. The boys teased her, trying to outdo one another at her expense.

After gobbling supper with their own families, they gathered together in front of the carport and glared at the kids across the street. Mickey, a boy from their school, was at the end of his driveway with his two cousins from Boston. The trio had the same dark shaggy looks, except the cousin in high school wore a cigarette tucked behind his ear. They were damming up water as it streamed along the curb from the old lady's rose garden at the top of the hill. The smallest cousin was busy plastering the rock stack with mud.

Whit, Lolly's older brother, walked over and kicked out the supports of the dam. The pressure of the rushing water sluiced most of the stones and debris into the sewer. Laughing, he ran back to the German Shepherds' yard, twisted Lolly's arms behind her, and held her like a shield between the angry cousins and himself.

"War!" Mickey yelled as Lolly jerked free from her brother and both groups tore out, whooping, toward a small stand of trees and brush in the median, picking up pinecones as they ran.

Mickey pumped one volley after another at Lolly, the missiles finding their target in rapid succession. She hollered and swore, but couldn't look up more than a second without getting her face pummeled. Because she had to keep her head down, she noticed the rectangular opening in the gutter she'd climbed through the previous summer to retrieve a runaway skateboard. She'd been surprised by the spaciousness of the brick-lined storm drain under the street, and at the light spilling in through small drains along the gutter above.

To save herself now, Lolly slid into the storm drain opening and over the lip of the wet gutter to safety, gratefully landing on her feet beneath the street.

As her eyes adjusted to the gloom she heard James talking above. "Lolly's a big fat chicken."

"Forget about her." Whit's voice became fainter as the boys moved off. "We didn't want her hanging around with us anyway."

Dusk was coming on, but Lolly could still make out the details of the long expanse before her – an arched space in which she could almost stand up straight. A few inches of rust-colored water flowed at her feet. She placed one sneaker on either side of the stream, bowed her head slightly, and walked toward the dab of light at the far end.

In the brighter sections below the drains, objects had color, and Lolly realized that the concrete floor she thought empty was littered with junk. She stepped over a lawn chair with only half its webbing, an anti-freeze jug, and a man's brown dress shoe.

She stopped to examine liquid seeping through the wall, wrinkling her nose at the sharp smell. A nearby splash echoed in the tunnel. She whipped around, but couldn't pinpoint the source of the sound. She spun forward again and squinted at the stretch of tunnel just ahead. A debris pile had formed against the curved wall, the largest mound of rubble in either direction. Another splash. The pile quivered.

"Who's there?" she called. "This is so not funny."

Lolly's shaking knees didn't knock like they do in scary movies, but her teeth did.

"Don't be such a baby," she said out loud. The only reply was the gurgle of flowing water.

She stepped closer to the heap, froze, then shook her head to clear it. In the murky rivulet just beyond a logjam of trash, bricks, and scraps of wood, a partially submerged girl floated next to a small overturned shopping cart.

In spite of her fear, Lolly rushed over to the motionless form. Several long strands of the child's butter-colored hair were wrapped around one wheel of the cart, another hank was tangled in the spokes, the rest drifted back and forth in the tea-colored water above her bare chest. Suddenly, the rail-thin little one struggled to raise her head and shoulders, wincing with pain.

Lolly fought the urge to call out for Whit as she pressed herself against the wall. She knew he wouldn't climb down into the dank smelly storm drain, even if he did hear her.

"What are you doing down here?" she asked instead. Her voice boomed in the tight space of the drain pipe, causing the girl to thrash and the overturned cart to jerk and scrape the bricks.

This was too much for Lolly who ran back the way she had come. Almost immediately though, she ordered herself to search the floor of the tunnel for anything she could use to cut the trapped hair.

"It's all right, sweetie. I'll get you out of here," Lolly called more bravely than she felt. Finally, she spotted a tuna can with its opened lid wedged inside.

She approached as gingerly as she could. "I won't hurt you, but I need to cut your hair loose."

The child didn't answer, just opened and closed her mouth, panting. In the light coming through a grate above, beneath the film of white covering the girl's enormous eyes, Lolly could see specks of green in her irises.

The hair felt like thick yarn as Lolly sawed the captured snarls with the sharp-edged lid. The girl reached up to feel each freed strand. Lolly unwound a few cut locks from the wheel, tucking them into her pocket. As the last piece was snipped, the girl sat up at the same time a large fin, a tailfin, rose up and splashed back into the water.

At the sight of the tail, Lolly lost her footing and sat down with a splash herself. She rubbed her eyes and stammered, "Wha … what are you?" She didn't really want to hear "mermaid." She didn't believe in mermaids. But then again, she didn't believe in a half-naked kid stuck to a shopping cart in a storm drain either.

"How did you get in here? And trapped by this cart?"

The child turned her head toward the circle of light at the far end of the tunnel. The fin, the color and glossiness of the grass in the Easter basket Lolly still had on her dresser at home, rose up again and slapped the water's surface – its swishing movement frightening Lolly even more. She could never imagine anything moving like that.

"Did the flooding last week wash you in here?" Lolly was soaking wet and shivering. The girl looked toward the light again, her pale lips trembling, too.

"Okay." Lolly gulped hard. "You want me to take you down there?"

As if to answer, the girl sank back into the water. Lolly approached and slipped her hands around the child's cold fingers. Walking backward was clumsy, and having to scrunch over to avoid banging her head, uncomfortable. She knew they would make better progress if she just picked her up, but the thought of getting a clear look at the tailfin again was just too scary.

The going got even more difficult. Lolly had to crane her neck over her shoulder to check the floor of the tunnel after every two or three steps. She stopped to shove a snarl of plastic soda bottles and yard clippings up onto the dry bricks bordering the stream, sick with worry because instead of fluidly moving as before, the creature's tailfin floated lifelessly near the top of the water. Lolly got a better grip and pulled the child along by her delicate wrists, but even though the creature's arms and shoulders were up, her head slumped back.

Lolly wanted her mother.

Suddenly, the water rushing to get out of the tunnel made everything go faster. Lolly twisted around to see how close she was to the end. Her heart sank. The exit was partially blocked with bulky rubble. She let go of the child again and struggled to drag a large branch out of the way.

She stacked some of the junk to one side of the opening so she could get a peek outside. The height of the drain was only a few feet above the creek, but there were several large rocks spilling from the bank directly below.

Finally, she cleared a narrow path to the end.

"Can you get down from up here?" Lolly asked, worried now that her struggles to this point had been for nothing.

The girl didn't answer, just floated, her face turned to the side, half in and half out of the water.

"Please." Lolly lowered her shaking hand and turned the pale face toward her. "You're almost free." She smoothed sodden tendrils back from the girl's forehead with her other hand so she could look into the cloudy eyes. "What can I do to help you?" Lolly was crying now.

Somehow she understood what she needed to do, but was afraid to touch the creature's translucent skin in order to turn her onto her stomach. She did it anyway.

The child pushed her torso up and locked her elbows. She wriggled back a few inches and with a wave-motion, shot forward. Just clearing the rocks on the bank below, she disappeared under the water.

Lolly bent over, put her hands on her knees and breathed in and out, in and out. Big gulps of air. Then, to stay above the junk and muck, she braced her back against one side of the brick enclosure, straightened her legs, and placed her feet on a wedged wooden crate. She leaned outward and waited, scanning the creek, straining to see details in the fading light. After a few minutes, small fish leapt high out of the water in an area to her left, and seconds later, more jumped to her right. Near the commotion she caught sight of the creature's tailfin cutting the surface, sparkling like an emerald in the last rays of the setting sun.

Lolly wasn't ready to leave the child, but knew she could get hurt walking through the tunnel in the dark of night. She turned and moved quickly but carefully toward the rectangle of light where she'd started, a destination fading grayer and more shadow-like as she stumbled toward home.

No one will believe this, she thought. She felt the strands of hair in her pocket, not sure if their existence made her feel better or worse. I saved the life of a mermaid.

As she climbed out through the storm drain she could hear Whit calling her name. She didn't jump right up, but sat on the curb watching him pump the pedals of his bike, round the cul-de-sac and catch sight of her. She noticed his relief in the sudden hiccup of his shoulders and in the way he jerked up his head.

"The streetlight's been on for almost an hour," he said as he got near.

The streetlight coming on signaled their mother's most steadfast rule — time for the siblings to go inside for the night.

No longer worried that his sister was dead, or worse, Whit was enjoying telling Lolly how much trouble she was in, laying it on thick, looping her in ever-widening circles with his bike as she walked home.

"What happened to you down there?" he demanded.

Lolly made an instant decision never to share her encounter. "None-ya."

He popped a wheelie and sped off, calling out one last dig with dramatic flourish, "You are soooo grounded."

Something amazing had happened that day after all, Lolly thought. She felt the strands of hair in her pocket again and looked back at the dark opening in the gutter. Maybe, sometimes, it only seems like we're alone.

AT THE WATERLINE
Terri Osborne

"It was the Law of the Sea, they said. Civilization ends at the waterline. Beyond that, we all enter the food chain, and not always right at the top."
Hunter S. Thompson

The smell of brine was still the warm embrace of home.

It was 1940. The Germans were giving the fish in what you call the South Atlantic plenty of places to play. They were hunting merchant vessels like sharks within a school of fish, and prisoners were filling their cargo holds.

I had been appointed by King Haakon VII as the official Liaison to the Royal Norwegian Navy. While he held the title of King, Haakon had actually been elected to the throne after Norway and Sweden decided they didn't want to play together anymore. Ever the politician, Haakon had the thought that seeing a woman in a position of power might be good for some of his commanding officers. Fortunately for him, the Nøkken had agreed. What Haakon hadn't fully comprehended, however, was the nature of the woman he was sending to the Navy. No one had told him that I was a mermaid. The Nøkken had ensured that one of their legal enforcers made the deal, who kept that particular detail close to his proverbial vest.

The Royal Navy wouldn't know what I was, either. That was one of the great secrets. Humans weren't the only ones fighting the Nazis. I walked among the sailors during the day, and patrolled the fjords at night, all to ensure the safety of the Nøkken's Realm.

One cold, February day, I found Rear Admiral Carsten Tank-Nielsen in his office, pouring over messages from the government back in Oslo. The electric light overhead reflected off his balding pate as I entered. His eyes were deep, as though he'd already seen the world and found it lacking. He was focused on a report in his hand. I had a feeling I knew what it was about.

There was a ship, a German tanker named the *Altmark*. It was known to have been assisting a small pocket battleship christened the *Admiral Graf Spee* in raiding merchant ships in the southern Atlantic. They were very good about striking in international waters. The raids had finally stopped when the *Graf Spee* had been scuttled off the River Plate near Argentina in December. There had been no merchant sailors on board, however. Where were all of the prisoners that had been taken from the merchant ships? That was the mystery the humans were trying to sort.

"Admiral," I said, "we need to keep watch for their supply ship. Intelligence from our allies in Argentina suggests that the prisoners taken by the *Graf Spee* might have been transferred to the *Altmark* for transport back to Germany."

His desk looked as though a paper factory had exploded. That surface must have been cut from wood as dense as a sperm whale. It was massive, a sculpted behemoth with curves worthy of Bergslien himself. I'd seen Tank-Nielsen dress down sailors half his age with a simple glare across that desk. He picked up one piece of paper, looking at me with a weary gaze. "We have similar intelligence, Astrid. However, these same reports show they were British sailors. Norway is neutral ground in their war. You know that as well as I. I've already ordered that any news of the *Altmark* is to come to me immediately. I am not certain what we will do if we find them, but we need to know if they approach."

British merchant sailors. The last thing anyone in the Realms wanted to do at that time was help the British. Still, these were human beings being held against their will.

"I will talk with my superiors, Admiral. There has to be something we can do to stop the Germans."

At that point the war was just beginning. Germany had invaded Poland the previous September. Great Britain had begun massing soldiers and teamed with the French – an idea that the shapeshifters in Europe had protested quite vehemently – to declare an ultimatum for Germany to vacate Poland. Germany, of course, ignored it. Chamberlain declared war the very next day. The rest, as they say, was history.

When my meeting with Tank-Nielsen finished, I slipped into some heavy boots and walked back to the shore at the Nordnesparken. The snow wasn't deep, but this form of water wasn't quite as welcoming to me as the oceans. Walking could be enough of a chore. Adding in the shoes simply bothered my inner ear. I was far happier barefoot than I ever would be in shoes, but that would never work in the snow. I wasn't particularly fond of frostbite.

I worked my way down footpaths to the shore. There was a stone outcrop at the northernmost point of the park where humans would occasionally fish. There were no humans there, not that day. The air had that wonderfully crisp aroma that only comes on a clear winter's day.

"My lord? May I have a moment?" The fact that there were no humans present kept me from looking like a madwoman speaking to no one. I suppose some might have thought I was praying to the god of the Christians. I'd seen humans speaking to the air when addressing their deity. Unlike those humans, I was expecting a response. This was the Nøkken, after all.

The water crept in and out with each wave, a lullaby for aquatics. In the corner of my eye, I spotted a mass of sea grass that should not have been that far in from the border islands.

"My lord?"

The gurgle of a clogged bathroom drain was followed by a groan. Under the sea grass, a body began to rise. It looked like a man, but if any human had been watching they'd have realized it wasn't one of them. The sea grass clung to the Nøkken's body like a heavy cloak, leaving only glowing yellow eyes watching me as he rose. "Mermaid." His voice was a rush of darkness, like the maelstrom of Moskstraumen given the ability to speak. "Why do you disturb me?"

I bowed, and then fell to one knee. Snow be damned, protocol was protocol. We weren't even in the wave pools of Gulen, let alone the palace. How else were we to keep order? "How stands our relationship with Britain, my lord?"

"As frigid as ever. The shapeshifters sent an envoy when war was declared, but they were turned away before they could cross the Channel."

"The Unseelies wish to ensure Britain's continued disassociation with the Realms?" I asked, slowly standing.

"By the sword's point, if necessary."

The Unseelies. Thanks to Lord Thomas of Malmesbury, those evil little creatures had done their best to ensure no creature of any Realm stepped foot onto British soil. If a foolish supernatural did make that mistake? Suffice to say that their stay would not be pleasant, and they were usually encouraged to leave with whatever weapon in the arsenal would most efficiently kill them. They had even developed a silver bullet loaded with splinters and holy water, which was then blessed by the Pope himself, just for the Coteanno family. If they were willing to do that for vampires, I wasn't sure I wanted to know what they had in mind for someone like me.

Peace offering after peace offering had been rebuffed. There had to be some way to try to break the standoff.

"What if we could rescue some of their humans?"

That took the Nøkken aback. "What do you mean?"

I took a deep breath, allowing the misty air to relax me a bit. "There is a ship, my lord. A Nazi tanker. The Mayup Mamman in Argentina believes it now carries prisoners of war."

"British prisoners, I presume?"

"Yes, my lord. Mayup Mamman believes the ship is heading north. It is trying to stay within international waters to escape mandatory boarding actions."

The Nøkken appeared dubious. At least, that was what I thought the sideways cant to his waterlogged head meant. "And what do you believe we could do, young one?"

I took a deeper breath. I was being tested. There was no doubt about it. Pass and I remained where I was. Fail and only the Nøkken himself knew what would happen.

"I believe we could keep a sea watch, my lord. If this ship takes the path of least resistance back to a German port, that move will undoubtedly bring it through your waters. The humans on board, all of them, both German and British, would then be under your charge."

He paused for a moment. In all of the decades I'd been in his service, this was the first time I'd been able to get a semblance of an idea being considered. Usually, I was simply too young to know what I was speaking about, so be gone with me. This time, though …

"They have declared war, Astrid. The humans involved are mutual belligerents. You know our role is not to protect them from themselves. It is no longer our job to play deity."

He was right. Part of the Treaty of the Realms was that the humans would be left to their own devices as much as supernaturally possible. We would be fellow inhabitants of the planet, but they had the right to choose their own path. Some humans had chosen paths that intersected with the Realms, but those unfortunate souls usually ended up in Italy with the vampires. The Scandinavian lands under my lord's protection had, thus far, been quite peaceful.

"Do you not also have the right to protect your subjects from the side effects of human belligerence? If humans fire against us, can we not protect ourselves?"

The sea grass covering most of his face rustled. "What are you considering, mermaid?"

I quickly shook my head. "Nothing, my lord. I am merely trying to understand the nuances of the situation in order to advise Admiral Tank-Nielsen accordingly. I wish to keep him from aggravating the Unseelies as well as the Germanic shapeshifters."

Those glowing yellow eyes stared back at me. There was a weight in my chest – no, in my soul – that said he was measuring my heart. He was measuring my truth; not the truth I was telling, but the truth of my being.

"Is that not the job you have tasked me with, my lord?"

"It is now," he said, punctuating it with what looked like a nod. "Know this, if there is an incident, it will be on your head."

I knew it was probably more "off with my head", but bowed anyway. Deference, always. "Understood, my lord."

"Swim. Watch the borders. I will consider what to do with the ship if it enters my waters."

"Yes, my lord. I will apprise you if the situation changes."

A rustle of wet leaves, the gurgle of a dead drain, and he was gone. I didn't like the situation at all. Still, I had my swimming orders.

When night fell, I headed out toward the west. There was a tiny spot near the shore where I had long ago dug out a crevasse in which to put my clothes while I swam. As soon as my legs hit the water, my tail re-appeared. It was the charm cast upon those of the waters who served. No, there was no pain. Not anymore, at least. My skin just turned back to the scaly texture I was born with, and it encased my legs to help me swim. Before you ask, no, it never happened when I took a bath. It only happened with the organic components of seawater. Simple saline water wouldn't do it. It was the life in the water that triggered the change. It was returning to my home, and being with my fellow ocean-dwellers.

When I got into the current, I simply swam. A grey seal accompanied me for a few hundred meters before breaking off to return to his pod. The seal's companionship helped me relax and think. Being back in the water didn't hurt, either. There was something about water flowing that just made thinking so much easier.

That, unfortunately, had been my first mistake. When I began thinking, the "what if's" began coming. What if the ship crossed into Nøkken waters? What if the Germans had British prisoners? What would the Unseelies do if we did help them? What would the Germanic shifters do if we attacked a Nazi ship? I'd heard reports coming out of Europe that the shapeshifters were trying to mount some kind of shadow resistance, use their abilities to help eliminate the Nazis from the area, but even a shifter's stealth only went so far.

For a long, long moment, I simply floated on my back and stared up at the stars. Cassiopeia was clear in those stars, her head dipping into the water as Zeus mandated. There was a rumble in the depths of the water, and I briefly wondered if the Kraken might be stirring. Taking a deep breath, I dove as deeply as I could, swimming until my lungs hurt from the pressure. The moonlight was barely reaching those depths. I let out the most melodic burst of singing I could muster, considering I wasn't a siren. My hope was that the song of a fellow creature might keep the Kraken from causing trouble. I pulled up short when I realized that the water temperature was changing. There wasn't any physical dividing line that could be seen as it was crossed. We knew where our borders lay. I wasn't in our waters any longer. It wasn't the Kraken I was hearing. It was the rumble of a ship in the distance.

There were no lights to give it away. The only sound was the engines pushing it through the water. It was a ship in hiding.

I swam closer, trying to keep my profile as low as possible. It was a solid ship, big as the Norwegian tankers in Bergen harbor. The hull above the waterline looked as though it had been repainted several times in recent months. Still, I could make out the white block letters that had been repeatedly buried. *Altmark.*

I quickly looked around. Where was I? How close were they to our waters? The ship steamed on, either not noticing or not caring about my presence. I pulled up alongside, swimming as quickly as I could. Not even a mermaid could keep up with a ship at full steam, not for long. I ducked in close to the lower hull. I don't know what I'd been hoping for, but I hoped. What would be the sound that told whether prisoners were on board? Just above the waterline was a row of dirty portholes. Crew quarters, perhaps? It was the single clean window, set by itself against the black of the hull, which held my attention. Why would one window …

A dark-skinned face peered out. Prisoners. The Nazis, with their obsessive racial purity, would never have a Nubian on a ship's crew.

I'd found the ship that the British fleet had been hunting for months.

They were taking the northern route home. *Altmark* was undoubtedly heading toward a northern German port. It would go through Norwegian waters. If it didn't go through our waters, they'd have no choice but to venture too close to British territory. The Brits would spot them and those prisoners would be in the middle of a firefight.

The sound of a male voice speaking German caused me to duck underwater and back off from the ship. I couldn't risk being spotted. I didn't understand what the man was saying, but I knew if he saw me, my chance of returning to Norway was lost.

I left a part of my heart at that ship that night. These were human beings, imprisoned and headed for certain death. Gathering my bearings, I headed back to Bergen harbor. I had a briefing with Tank-Nielsen the next afternoon. I needed to talk to the boss.

I was back at the park the next morning, my coat pulled tight against the chill. "My lord, there's been a change."

A gurgle near the water's edge once again announced his presence. Wet leaves slipped across the shore, and once again I was looking into those yellow eyes. This time, there was a burst of steam from his mouth as he spoke. "What is it, mermaid?"

I bowed. "My lord, while patrolling last night, I found them."

"Where?" he said, emotionless.

"They were bearing east-southeast near the Faeroe Islands. They are not in our waters yet, but they are coming our way."

If water could laugh, that might have approximated the sound I heard from my lord's throat. "How can you be so certain?"

I folded my hands behind my back. "My lord. The trajectory of the ship's travel takes her to the fjords north of Bergen. I was not able to stay with her long enough to get an accurate assessment of how fast she's traveling, but if she keeps her current course, I believe she will be in our waters within forty-eight hours."

His eyes turned to the water. "Forty-eight hours?"

"Yes, my lord."

"Have you shared this with the humans yet?"

"No, my lord."

"Good." For the first time since I'd been in the Nøkken's service, I saw him pace. He began walking along the shoreline, one sea grass-covered foot in front of the other. He looked like a wet hill had come to life.

"My lord, the humans. If they see you ..."

"That is not your concern."

Well, it was, because if he was exposed to the general population so was I, but we had bigger problems on our plate at that moment. "Of course not. What is your plan?"

His head turned with a slowness that rivaled a sea horse. One thing I hadn't noticed when we'd spoken the day before grabbed my attention: the clear, crisp smell of the winter's day was fading away. Replacing it was the damp, almost musty aroma of soil. It was like being in a greenhouse right after the farmer had watered the seedlings, but without the heat. "My plan?"

I had a very bad feeling about that tone. "We could attempt to save the prisoners. I saw a Nubian looking through the porthole. Apedemak would be indebted if we saved one of his."

"He would be unable to assist us if the Unseelies took umbrage. And the Unseelies will take umbrage."

A vision of the Unseelies being publicly embarrassed by another Realm saving their humans appeared in my mind. The incident with the Coteannos had driven them toward isolationism a century before. The British teaming with the French in the human war probably already annoyed them. An annoyed Unseelie was not something for the faint of heart. The dark fae could take a lower supernatural apart with a thought.

"Have we been able to get an operative into Scotland to infiltrate the Unseelies?"

My lord shook his head.

"Not even the freelancers?"

"They were the first to run away. The cowards."

"What would you like me to do my lord? The admiral will wish some guidance."

The Nøkken stared out over the water. I followed his gaze to the horizon, where I saw a ship heading out into the North Sea. "We allow the humans to do as they will. This is their war, not ours. We cannot risk the Unseelie becoming involved."

"My lord, what about what I found last night?"

"What of it?"

I could believe what he was saying. "You would leave those humans to die, my lord? If that ship reaches German shores, the Nazis will imprison them."

He stared at me, those eyes glowing like yellow diamonds. "Humans are to be left to their own devices. We agreed to that centuries ago."

My stomach turned. I understood the logic, but it was so cold, so heartless. I had never seen him act like that toward the humans. Even during the last war, when Norway had tried so hard to remain neutral, the humans had received a modicum of compassion.

"Mermaid, the humans will find that ship on their own. Do I make myself clear? You will not give over this information."

My heart started racing. What was I supposed to tell Tank-Nielsen? He'd ordered that any information on *Altmark* be immediately passed on to him. I opened my mouth to protest, but closed it when I realized that the Nøkken's order were sacrosanct. I was to liaise with the humans on behalf of the

Realm. We were supposed to cultivate a unity of effort, not stonewall the humans. These orders went directly against that mandate. Tank-Nielsen's orders had been to his people, not me.

It was my responsibility to find a way to resolve that disparity.

"Yes, my lord. I understand."

He slipped back into the water, disappearing into the depths without so much as a dismissal. It couldn't have been an easy call. If it were an internal dispute, confined to the humans of his Realm, I was fairly certain his response would have been different. However, the British involvement was the problem. We had no idea then that the Germanic shifters were involved with the Nazis. They were territorial creatures. If the British humans fell to the whim and fancy of the German shifters? I didn't want to imagine.

I walked back to the coast. I had already missed the scheduled meeting with the admiral. I wasn't ready to talk to him yet, not at that point. I put my clothes into that crevasse, and dove into the water. I needed to do a lot of thinking at that moment. I swam back out west. There was something in me that needed to see that ship again, during the daylight this time. I had to see what flag it flew. I had to see the repainted hull in the light of the sun.

I needed to know if putting myself on the line was worth it.

I swam around for hours, while the sun passed directly above and began the trek toward its evening slumber. Question after question ran through my head. Didn't we have stewardship of the planet? Didn't we have a responsibility to guard the lower supernaturals? Didn't we have a responsibility to help those who could not help themselves?

My conscience was screaming at me to go back and tell Tank-Nielsen what I'd seen. If the tables were turned and I was in that prison hold, would I want humans helping me, or leaving me to my own devices like an abandoned animal?

But the Nøkken was right. From his own perspective, the leaders of the Realms had agreed that humans would be left alone. We would no longer interfere in human development. We would no longer play at being deities. If one Realm contravened, it opened the door for the others.

However, the Nazis were proving to be such violent oppressors that someone would need to step in. If we insisted upon remaining neutral, how were we not aiding and abetting those oppressors? Was it possible to remain neutral in the face of a power that thought it perfectly fine to just walk into a neighboring country and take it over?

Theoretically, the Realms could not get involved in the humans' war. What could not be ignored was that we already were involved. How could we possibly not be? Nobody knew how big the war would become at that point, but one thing was clear: Hitler wanted as much territory as he could take. If this war kept up, how could it not eventually engulf the Realms? There were Realms who took a more protective, parental stance regarding their humans. Those Realms would inevitably get involved against the Nazis. I couldn't stop that from happening. I was just one mermaid in an ocean.

There had to be a way to help those humans in that prison hold that didn't involve telling Tank-Nielsen that I'd seen the ship. There had to be a way where I wasn't damned if I did, or damned if I didn't.

I kept swimming as the sun slipped lower in the sky. It was near dusk when the rumbling began again. I quickly looked around. Even though it was fading, it was still daylight. Where was it? A ship that big had to be visible.

Gears ground in the distance. Winches and machinery belched smoke into the air. I ducked under the surface, making my way toward the sound. The hull cut through the water toward me, darkness incarnate. Backing away to a safe distance, I surfaced and tried to find the name on the upper hull. The encircled black and white swastika on the red background of the Reich Service flag caught the light. The name painted on the hull sent a chill down my spine. It was the *Altmark*.

I went to the single clean porthole and listened. There were voices, so many voices. None of them bore a German accent. Welsh, Scottish, English, most of those accents edged the voices I heard. The rest must have been the Nubian sailors. The ship was full of imprisoned humans, and they were getting closer to Norwegian territorial waters. They were already in my lord's waters. They were coming. There could be no doubt. And I was likely still the only person who knew they were on the way.

I watched them steam off toward the night. What was I going to do?

The next day, I walked into Tank-Nielsen's office right behind his secretary. "Admiral, we need to talk."

Tank-Nielsen looked up from the papers on his desk. "They just crossed the borders into our waters two hours ago, Astrid. They're close to Halten. Oslo is desperately trying to figure out what to do. The last thing we need is another Westerwald incident."

I remembered that incident. It had only been a few months before. "They won't refuse to be searched, Admiral. They might try to hide the prisoners from you, but I suspect they will want to pass as unnoticed as possible."

Tank-Nielsen ran a hand over his balding head, the only giveaway of his stress. His necktie was still tucked perfectly against his throat, the points of his collar perfectly white against the tie's darkness. His uniform jacket was spotless and wrinkle-free. The ring of the telephone clattered through the room. The admiral picked up the handset. "Tank-Nielsen."

The voice on the other side had a frantic measure to its speech, but I couldn't hear specific words.

"Trygg gave them a pilot? Taking them to Alesund? Did they perform a thorough inspection? And they did not find prisoners? They searched the entire ship? Keep the escort on them. I will contact you with further orders."

I brightened at that point. It was the perfect opportunity. "Admiral," I said as soon as he hung up the phone. "This is the chance. I'm sure if a thorough search of the ship is performed, you will find the prisoners."

He stared at me, and I understood how the lower officers withered under it. "How can you be so sure, Astrid?"

"I know…" Instinct cut me off at that point. Taking a deep breath, I pressed on. "I know that if there are prisoners on that ship, Admiral, someone with your dedication and tenacity will find them. You will, of course, need appropriate intimidation. You know as well as I that the Nazis do not surrender to defeat. Not without a battle that would rival Ragnarök. The tanker has portholes, does it not?"

His brow furrowed. "How do you know that?"

I covered with a confused look. "Our tankers have portholes. I assumed the same design. If the prisoners are being held above the ship's waterline, then they will have to be in a modified cargo hold. Our tankers have at least one porthole in the cargo section to allow air into dank holds, do they not?"

It was a stab in the dark, but I had to try. If I couldn't tell them the information outright, perhaps I could guide the searches? That one clean porthole against the dirt was becoming my beacon of hope in the Norwegians finding the prisoners.

"This design of German tankers has portholes, yes."

"What is a supply tanker most afraid of?"

Tank-Nielsen paused, then smiled. "Either fire or sinkage. We are able to bring both to them."

He picked up the phone. "Get me the Snogg. Yes. Good. Captain Simensen, excellent. This is Tank-Nielsen. I want you to escort the *Altmark* toward Bergen. If she so much as blinks, you have your torpedoes. I will send a destroyer to assist as soon as they are able to reach you. The *Altmark* is only to move through the Bergen Defended Area during the daylight. I do not wish a Nazi tanker in my fjords unless it is an emergency. Do I make myself clear? Good. You have your orders, Captain. Notify me and me only if there is any change in the situation."

He rang off, returning the handset to the base. "I'll send the Draug. She may not have the firepower, but I know her captain will not be satisfied with anything less than a thorough job."

That was all we could ask. If the humans conducted a thorough search on their own? I knew they'd find the prisoners themselves.

They performed repeated inspections of the *Altmark*, and still did not find the prisoners. The German Captain Dau had been a conniving sort. According to almost constant flow of telegrams coming into Tank-Nielsen's office at that point, Dau had not allowed them to inspect the cargo areas. He'd used some line about secret cargo that could not even be seen by his own people, and the humans had believed it. The deckhouse, the bridge, navigation rooms, those were all searched time and again. Reports were that the same steam winches I'd heard days before had been going the entire time.

"Why would they do that?" I asked the Admiral over tea. "If they are being inspected, why do something to make that much noise? Why can no one inspect the cargo hold? What is this 'secret cargo' if not the prisoners?"

The ship had reached Sognefjord at that point. They were making good time down the coast. We weren't going to have much more time before they made their escape to German waters.

"I do not know," he said, "but I intend to find out. I will not have a ship carrying prisoners of war pass through my waters unchallenged. I have ordered the Garm to conduct another inspection.

"I have confidence that the ship is what our reports suggest. Perhaps a woman's presence might make the captain more amenable. May I accompany them, Admiral?"

That got a slight smile from him. "I am afraid this is not a situation for a lady, Astrid. While I appreciate your counsel, this is a job for the soldiers and the diplomats."

I hated being talked down to by humans, but this was their culture. I wasn't supposed to tell them what to do. I was there to protect the Realm's interest. If I told myself that enough, I might eventually be able to believe that point. I hadn't reached that stage, yet. "That's fine, Admiral. I shall consult with my people on what to do about the situation."

Placing his teacup on the desk, he stood and carefully donned his uniform jacket. The commendation ribbons stood vivid against the fabric's darkness. He was, as always, perfectly pressed. "I shall speak to you this afternoon, Astrid."

I realized at that point that I was being dismissed. "Oh, of course, Admiral. Please feel free to call the legation when you are ready. I will await your report."

Placing my teacup on the desk, I quickly stood. Pressing down the fabric of my skirt, I walked toward the door. It was time to find out just where the Garm was, and see what I could do.

When I caught up to the Garm, it had pulled up alongside *Altmark*. I swam close to the Garm's hull, but tried to stay as far out of sight of the prisoners' porthole as I could. They might have seen me as a hallucination, but I didn't want to take that chance.

I could see the captain; his dress cap perched atop his head as he crossed with the other officers in the party.

While the humans tried diplomacy and possibly intimidation, I swam over to the *Altmark*'s unmoving hull. Since I didn't need to keep up with the ship this time, I could manage some alternative means of investigation. While the Norwegians were on board, if the prisoners were going to try anything, that would be the best time to do it.

A scream of steam later, the winches started up yet again. This time, though, someone was in the right place to hear why. Clanking and banging on the hull rang out from under the waterline. I covered my ears when the whistles began crying out S.O.S. How could the humans not hear this?

I swam over to the clean porthole, putting my ear to the hull plate directly under it. The din was astonishing, even with steel between us. The prisoners were screaming for their lives, praying someone heard them. "I hear you," I whispered. It felt as though I had been kicked in the chest. They were there, and they were desperately trying to be heard. I had been ordered to do nothing.

With the realization of how restrained I was, I swam. I swam for at least an hour to the west. There were prisoners on that ship. They were headed for prison camps at the very least. Could I just sit by and have whatever happened to those men on my conscience for the rest of my life? What would the German shifters do if they got their hands on British prisoners of war?

There were too many questions, and not nearly enough answers.

I wasn't given a second more to consider the subject, though. Engines roared in the distance. These weren't ships. They didn't cause the waters to rumble. These were airborne. As the fighters zoomed over my head, I could see the Union Jacks on each plane's wing. My stomach tied itself into knots.

The British were coming.

Six British ships had entered Nøkken waters: one cruiser and five destroyers. It was a strike force. The fact that they had air support? The British were here for their men, and they knew they were on *Altmark*.

I was allowed into Tank-Nielsen's office as he was on the phone with Oslo.

"I do not know, sir. The British have been searching for this ship for months. Yes, sir. I agree. We cannot allow them to battle in neutral territory. The *Kjell* and the *Skarv* are on the scene. *Altmark* is being shepherded into Jøssingfjord. It will enable us to remain between the combatants as well as not allow *Altmark* to go until she lets us search the cargo hold."

Now that the British had arrived, it was past time to put the prisoner situation to bed. I had to agree; the idea of moving the ship into an aquatic cul-de-sac was a good one. Unless, of course, the British decided that our ships be damned, they were going in for their people. In that case, we were probably in trouble.

"Yes, sir. I am aware that the British want their people. In their situation, I would feel the same. They've what?

A knock on the door behind me preceded his secretary walking into the room with a handful of telegrams. She put them on his desk, and disappeared back to her own space. Tank-Nielsen began flipping through them as he listened to his superior officer talk. "Admiral," he began, "I am sorry, but I have received word that there have been confrontations between the British captains and our ships. We have inspected the ship repeatedly, but they refuse to accept that."

That was because they rightly suspected our inspections had been useless.

"They have contacted London, sir. Churchill will not be pleased unless they come back with a prize." There was a long silence from Tank-Nielsen, and then, "Yes, sir. I will. I have already ordered the neutrality to be aggressively maintained. We stand between them now, but we cannot intervene."

I was right. We were in trouble. Even if I told him everything I knew, I wouldn't stop the British. I quickly put my coat on and headed back into the frigid night. There was a layer of ice over Jøssingfjord. The ships would have to crack through it to make any headway in their retreat from the British. The Germans were backed against the wall, and we were standing right in front of them. If I swam at top speed, I might be able to get there before the situation exploded. I hoped it wouldn't be literally.

When I finally reached Jøssingfjord, saying it was frigid would be understating the scenario. The ice was dense, but a ship – *Altmark* judging by the size of path of broken ice – had made a path into the fjord. Inside the mouth of the fjord, a British ship waited. It was a looming, overwhelming hulk of a ship. The Norwegian gunboats stood by, waiting for one side to make a move.

I ducked under the ice and swam up the fjord, wishing the dense skin of my tail would somehow cover the rest of me. I ran low, hoping the ships wouldn't think I was a torpedo. When I reached the propeller blades of *Altmark*, I realized that there wasn't much room between the hull and the shore. She was in the fjord tight.

A sloshing of water behind me caused me to turn. I was starting straight at the bow of the British cruiser, and it was coming at me fast. Ramming speed. I swam out of the way as quickly as I could.

Before I realized what was happening, I heard a cracking sound from the surface. It wasn't the long crack of an ice floe breaking. This was a pop-pop of something else entirely. I surfaced at the stern of the cruiser, just past its quieting propellers.

The ship had forced *Altmark* to ground. The sounds I was hearing were gunshots. The British were boarding.

I swam to a secluded spot in the fjord that wasn't coated in ice, and worked my way onto the surface. When my legs returned, I snuck to a nearby house and found some clothes in a back room. It wasn't anything flashy, but it kept the cold at bay. The Nøkken would repay the humans, I hoped.

I sprinted across the thin ice to where Germans were jumping off of the ship. Some were even still alive. I found one soldier scrambling on the ice to get his footing. A Nazi soldier on Nøkken land. That would not be allowed.

The residents of the area around the fjord were watching the battle. It wasn't often that a war came to your front yard. When one man came over to the Nazi soldier with a revolver in his hand, I couldn't stop myself. I reached out and grabbed the gun.

"No. Let him go."

The man's eyes turned to me, and I realized that he wasn't human. Those eyes were a golden, luminous yellow. "My lord," I said, dropping to one knee on the ice. "I am sorry."

The Nøkken had the capacity to appear human, but I hadn't seen him use it for years. I'd forgotten what his human form looked like. He raised the gun once again to the German soldier, who was staring at both of us in fear.

"It's all right," I whispered to the young man. "We are here to protect Norway."

I heard the hammer on the revolver cock and the barrel turn so a bullet was readied. "My lord, if we allow the human to live, who would believe his story? A Norwegian man with glowing yellow eyes tried to kill him? And a woman kept referring to him as 'my lord'? Not even our humans would believe that. Please. Isn't there enough blood being shed tonight? They are not of your Realm. Why should we add to the toll? If we anger the Nazis, they will retaliate, my lord. If they come, the shapeshifters will not be far behind."

I couldn't believe it, myself. I was arguing that a Nazi should be spared. At that moment, though, the young man wasn't a Nazi to me. He was a human being. He would have to live with what the *Altmark* had done to those men for the rest of his life. I had no idea if he'd been a warden or an innocent bystander on the tanker, but I knew the British would leave with those prisoners this night. The Germans were being humiliated with the boarding. I could hear the British voice calling for a gathering of the Germans on the deck. Would they take the crew of *Altmark* back to England? Only their captain knew. The Unseelies might be quite happy with their prizes this evening.

"My lord. If the Germans fired the first shot against us, would you not demand retribution from the shapeshifters? If we are to remain neutral, we must restrain ourselves."

The Nøkken cocked his elbows until the gun was pointed at the sky.

"Go, now," I whispered to the German. With a scramble of feet and hands, the young man disappeared into the icy woods.

"Mermaid. Why are the British in my territory?" His voice was a growl. Human vocal chords couldn't manage the maelstrom of his true form. "They have violated my waters. Did you know they were coming?"

I gulped. I hadn't told him when the fighters had flown over me while I swam. I'd been too worried about the prisoners and what Tank-Nielsen might do. "Yes, my lord. There hadn't been time to tell you."

He turned on me, the gun pointed at my head. "Yet you are here, with the humans. You violated my orders."

"I swear to you! I did not tell them anything, my lord. They found the ship on their own. The British fighters gave them eyes I did not anticipate."

"Then they violated our air."

I nodded. "Possibly, my lord." It didn't matter. I was still staring down the barrel of a revolver. My lord, please. They were searching by air and sea. They had an advantage."

Those golden yellow eyes flared, and suddenly Tank-Nielsen's glares didn't seem quite as intimidating. "You may live, but not here. I cannot have servants whose word I cannot trust. I cannot have a servant who does not put the Realm first. Go. Now. Never return."

My heart hammered in my chest. The gun didn't move. If I didn't leave, he was going to shoot me on the spot. I could die, or I could live in exile, all because of three hundred humans. While the chaos continued around me, I dove into the water. Removing my clothes, I left them piled on the ice. My tail re-formed around my legs, and I began swimming once again. I went west. I didn't know where I'd end up, nor did I care. All that mattered was that I would never see my home again.

TO REACH FOR DISTANT SHORES
A Tale from the World of the Silver Moon

Danielle Ackley-McPhail

The answers to my dreams came by a flash storm that rolled up from the south off the sea — violent, sudden, unexpected. The winds rarely drove from that direction, but when they did it was gloriously primal. I could feel their distant effect on the sea in the fine bones of my body, like the warning my whisker hairs sent when something dangerous loomed close by.

While my sisters and brothers dove down deep at the threat of the storm, I wended my way upward. I broke the surface to peer from the lee of the rocks jutting from the slapping waves, my eyes trained on the water's surface and the skies. I avidly watched for the signs that would come swift and sudden and much too late for any about on the surface to heed. In the distance, barely heard, the air rumbled warning of the tempest's approach. With vague interest I noticed a narrow, oblong bladder high up in the sky, floating like the jellies beneath the waves, right down to the tendrils dangling from its core. Tiny trailers of electric static crackled like an eel's warning across the bladder's skin before the energy was gone, dispersed on the quickening wind.

Again my bones shivered as the storm drew ever closer. This was the moment when down close to the water the air fell too still. My eyes scanned the sea, drawn by vibrations on the surface. To my left, a large mass drifted by like a rare leviathan risen from the depths. It was a made thing, a ship, filled with man-things scurrying about at this first hint of the coming storm. I ducked low, eyes just under the water, so the man-things would not see me. As the vessel passed, thunder rumbled faintly in the distance, popping closer and closer. The rapidly darkening clouds lit up, and sudden trails of lightning danced down from the sky, colliding with each other and the mass on the water, high up where thin, straight branches reached like webbed fingers to touch the air.

I rose just above the water as the mass moved by, my breath barely rippling the froth on the waves. My hands gripped tight to the algae-coated rocks as my fins were nibbled clean by the tiny fish living in the shoals. I remained poised, ready to escape beneath the depths when the heavens finally crashed down to whip the waves into a frenzy. I left my leaving long, clinging in place as the air charged and crackled and thunderclouds of a sudden boiled up on the horizon. With a gleeful laugh I dove deep and fast before the storm front blanketed the world above.

None on water or in air saw mercy from that tempest. I came up to the shallows when the worst passed, eager to see the evidence of the storm's might. With care I darted from mass to mass, just beneath the water. Everything I found was broken by the punch of the waves and wind, bitten by the power of the lightning. Fragments of those odd conveyances rained down: rough, oily strips of the bladder, severed lengths of ropy tendrils, jagged planks torn from the massive ship, all caught and cradled a moment before being swallowed by the sea.

I turned my attention to the masters of those vessels. The dead I left for the currents to slurp down, or batter upon the distant sands as they may. There was one I came across with warmth yet in his veins. I wrapped both arms around and drew him down with me. Beneath the runnels of blood and scraggled hair there was something of his face that spoke of fear. He jerked and thrashed as the waves closed overhead, his odd, split tail flailing uselessly against my single powerful one. I murmured reassurances in his ear, but he continued to struggle. Grimacing, I tightened my grip and swam more swiftly to gain us the sanctuary of my private grotto.

I held an eager breath. Never had I had this chance before. To speak to one who made their home above the water. One who knew of the sky jellies. There was little doubt of communication between us. In my long life I had travelled far and listened well; I was certain I could speak and understand every language the man-things spoke near the sea — which was to say all of them.

I knew what I would ask him. The only thing I cared to ask him: How? How do you reach the sky? It was my dearest dream to take my place up there, to gain those distant shores and swim the waters of the unseen moon. I dreamt of dancing with the lightning, of climbing its jagged bolts into the heavens. There were oceans there. I could not see them, but I could feel their call in the shivers down my scales and the tremors through my whisker hairs. I had no doubt those waters were there. After all, look how much spray rained down to mingle here below.

The lightning climbed up into the sky. Those like the one wrapped in my arms rode the winds. Perhaps the air jellies were the key to gaining the clouds. This one held the secret. He would give it up. My egg sibs scoffed, but I would not rest until I was as cradled by those waters above as I was by my own sea.

And here was my chance to discover the secret to making this so.

But my effort was for naught. By the time we shook off the water's clinging, and I drew the stranger from above up upon my own hidden sands deep below, the warmth had fled him. I stared at his peculiar face, and my teeth gnashed, jagged edge against jagged edge. I traced the plump curve of his now-blue lips and peered into strange, near-flat eyes, gone blood-shot and lifeless, as if my answers were written there. They were not. But something did glitter slightly lower. I reached out, pushing aside the odd flaps that covered his chest like a skin torn loose and let flop to either side. Beneath was a wonder. It was an object like lightning-struck sand only smooth and straight and clear. Something encapsulated within glowed faintly. I lifted the thing away, breaking the thin strap it hung from around the dead one's neck. And none too soon.

A splash behind me betrayed an intrusion. "Your bottom-feeder tendencies are showing, Cochina."

Phin. Like a case of scale rot, that one had plagued me ever since we were fingerlings. Even in the sac he was rotten, I was sure. Someday, when I spawn my young, I would eat any eggs that held darkness such as his, for Phin had one goal: by word and deed, inflict what harm he may and often. His disdainful tone sent my lips into a snarl. As if I would feed upon a thinking being.

Before he spied it, I slipped my prize into the kelp bands I'd strung about my waist for carrying such things as I did not wish to hold in my hands. I then turned and glared at where he lounged, flukes in the water, arms on the sands, bracing him up. As ever, his eyes were mocking.

He could not have noticed my expression.

Not when he was too busy staring up and down the length of me, eyes lingering in the region of my pelvic fins. Hissing with annoyance and distaste, I heaved the strange one to my shoulder. With a wiggle of my fins and tail I shoved past my egg brother — we were sheltered in the same nest, though not spawned from the same source — before sliding into the water, hauling the corpse to the grotto entrance where I let the current reclaim its prize.

Unburdened but still weighed down, I undulated upward. The surface was choppy yet, dotted with flotsam not claimed by the depths, but the clouds had vanished as quickly as they'd come, leaving the sky deep and dark and finely speckled, like a dolphin. I let my head fall back, eyes closed, and breathed deep of the cleansed, ozone-scented air, savoring the lingering taste of salt water tinged with fresh-churned kelp on my lips. Slowly my muscles unbunched. My eyes opened to scan the sky. To the left, high up, there was a patch seemingly void of stars. A dark cloud? One of the sky jellies? With a few powerful strokes of my tail I swam again toward the rocks, hauled myself up, and let moonbeams caress my skin. I looked up to the larger moon, the one all could see. Its touch was cool, soft. Pleasant, but nothing more. The other…the unseen moon…my skin and scales glowed with the charge it imbued. Warmth bathed me on the inside, despite the chill of the night.

Someday…. Someday I would gain that vaunted moon's shores and swim in its vibrant seas.

Forcing my gaze down and away lest I remain mesmerized for longer than was safe, I looked down to the object tucked within my kelp bands. My hand trembled as I drew it out with care. It was fine, more delicate than I would have thought possible. I could imagine neither its purpose nor manner of creation. I kept it, for it seemed a treasure, something of value to the lost soul I had claimed it from. Perhaps it would serve a purpose for me, as lure or boon to one from his world who might aid me. I secured it once more, lest the jealous waves snatch away my prize.

That was when I heard it. A broken sound. A weak one. It was foreign even to me, who had ventured forth through all the earthly seas available to me — which was to say, all of them. I was a powerful swimmer.

My dorsal fronds stiffened, not quite billowing as they would beneath the waves, but nonetheless they snapped at the air. This was a new thing. I angled my head to capture the sound. To pinpoint the source. It had something of a seal's bark — were the seal half dead. And something of the seagull's caw, only much less demanding. I could not for a moment imagine what made such a sound.

My flesh rippled at each sounding, my muscles tensed. I drew myself across the rocks, up through the crevice that split this oceanic outcrop. I was silent as I moved, the muscles in my tail bunching to push against the rock, aiding my arms as they may. As I drew closer to the sound, I slowed my motions. A tall, thin spire of rock jutted high overhead. With care, I placed my webbed fingers against its jagged mass and pulled myself up to peer around the bulk of it.

The water glittered in the moonlight as it could not hope to beneath the sun, else I would not have noticed. Breaking up that liquid shimmer was an odd form clinging to the base of the outcrop, half in and half out of the waves. It humped first large, then smaller, holding to the rocks as tight as a barnacle did.

I almost lost my grip and tumbled down as suddenly a different, higher wail rose, piercing my delicate ears clear through. And then I saw the one form was two, small huddled against the large. My pelvic fins fluttered instinctually. I watched as the bigger of the two pulled the other close to shelter against her…for her it was, I could see as the moon now caressed the paleness of her face. The little one looked up and a sound escaped me. It was a boy-thing, little lips full and flat eyes familiar, though lacking the tinge of blood-red last seen upon the eyes of another face. Were the sea kinder, this one might grow into the man-thing I'd gripped in my arms not long ago.

Perhaps it was my earlier thoughts of spawning, but an ache settled in my chest. How could I leave that young one at the mercy of the sea? I leaned closer, my head tilted for a better view, my ear hole angled toward them to pick up words drifting on the night's breeze.

"He said that he would find us…he promised. If anything happened to the ship," the woman-thing murmured through cracked lips. Her words drifted, broken and as faint as the sounds she'd first made. "Find a place of safety, he said, and signal him. He will come. He promised. But the flare… it's gone." Her one hand came up briefly to touch an object around her neck. From a familiar strap hung the fragments of what seemed the cousin to the object hidden in my kelp bands. As the woman-thing slid deeper in the water, she scrambled to cling to the rocks.

More of the tortured sounds, point and counterpoint, high voice and low. Though the sounds hurt my ears, I remain perched in my crevice, unable to draw away from the scene below. As I stayed there, the night air brushed over my form, gentle but persistent, until my skin and scales itched and twitched and tightened enough to bring me close to wailing myself. The depths called to me, soothing and wet, cool and dark, and yet I remained until I spied the boy-thing slide into the grip of the waves.

The woman-thing cried out and dove after, in several long moments surfacing with her sputtering young. He choked and gasped as I have never heard a creature come from the sea. Great wracking coughs spewed water upon the rocks. My gaze went to his neck. I drew a sharp breath and my gills twitched as realization dawned: as the fish remained ever below, these man-things thrived only above. My heart ached with remorse as my eyes were opened to what I had done in drawing the man-thing down beneath the waves. I had borne no malice, yet like Phin I'd wreaked great harm. Even could I reclaim the man-thing from the sea the deed could not be undone. He would not breathe again, nor return to these steadfastly waiting.

But there was one thing I could do in restitution. My numb fingers slid down to grip the rod still lodged within my now-dry kelp bands. It had clearly held import for him, kept, as it was, hidden against his breast. Could this be another of the flares the woman-thing worried over?

I knew what I must do.

Sliding back down the outcrop, the rough rock scraping at dried scales, I slipped with a sigh back into the sea. Powerful twitches of my tail sent me around the rocks to where the two still clung. From this new vantage point, I could see they perched because they could not climb higher against the algae-coated rock. This I could fix.

The waters would not have them.

The night air splintered with their shrieks as I braced against their bottoms, first the boy-thing, then the woman-thing, and with powerful thrusts of my tail surged forward, propelling them from the sea and up onto the rocks. They scrambled higher, clutching each other in as tight a grip as I'd held their man-thing when I drew him under the sea. I bobbed there where they had clung, merely watching. I met the gaze of the woman-thing, remorse in my eyes, though my tongue remained silent.

I had not the words to make my deed right, none to excuse it. I bowed my head as I slid my hand into the kelp band, working the object free. It glowed in the moonlight as I brought it forth, and the terror in the woman-thing's expression gave way to a gleam of hope. Like a crab, she sidled toward my outstretched hand, snatched my prize, and scurried back.

Without a word, I turned away and dropped beneath the waves, but not before I glanced a fleeting moment up into the sky. Someday I would dance with the lightning, and climb its jagged bolts into the heavens. Someday…I would reach those distant shores to swim the seas of the unseen moon.

But not today.

HOOK, LINE, AND SINKER

A Detective Sorrow Casefile

Patrick Thomas

The rot of death has never really affected me. It's been a part of my life ever since I was a little girl. You might say I'm an expert on death, both by genetics and profession. One thing however I never could stand was the stench of fish.

This case combined the two in a most unpleasant fashion.

This was a bad one. Even Micky Summers, a grizzled veteran cop, looked like he might blow chunks any moment. Just my luck to draw this one.

"Summers, what've you got?" I asked.

"What you see is basically what I got," the leprechaun said. "We had a call from a neighbor about the smell. We knocked on the door, no answer. This is what we found. The vic's name is Sandy Fishman. Comes from a big fishing family."

That much was obvious. "I take it she didn't live here?"

"Nope. Apartment's supposed to have been vacant. The killer probably knew that," Summers said.

"Or got real lucky," I said.

Summers laughed harshly. "Ain't no such thing as luck."

"Odd view for a leprechaun to take," I teased.

Summers and I had danced this dance before.

"If leprechauns could really control luck and grant wishes, do you think I'd be walking a beat instead of living the life of Riley?" Summers groused. He did that a lot and I couldn't blame him. He's been on the force since the fifties. After WWII and the Limiting, magical beings were forcibly relocated to nine spots on the planet. Those of us in North America got the city of Purlieu and the rest of Arcane County, Mississippi.

Most of the magic races barely had any time to get personal belongings, let alone dig up hidden pots of gold. Summers lost a fortune. Still won't tell a soul where he buried it. Figures the Limiting might end someday and he'll be able to go back and get it. In the meantime, he's a working stiff. As opposed to the type of stiff we deal with at work.

Summers took a deep breath and held it, trying to get control of his rebelling guts.

"Sorrow, you know the officer on the scene can't make the call about whether a death's a homicide." Mainly because sometimes it's an accident or a suicide. "That's the Medical Examiner's call. Oh yeah, and I called the crime scene folks."

I chuckled. "I'd say it's pretty safe to assume that the mermaid didn't ram the giant hook through her own mouth and through the top of her skull."

"Tis what I figured. I have picked up a few things after more than sixty years on the force. I leave you to your investigation and other things above me pay grade, Detective Sorrow."

Summers didn't go far, standing with arms crossed by the door. The leprechaun was the paranoid type. Most of his people are. Makes sense when everyone you meet is trying to capture you and steal your fortune. And because of an age old curse, they are forced to give it to them. Magic ain't always pretty.

However the mermaid probably had been quite pretty, back before someone mistook her head for bait. She was Caucasian and blond, although judging by her roots it was a dye job. Well-endowed on her human side. Big, green and scaly on her fish side.

Whoever did it was strong, although not necessarily ogre or minotaur level. Merfolk were pretty powerful. Had to be, all that swimming around and living under the pressures of the ocean. But one of her kind was not likely to be our perp. Those tails make it real hard to climb stairs.

How had the mermaid ended up in a third floor walkup? The bloodstain pattern and pooling made it pretty clear she was killed there. Was she carried? Or did she scoot up on her butt like a toddler?

The killer or killers had the strength to string up a several hundred pound mermaid like she was a trophy catch. It didn't point to a weakling, although a few weaklings working together might have managed it.

The poor woman was naked. The media and entertainment industry like to portray mermaids as going around eternally topless, but it's just not true. For one thing, outside of the water gravity works twice as hard pulling down on them. For another, no woman of any race likes men constantly staring at their chest. There is an entire line of bathing suit tops and wardrobes designed for the water set.

There is jealousy toward mermaids and the like by some land dwellers when it comes to their female attributes. Living in the water can offset the effects of gravity to a great degree so that even elderly mermaids can remain perky. I hoped that wouldn't be enough for someone to commit murder, although people have been killed for far less.

Her killer obviously had some big time issues with her breasts, having rammed a smaller makeshift fishhook through each of them. The cruelty and perversion didn't stop there. There was a broomstick with dried blood on the floor. There was matching blood around Ms. Fishman's groin, leaving little doubt what the stick was used for. Still the crime scene unit and the ME would tag it, bag it and prove it was used on the victim.

It may sound callous to say, but that might be a good thing for the investigation. It's a horrible thing to have happen and a terrible tragedy, but her attacker may have left behind some DNA if he used more than just the broomstick. Here in Arcane County and the city of Purlieu we have some investigative advantages over the rest of the country. Sure, magic and the beings who depend on it for survival may be trapped here by the Limiting, but that same magic puts our crime scene unit far ahead of anything the rest of North America can manage. Most departments can only use DNA to identify. Our police witches can use it to track down the sick bastard who did this. In the 13th Precinct we had the best, Karen Vorlocke, the city witch herself. If she couldn't track DNA, it couldn't be done.

My gut told me even Karen couldn't do much to help here. Sure, there had been a struggle. All the furniture nearby had been crushed or smashed, consistent with a mermaid's tail trashing about. Blood covered everything, but it smelled like only mermaid blood. Yes, I can separate blood types by scent. My examination of the corpse and the rest of the crime scene lead me to one sobering conclusion. The attacker didn't leave any tissue behind. The victim's fingernails were clean. Maybe the crime scene unit would find something I missed, but I doubted it.

It was time to show why they paid me the big bucks or at least why I wish they did. Detectives don't do bad, but I'm far from rich. Like many of the folks in Arcane County, I might look almost human, but I'm not. I'm a banshee so I know a bit about how the Reaper works. All my senses were attuned to death. I could see it coming, sometimes even hear or smell it. On rare occasions taste it. These skills come in handy working homicide. Depressing on a personal level though. I know how everyone I meet is going to die. Not necessarily when, but I can sense the details.

Take Officer Micky Summers for instance. He's a gruff and crude SOB, but I like him. He's going to die on the job and meet the Reaper saving a whole bunch of people, a real hero's death. There is no truer measure of someone's mettle than how they choose to meet death, be it with defiance or on their knees whimpering. Summers spits in the Reaper's eye by stopping him from claiming many others. A brave death, so I cut him some slack when it comes to other things.

My gifts works best on the living. On the dead, its effectiveness decreases the longer the person has been a corpse. Sandy had been dead about two days. I knew I wasn't going to get much, but there was no harm in trying. I'd been wrong before.

I closed my eyes and let my mind reach out to the corpse of the mermaid and saw her brutal death. It was as bad as I deduced it was. I couldn't see the killer, but could sense enough to know there had been only one murderer. Beyond that, nothing useful.

I stepped outside for a smoke. Yeah, I know they're bad for me, but I also know how I die. Cigarettes have nothing to do with it. Summers pulled up alongside me to bum a smoke. Gave him one too. Won't affect his death either.

"Want me to notify the family?" Summers offered while blowing smoke. I shook my head. "I'll do it."

It's never an easy job notifying the next of kin. It's especially difficult in the case of a murder with no suspects. The family is always demanding that whoever did the crime be punished. They don't want to hear that an investigation is under way. They want the cop in charge to tell them that their loved one is going to get justice. And the sad truth is justice is rarely a given.

Sandy Fishman's father owned Fishman's Seafood. Their business offices were on the gulf side of Little Atlantis and had a stereotypical trident as their logo. Sea folk have obvious difficulties living in a city, but Purlieu had adopted well. Back in '55 Hurricane Titania blew through, devastating the first quarter. Purlieu, like much of the surrounding gulf coast, was mostly below sea level. It had always gotten flooding, but Titania pretty much sunk whole sections of it. So when they rebuilt, some city planner had the bright idea of adapting that part of the city for those folks who were dependent on water as much as magic. Helped with future storms too. With the Limiting, the safe area where magic is still in play is only a little more than five miles out from the coast. For creatures that were used to the whole gulf or even the whole ocean to play in, that isn't a whole lot of swimming room. Folks like mermaids, selkies and fish folk did exceptionally well adapting. But there were others who weren't going to have anything to do with us land lovers. There is a small underwater city about three miles out, but they don't much like having air breathers visit.

Apparently Fishman Seafood shared the same prejudices. I walked in the door and was promptly ignored by a mermaid in a business suit, her red hair pulled up in a ponytail. Instead of glasses, she wore prescription goggles, which were much more practical for life under water.

I can do polite if I have to. I waited a moment, then cleared my throat. The mermaid had been filing her scales. She paused and looked up at me, narrowed her eyes and then went back to working on her tail. Although her top half was clothed, the bottom half was not. The office floor was covered in about four feet of water, with weighted plastic furniture, including the desk and the chair she was using. There was a narrow walkway for those with legs, barely wider than a two by four. Nothing like making the land dwellers feel at home. That or maybe it was narrow enough that someone periodically took a tumble into the water and it tickled their funny bone. In the background, Maxine Siryn was playing. She was the merfolk's cultural equivalent to Frank Sinatra. A little too smoky room for my taste, but not bad.

"Is Jacob Fishman in?" I said.

"He is booked solid all day. No openings. I might be able to fit you in a week from Tuesday," she said, not even bothering to hide her disdain. More than three quarters of a century of us all being forced to live together and some people still can't get along.

I flipped open my badge. "I'm Detective Sorrow. He'll see me."

"Nice try, Detective, but we're all paid up," she said with a scowl.

I don't like the sound of that. "Really? Who did you pay?"

"Like you don't know that Cooke picks up his money every week."

I didn't, but I was going to pass it along to somebody who might be interested.

"Actually I'm a homicide detective and I have to speak to him." No reason that the guy's secretary should know about his daughter before he does.

The receptionist grumbled, but picked up her waterproof phone, used it to call her boss then pointed with her chin towards a door. I walked along the plank and opened the door myself, since the secretary obviously wasn't going to. I looked down and noticed they had a small circular hole under the water between the office walls that they could swim through.

Jacob Fishman reclined behind his wooden desk. Most of it was submerged, a sign of wealth. It looked like the desk was made out of driftwood that had already proved it could survive the dampness. He was on the less opulent side of plump and had hair down to his waist. It was a fairly common custom among merfolk. It's said to be very attractive flowing freely in the water. The killer had lopped off most of Sandy's locks and parts of her scalp.

Judging by Fishman's expanse of belly, he didn't spend much time in open water. Those that do rarely get fat because they are constantly moving and swimming.

"Coral already told you that we are paid up," Fishman said.

"That's what I hear, but I can't be bought off," I said.

"Oh, so this is some sort of new shakedown? I pay Cooke. It's bad enough that I have to deal with a parade of the crooks who claim they are still working Inman's game even though he's in Iron Bars."

Inman was a demon crime lord that we had managed to put away a little bit back. He ran everything illicit in Arcane County or at least had tributes paid to him by those that did. His imprisonment had left a vacuum and a lot of people were trying to fill it.

"At least Cooke gets them off my tail. But paying off two cops? That I ain't gonna do. I'm calling Cooke so you can get the hell out of my office and settle this with him."

"Sir, if you just let me …" My polite face was being strained.

"What part of get the hell out of my office didn't you understand?"

My polite face was down, but remembering what he was about to learn regarding his daughter kept my tone civil. "Sir, you are being an ass. I suggest you shut up and listen to what I am trying to tell you. I'm not here about extortion. I'm here to talk about your daughter."

Fishman's face stopped mid rant. "Sandy? What happened to my little fry?" Slang for baby sea folk, not a reference to cooking them.

"I am afraid she's been killed."

"No…" Fishman's tail smacked his lounge chair out from under him and knocked his desk into the wall. "No! What happened? Who did it?"

"It was a very brutal crime, sir." I gave him the details as vaguely as I could, but it was damn hard to sugarcoat the fact that someone had put a hook through his daughter's head. "As to who did it, that's what I am here to talk to you about. Did Sandy have any enemies?"

"Everybody loved Sandy. She was even engaged to a selkie, I didn't exactly approve, but he made her happy."

"What is her fiancé's name?" I said.

"Bobby Honken. He's an accountant." Fishman gave me his info.

"When was the last time you saw Sandy?" I said.

"Sandy, her mother and I had lunch two days ago and went over wedding plans."

I asked some more questions about her work, friends, habits. The usual stuff. "Did she have any reason to be near 4th and Wolfbane?"

"None that I know of," Fishman said. "I want you to find out who did this to my little girl."

"I'll do the best I can," I said and left.

Turns out that Bobby Honken worked in the factory district for Stonewood Furniture. Because Purlieu was the only place on the North American continent where magical beings could survive, we had trouble getting all of our furniture from manufacturers outside of Arcane County – they tended to mark things up a bit high, blaming it on transport costs – which translated into a thriving local furniture district. After all an ogre wouldn't fit into the same chair a bogart would, at least not comfortably.

Honken was Stonewood's accountant. My badge got me past security and led into Honken's office.

The selkie looked up at me confused when I came through his door.

"Mr. Honken, I am afraid in have some bad news. Your fiancé …"

"You mean ex-fiancé," he said, cutting me off.

"Ex?"

"I called it off with Sandy two days ago," Honken said.

"Why?" I asked.

"Sandy was cheating on me with another selkie," he said.

Sandy appeared to have a type of man she was attracted to. Don't get me wrong. In Arcane County there are all sorts of trans-race dating and marriage. I honestly don't think there's anything wrong with it, although I prefer my men humanoid. Had a blind date with a centaur once. Didn't work out for many reasons, not the least of which was when I shook his hand, I had a vision of him causing a kid's death by running away from a danger and leaving the child to fend for himself. One of those times I wish I had more control over figuring out the when, but typically my window for knowing the time of death is less than three days before it happens. Often closer to a day.

"Do you know with who?"

Honken looked at my badge. "One of you. A detective named Darren Cooke. Apparently she managed to steal his skin."

Cooke again. Interesting. "Is that why you were going to marry her? Did she steal your seal skin too?" Selkies are seal people. Unlike changelings, dragons, and other shape shifters, their abilities are not innate. They can only change into their seal form by putting on their skins. Once destroyed, the skins can never be replaced. Most selkies are extremely protective of them, so it didn't make sense that a cop, even a dirty cop, would let someone get a hold of his.

"Sandy didn't need to steal my skin. She had already stolen my heart," Honken said with enough saccharin sweetness to make me want to put my finger in my throat and pretend to gag. Since I was on duty, I refrained. "But as much as I loved her, I wasn't going to let her run around on me with another guy. I broke up with her and told her if she wanted me, she'd have to dump Cooke. So what happened? Did Cooke drag her into something dirty?"

"Unfortunately nothing that simple. Sandy was murdered," I said.

Honken leapt to his feet. "Oh sweet Poseidon. He killed her!"

"Who? Cooke?" I said.

Honken nodded. "When I confronted Sandy about her cheating, she told me that she was only doing that to see if what they said about the seal skins were true: that anyone who held them controlled the selkie it belonged to. I told her it was, but that wasn't enough. Sandy knew Cooke was a dirty cop and how much money he was taking in over at the waterfront since Inman was locked up. She thought if she controlled him, she could control the money."

"So what did she need you for?" I asked.

"She figured since I knew finances that I would be able to take the money she got from Cooke and grow it into even more money. Sandy wanted to get out from under her father's control. She figured the money would let her do that."

"Of course, knowing the love of your life was cheating on you with another selkie must have made you crazy," I said.

"You bet it did."

"Maybe even crazy enough to kill," I said. "Sandy's murderer had a lot of anger, even rage. Hard to get that worked up over a stranger."

"Wait a minute. I didn't kill Sandy. I was hoping she'd come to her senses and return to me," Honken said.

"Where were you two nights ago?" The ME would probably get a more exact time of death, but my banshee abilities were pretty accurate, as least within a few hours.

"I was here working all night to prepare for an audit. Ask my boss," Honken said.

"I will."

And I did.

"Unusual for a Meliae to be in the furniture business. As least wood furniture," I said. Sam Stonewood was a Meliae. They're ash tree dryads, bound at birth to protect a tree. Think human tree huggers are bad? You ain't seen nothing until you see someone try to hurt a Meliae's tree. In fact, they were one of the races that suffered the most causalities percentage-wise during the Limiting. Only a handful would leave their trees. Some tried to move them. Others took something with them from the old tree to grow a new one. Some were simply drugged and removed forcibly. Most died standing guard at their posts as the magic was forced from their bodies.

"Yeah well, me and Ashley never got along. Still, I ain't lonesome. I brought her with me," Sam said, patting his desk.

"You made your tree into a desk?" I said, shocked.

"A desk, chairs, entertainment center, a couch, bookcases, baseball bats. Even a butt load of toothpicks." The dryad held out a box. "Want one?"

Sentient trees are rare, practically extinct since the Limiting. Using that toothpick would be equivalent to using a finger bone to clean my teeth. "No thanks. What were Robert Honken's hours this past week?"

"Bobby? Pretty much 24/7. We had an IRS audit yesterday. Passed with flying colors, thanks to him," Sam said.

"What about two nights ago?" I said.

"Pretty much all night. He slept in his office," Sam said, picking his teeth.

"You're a sick bastard," I said.

The Meliae smiled. "Maybe. You work what, forty hours a week? Maybe fifty with overtime. You decided to take the job and get paid for doing it. Me, I was bound at birth to serve something every hour of every day for my entire life. You don't like being a cop, you can quit. Me, not so much. If I quit, I died because the tree controlled my life force. Ashley made it clear that my walking away was a death sentence." He rapped on the desk. "Ashley here was centuries old. Centuries! What, you think all trees are nice? Control of my life-force meant she could make me collapse with a thought. Ashley was a sadistic bitch who made me jump through hoops just because she could. The Limiting broke her hold over me and I got while the getting was good."

"Stopping only to get a chainsaw," I said.

Sam shrugged. "Say what you will, I brought her with me. I never sold one scrap of her wood. It's all in my house or office. Ashley was going to die. Not her body, but her mind. She may have tortured me for centuries, but I wouldn't have lived past one without her power sustaining me. I owed it to her to make it quick. It was a mercy killing. And if I enjoyed it a little more than I should have, so what? There's no law against it, is there?"

"Not since it happened outside of Arcane County," I admitted. In Arcane sentient trees are protected by law and usually multiple dryads who lost their own trees backing up the locals. More than a few have even formed gangs.

"Anything else, Detective?" he asked.

"No," I said.

"Can I interest you in a kitchen or bathroom set? Always ten percent off for members of Purlieu's finest," Sam said.

Without a word, I left. And if I enjoyed seeing the vision of the Meliae's ironic death sometime in the future when a piece of his Ashley made furniture falls and stakes him through the chest a little more than I should have, so what? There's no law against it.

I tracked down Detective Cooke using the GPS in his department issued sedan. For some reason his department issued smart phone was turned off, making it impossible to track him personally. A violation of protocol.

Like me, Cooke worked alone. Purlieu PD doesn't insist that detectives have a partner. Some of us work better alone, while others are just too difficult to get along with. So long as the detective was able to pull his or her own weight and clear cases, working solo was permitted.

Cooke was inside a restaurant when I found him. I watched through the window as he ate a huge meal. As he got up, the waitress, one of the fish folk, didn't give him a check, although she did seem to be trying to give him a lap dance. Interesting people, fish folk. Claim to have started out as human then got all scaly. They've been called Deep Ones in some circles. As Cooke got up, the maitre'd handed him a thick envelope. Before exiting, the dirty cop pulled the green and scaly waitress into a corner that would have been out of sight to those in the restaurant, but was clear to anyone looking in. Cooke pulled down certain of their clothes, made some repeated thrusting movements, convulsed and let his eyes roll back in his head, then pulled his trousers up and left, stopping to slap her green fanny before leaving. A real romantic.

His car was parked in front of a fire hydrant. I leaned against the passenger door with my arms crossed in front of my chest and waited for him to notice me.

"That's my car. Get off it," Cooke said, still holding the envelope in his hand.

"Actually it's the department's," I said, unfazed. That caused him to do a double take. He looked closer at me and his eyes narrowed and he stuck the envelope in his suit jacket's inner pocket rather quickly.

"I know you. You're the City Bitch's pet banshee detective."

Working out of the 13th Precinct has its advantages and disadvantages. Our commanding officer was Karen Vorlocke, the City Witch. A finer woman I have never known. Purlieu has its own celebrities and the City Witch was bigger than any pop star, movie star or reality TV star rolled together. If she arrested a jaywalker, it made the news. She and the cops around her have been caught more than once in the sights of the paparazzi. All of us have made the papers at some point or another, usually in the background of Karen's pictures. A good detective, or even a bad one, tends to notice things like that.

"The 7th Precinct is off your beaten path. What can I do ya for?" Cooke asked.

"Wanted to talk to you about a woman named Sandy Fishman."

Cooke chuckled and got a look on his face best described as a sexual leer. "Yeah, I know her. What do you want to know about her?"

"For starters, I heard she had your skin. That she was pulling your strings. Have you been compromised?" I said. In Arcane County, there are all sorts of magics that can be used to control people. Most of them are evil, dark things. Department policy mandates anyone who thinks they have fallen under anything of the sort to report it. Every precinct has its own witches and if they can't handle it, then it's bumped up to the City Witch. The system is designed to keep our cops honest. Unfortunately, sometimes we needed more than that.

"Did she tell you that?" Cooke said chuckling.

"No, someone else did. Is it true?" I asked.

"I realize we don't know each other, Detective Sorrow, but I hope you'd think better of me than that. My skin is in a safe deposit box at Wizard City Bank."

"Then how do you explain what I heard?" I said.

Cooke shrugged. "It's a little game I play with the ladies. A lot of them have heard the legends and it gives them a thrill to think they can control a man like me." Cooke walked to the trunk of his car and pulled out his key. I didn't exactly reach for my gun, but I got off the car ready for anything that he could pull out. Or so I thought.

Cooke lifted up something grey and furry. "It's a regular seal skin. I've got a dozen of them. I buy them from some hunters up in Alaska. When I

meet a sexy lady, I don't waste time with pick-up lines. I accidentally let
her see my skin and more often than not she'll pick it up and a few minutes
later I've got all the action I can handle. Sandy was happy to do the same
and let me tell you, she's a great piece of tail." Cooke raised his eyebrows
and grinned like he had made the funniest joke in the world. Seemed disappointed when I didn't laugh. "A few seals get clubbed so I can get laid. Who
cares?"

"That's cold. Don't you feel any affinity towards the poor creatures
you're having skinned for your sexual pleasure?" I said.

"You're humanoid. According to the scientists that makes all of us re-
lated to monkeys and apes. Would you go and arrest someone for killing a
lab monkey?"

"If the monkey was sentient it and the crime happened on my beat,
you're damn straight I would," I said.

"Good for you, Detective Sorrow. I guess I'm just not made of the same
moral fiber."

"I knew that as soon as I saw you walk out of the restaurant." I said and
let my eyes wander to his breast pocket. Cooke shifted uneasily. Unlike
the 7th, the 13th had a sterling reputation. Sure there were bad cops every-
where, but the ones in my precinct were punished for it. "Were you on duty
two nights ago?"

"No. Why do you ask?" Cooke asked. He was no dummy.

"Sandy Fishman was found dead. A piece of metal rebar sharpened and
bent to look like a fish hook was rammed through her skull and other places."

"I didn't kill her. That's all I'm going to say without my PBA lawyer
present. You want to talk to me, talk to my lawyer," Cooke said, getting into
his car and speeding away.

As I stood on the curb trying to figure out the best way to interrogate
a fellow cop with a cop lawyer, the waitress who dropped her panties for
Cooke came out the door to glare at me.

"What do you think you're doing with my man, bitch?" said the fish
maiden. Fish folk were different then mermaids. For one thing, they had
legs. For another, the scales that they had for skin wouldn't let anyone mistake them for human, even above the waist. Of course they had normal human female attributes and proportions, along with webbed hands and feet
thrown in for good measure.

"Excuse me? Your man?" I said, playing along. "Darrin never mentioned having a girlfriend."

"You heard me right, you banshee whore." Banshee skin is a bit on the pallor side of pale. Not hard to pick us out in a crowd. "Don't think all that death vision crap is gonna scare me off from fighting for what's mine. Don't think I didn't see him show you his seal skin. Well I've got news for you. That's just an old scam he pulls on hos and skanks. It ain't really his skin. It's a fake. He just does that to …" The fish maiden paused.

"Just does that to what? Get laid?" I said.

"Don't you talk about my man like that. He's loyal to me. If he ever cheated on me, it would be because someone was making him do it. Someone hypnotizing him with one of those fake skins. Don't even think about trying it. Last bitch that did that got what was coming to her," she said.

I took a step back pretending I was intimidated by the fish maiden. "What do you mean?"

The fish maiden grinned, showing a mouth full of sharp teeth. It made it easier for them to catch fish in the water, not to mention defend themselves. Sharks were afraid of the fish folk. They've been known in times past to eat survivors of shipwrecks or lone swimmers that ventured out too far. At least the bad fish folk. Like any race they had their good, their bad, and their ugly.

"Let's just say she tried to get her hooks into him, but it ended up working the other way around," she said.

"Are you saying you killed the last woman who tried to sleep with your man? And you'll kill me if I try to do the same?"

I was hoping for a confession, but instead all I got was a smile. "I guess you'll have to find that out for yourself, bitch, if you ain't smart enough to stay away from Cooke."

"Actually I find this line of reasoning fascinating and I think we should talk more about it back at the 13th Precinct." I flashed my badge. "You're under arrest."

"Oh no, I ain't," the fish maiden said rushing at me, slashing toward me with her webbed hands and claws. I side stepped her, then put my knee in her stomach, grabbed her arm and pulled it behind her back. I twisted her shoulder to try to put her down to the ground, but fish maiden shoulders are more flexible than most of the people that live on land so it didn't do the trick. Kicking her knees out from under her did however.

I had both of her hands cuffed behind her back when she turned and tried to bite my face off. I grabbed the back of her head and smashed her face into the sidewalk three or four times. I may not have technically had to have done it the last time, but better safe than sorry. And let's be honest, sometimes that sort of thing feels good.

Purlieu cops carry more than just handcuffs. We have tail cuffs, foot cuffs and the ever popular face cuffs. I called for a patrol car to take the fish maiden to the 13th Precinct to be placed in an interrogation room.

My suspect's name was Koral. Like many of the folks in Purlieu she didn't have a last name. Last names were human traditions that not everyone had adopted. I wasn't one of them. My first name is Deidre.

"Koral, we know what you did to Sandy Fishman. We're combing through footage from the surveillance cameras in the area," I said.

The fish maiden snorted. "Who you kidding? There ain't no cameras in that neighborhood. All residential, no business."

"What neighborhood?" I said.

"Whatever one you're talking about," she said.

"Ooh, nice cover. I'll never see through such an amazing recovery. Stop kidding yourself that you are good enough to get away with it. You're not. Come clean now and I'll do my best to get you a deal. The crime scene techs have been all over the apartment. Once they find proof, I would be able to help you," I said.

"I don't want any help from you. Ever. So screw you and your deal," the fish maiden screamed.

"Sounds like an activity you are very familiar with, judging by your activity with Cooke in the hallway at the restaurant. What's the matter, you weren't good enough for him to take the extra thirty seconds to go into the rest room or the coatroom?" I said.

Koral smirked. "You wish someone was hot enough for your death seeing ass that they couldn't wait to have you that bad."

"You think it was you serving him his food that made him hot? Men love the slave girl fantasy. Or maybe the envelope with the payoff money got him so horny that he nailed the first easy thing he found? Or are you just part of his payment? Wait, I bet you're the special of the day and all the customers who order dinner and dessert get to bend you over before they leave?" I said, trying to get her rattled and angry enough to say something she shouldn't. "Explains why business is down there."

My plan didn't seem to be working. Instead of getting angrier, Koral just leaned back in her chair and crossed her arms. "This was fun, but we're done talking. I want a lawyer."

Unfortunately that meant I had to stop until her attorney showed up.

To fill the time, I checked in again with the crime lab. Nothing new by way of forensics. The rebar was the same kind you could find on any construction site and there were no tell-tale signs of DNA of any sort.

Of course forensics was made a lot more difficult in Purlieu by the fact that you could buy magic gloves. These magic gloves were marketed primarily for household cleaning as they protect the wearer from getting any dirt or liquids on their hands. They're also used by surgeons and other medical folk, so they're not terribly hard to get a hold of. They're also sold in varieties that go up to the shoulder. Smart criminals tend to wear them so they don't leave anything behind. Of course we had witches that could use spells to find out who had touched things. The problem is the courts tend to allow that as a starting point to find other evidence, but rarely convict on that alone. Based on what Koral said to me we had enough for a search warrant for her home. We sent a couple cops over and they tossed the place with a couple of crime techs. We didn't get lucky. None of her clothes had any signs of blood on them.

We chatted again when her lawyer arrived. I got less than nothing. I was expecting a public defender, but she had a high priced lawyer whose suit cost more than I made in a week. Where did a waitress get the cash to hire that kind of high priced legal talent? I made a note to pull her financials.

We could hold her for seventy two hours and charge her with resisting arrest, but she'd get bail. Basically we'd have to let her walk if we couldn't make a case by then.

The trick was making a case that would hold up. It would take a very good detective to pull it off in this case. Or maybe a very bad one.

The next morning, Detective Cooke showed up at Fishman's Seafood for his weekly payment. He brushed right past the secretary without even talking and went into Fishman's office. He saw the merman sitting at the desk.

"I'm sorry to hear about your daughter," Cooke said. "I liked Sandy and because of that I will take half off this week." The merman behind the desk opened the envelope and took out half of the money and gave it to Cooke. "Pleasure doing business with you as always, Mr. Fishman."

"Well that's going to be the last extortion business you'll ever do," Fishman said, before suddenly morphing into Karen Vorlocke. A simple glamour spell was nothing for the City Witch. She also dropped the cloaking spell she had on me standing in the corner, my gun drawn. Next to me was a video camera on a tripod.

"I'd advise you not to move. Put your hands behind your head and lock your fingers," I said as I walked over and took his gun out of his holster and then proceeded to cuff his hands behind his back, then read him his rights.

"I hate dirty cops," the City Witch said. "Nice job, Sorrow."

"Thanks boss."

We took Cooke back to the 13th and booked him on a slew of charges. Thanks to recording the whole sting, we had Cooke by the short and curlys. There was no way he was going to walk.

Time to see if we could make him flip on his number one girl.

I made Cooke wait in the interrogation room for twenty minutes before I went in and laid out what I was offering. Figured he might have a different appreciation of the process when sitting on the other side.

"Let me get this straight – you want Koral for Sandy's murder and you want me to help?" Cooke said. "And you want me to wear a wire? What else did you ask Santa Claus to give you for Christmas?"

"Funny, but basically that's the deal on the table," I said.

"What's in it for me?" He said.

"The knowledge of knowing you did the right thing," I said. That got a smirk. "How about the City Witch doesn't use a truth spell on you to find out what other things you've been involved in."

He made a face. "She can't do that. I know my rights."

"You lost most of when we caught you extorting Fishman," I said. "You know damn well Vorlocke hates dirty cops. She'd have no problem using the spell. Are you so squeaky clean that we won't find something else that will add 10 or 20 years to your sentence?"

"I do this I get time served and walk," he said.

I laughed. "Not a chance. You're going away, all that can change is how long. You do this, Vorlocke doesn't fight the ADA offering you a deal. You also sign away your pension."

"I worked a long time. I ain't giving up the pension. Maybe I just ask for my PBA lawyer now."

I shrugged. "Once you're convicted you'll lose the pension anyway," I said. Happened ninety-nine percent of the time. Didn't want Cooke to manage to be part of the one percent. "You ask for the lawyer and this deal is off the table and Vorlocke makes your case her media darling. The public will be so riled up that the DA won't be able to go for less than the max. Or you can sign here and help me nail Koral."

"She's a crazy bitch," he said, reading over the deal.

"You're the one sleeping with her," I said.

He shrugged. "She's great in the sack. Sometimes that's worth a little crazy."

"Charming," I said.

He shrugged. "I make no apologies. I am what I am."

"Aren't we all. At least what most cops are doesn't make me want to puke up my last meal."

"Hope it was an all you can eat buffet. I'll wait." Our eyes met. Cooke looked away first. "If I do this thing, I want full immunity for anything that may come up in conversation with Koral."

"Blanket immunity for unnamed crimes? You're delusional. There's no way you're getting it. You know what happened to the last crooked cop Karen took down, right?"

His eyes narrowed and his jaw tightened. Every cop knew – guy was doing thirty-five to life in Iron Bars with no chance of parole for at least twenty years. The city witch is not afraid to use her influence with the DA's office. Karen is also very charismatic so when she testifies judges and juries pay rapt attention.

"Besides, you're claiming this extortion thing is your only crime. That means you don't have anything else to worry about, right?" I said.

Cooke sighed. "Right," he said, but I can tell he wasn't telling the truth. No magic power, just years of being a cop. "I'm eligible for parole in five?"

"With good behavior," I said. I hated the idea of him getting off so easy, but hated the idea of a murderer walking free more.

"Fine, I'll sign," Cooke said, wriggling a pen over the dotted line.

I checked to make sure he signed his own name and didn't try to pull a fast one. It's happened. "Anything else you'd like to tell us before we send you in there? If Koral did kill Sandy Fishman, she's a certifiable psychopath and dangerous as a vampire after a thirty day cleansing." A technique they use to get off blood. Works about one in ten times. The other nine it makes them starved, crazy, and more deadly than a swarm of chainsaws. "Koral's also a hell of a lot stronger than you are." Cooke looked insulted, but I didn't have the time or the patience to deal with his wounded ego. "I'm asking you again – is there anything else that we should know before we send you in?"

"Not a thing."

We waited until the clock ran down on the psycho fish woman. We didn't want her to think we had anything going on that she'd have to worry about. If she thought she was free and clear, she'd be more likely to incriminate herself.

We wired Cooke up with the latest in surveillance jewelry and sent him out on his booty call. Since he was no longer in the PPD once he signed the deal, Cooke didn't feel any need to follow the professional code of ethics, so those of us in the van outside got to listen to and watch a twenty minute video feed of his amorous affair. I didn't begrudge him his nookie. This was going to be his last shot at it. Fortunately the watch with the camera was pointed at the wall for most of it.

When the screaming and spanking was done, the pillow talk began. I guess Cooke figured it'd be easier to get information during the afterglow.

"Looks like you got away with it," Cooke said.

The fish woman's giggle was almost a gurgle. "Honey, you knew I would. No one messes with my man. Was awful good of you to tell me about her."

Now this was beginning to get incriminating, at least for Cooke. Probably why he wanted immunity. But why the hell would he agree to this if he knew Koral was going to implicate him on things not covered by his deal? Cooke was too smart for that. He had to have another angle.

"I never told you to kill her," Cooke said.

"Come on now, I didn't do anything you didn't want me to do. Otherwise why would you tell me about you and her? I know you get a little something elsewhere from time to time, but you never told me about any other skank. When the skin stealing thing didn't work like she thought it would, she tried to blackmail you by threatening to tell the other cops about your sideline. You didn't have to tell me what you wanted done – I knew. True love is like that."

The combination of sickly sweet and psychotic made me sick to my stomach.

"Even so, why'd you go so wild on Sandy Fishman? No way to make it look like an accident."

"Skank was messing with my man in bed and messing with my man's business. Mermaid whore tells everyone that she had your selkie skin. And we both know I figured out your booty scam a long time ago, but I showed you. I found your real selkie skin and made you my man and my bitch. So not only was the whore messing with my man's business, but she's trying to take money out of my pocket since you give me three quarters of everything you collect."

"You really didn't leave me much choice," he said barely keeping the bitterness out of his voice. At least we knew his angle. Koral goes to prison, she loses his skin and it gets returned to him. Mystic folk live longer than humans. Five years would be an inconvenience.

"On, honey, don't pretend you're upset over a little homicide since it lets you hold onto the teeny bit of cash I let you keep."

"How'd you do it so the cops couldn't pin it on you?" Cooke asked.

"It was easy. I waited in the canal for her to swim home, snuck up behind her and knocked her ass out. Then I dragged her scaly tail up to that vacant apartment and had my fun."

She went on to describe the crime in sickening detail.

"I think we have enough." I said over the radio. "As soon as Cooke leaves, we move in."

"Darren, why do you keep angling your watch towards me?" Koral said.

Damn it. "She may have found the camera," I said over the radio. "Get ready to move in on my mark."

"What happened to the Rolex I gave you? Where'd you get that piece of crap? Another shank? I may look the other way on occasion, but I ain't going to let you rub my nose in nothing by wearing some ho's cheap watch."

"It's work issue. Supposed to keep track of us. Some citizens group sued and now all cops got to wear one," Cooke said.

"Hey, what's that little circle on the dial? Is that a camera?" Lot of races have enhanced eyesight. Fish folk are one of them. Probably helps when swimming in murky water. Personally, I'd have to have it up to my face to see the lens. "Are you filming me talking about killing your shank?"

"I'd never do that baby," Cooke said. I hoped he'd talk his way out, but the picture showed him moving away from her, a little too heavy on the fish maiden full frontal visual.

"Everybody move in!" I yelled over the radio. Even as I ran inside, my earpiece was still picking up their conversation.

"Then let me see it," Koral said, grabbing his arm.

"Let go," Cooke said. "I'll shoot your ass." Cooke probably pulled his service revolver, but it was a bluff. It was empty. I wasn't about to let him bring live ammo that he might use against good cops. The same good cops who were supposed to be protecting him.

I was going all out, but Officer Summers was first one in. Leprechauns can really haul when they need to. I wasn't far behind and was just in time to see that things had gone from bad to deadly all too quickly.

The fish woman had her hand around what looked like sealskin and from the look on Cooke's face it was probably his real one.

"Go down on your gun, you bastard. Put it in your mouth and suck it," Koral said. Cooke obeyed, rage in his eyes fighting the tears running down his cheeks. "You wear a wire to send me up the river? It's one thing to betray me with another woman, but it's a whole other thing to do this. It's over. You keep the gun in your mouth and don't stop pulling the trigger until you're dead."

"Freeze. Belay that order Koral or I will shoot you," I said. However it was too late. Cooke pulled the trigger, but his empty gun just went click. I smiled, thinking I beat the Reaper, but old Grim is a hell of a better chess player than me.

Koral pulled a twenty-two out of drawer on the bedside table. "Darrin, use this gun instead." Summers and I opened fire, hitting the fish maiden a half dozen times, but we were still too late. Koral tossed the gun to Cooke before she fell.

"Cooke, don't do it," I said, helpless. Cooke was fighting the order, tears and sweat fighting to see which could soak his face more. The disgraced detective wasn't strong enough to beat the magic that bound his race to their seal skins. And it wasn't like I could shoot him to stop him from shooting himself.

Or maybe I could. I put a slug in his right elbow which forced him to drop the gun. Cooke fell to the ground, but still bound by the order the fish maiden had given him grabbed the revolver with his left hand.

This time I didn't have a clear shot. If I fired it would kill him just as dead as one from his own hand.

Summers dove on the fish maiden and wrestled the seal skin from her. He socked the wounded Koral once in the jaw and she lay still. The leprechaun stood up holding the selkie's true skin it in his hands. "Cooke, I order you to ..."

Summer's plan was brilliant, just too late. Bam. The twenty-two fired once, splattering Cooke's brains all over their little love nest.

Summer checked Koral's pulse, shook his head and came over to me. "You okay, Sorrow?"

I nodded trying not to cry. Ruined the tough cop image.

"Should I call the meat wagon?" Summers said as other officers secured the crime scene.

"And an ambulance. The fish maiden's still alive," I said.

"She don't have a pulse," the leprechaun said.

"Fish folk have a hibernation state when the seas get too cold. Helped them survive the bitter arctic seas. She just slowed her metabolism down. She's not going to die tonight," I said.

"I guess you'd know." Summer said. He made the call on the radio, then looked down at Cooke. Never one to beat around the bush when he could trample through it, Summers pointed his chin at the former detective who was minus some skull and brains. "So you knew Cooke was going to buy it?"

I nodded. "Yep, as soon as I saw him tonight. Even tried to save him, not that he deserved it."

Summers looked at me.

"On the very rarest of occasions a banshee can help someone cheat the Reaper," I said.

"How rare?" Summers said.

"My grandmother did it. Once."

"You ever do it?"

"Nope. Never heard of anyone else who ever did except my Maimeó. But I'm going to do it someday," I said. "And once I figure out how, I'll keep doing it."

Summers nodded. "I believe you will. What did you do for Cooke?"

"I saw he was going to eat a bullet, so I made sure he didn't have any. I figured he might do it out of shame later, so I was going make sure the cops who took him back to jail had no sidearms." I knew beyond the shadow of a doubt that had Cooke not gone on the sting, a gun would have ended up in his hand and mouth some other way.

"I would have guessed Cooke would get sent to meet his maker by a jealous husband," Summers said, lighting up a pair of cigarettes and handing me one. I took it and nodded my thanks. "Hey Sorrow, would you do me a favor?"

"Probably," I said.

"If you ever get the chance to try to beat the Reaper for me, will you give it a try?"

I nodded, knowing that despite my bravado I probably wouldn't be able to. At least with Summer's death something good would come of it.

EMT's had gotten Koral on a stretcher and were rushing her to the ambulance. Summers and I watched her go, then stood nearby as they put a sheet over Cooke.

"Cooke may have been a crooked cop, but he was still a cop. I hate cop killers," Summers said. All cops did. "I know you don't like to talk about it, but how does the scaly bitch buy it? She get the death penalty for this?"

"Not sure, but let's just say no matter how long she gets in prison, it's going to be a life sentence," I said.

Summers nodded, almost smiling. "Fight over cigarettes?" he said, waving the coffin nail in his hand.

I smiled. "One of Cooke's other women evening the score."

"Poetic, I like it. You going to tell the warden?"

I shrugged. "Won't make a difference. The warden might even be the other woman. Besides, Koral told me when I arrested her that she didn't want help from me. Ever. And you know me Summers – I aim to please."

And sometimes to kill.

LOCAL CATCH
John L. French

He sang of joy – joy of life, joy of the sea, the joy he would find at the end of his journey. There he would meet his mate and he would know her by her song. Bonded forever, they would raise young and teach them the old songs and help them create their own.

His had been a long trip, one that was nearly over. Looking toward its end, he failed to sense the danger around him. Ensnared, he was lifted up into the harsh light of the Above. Blinded at first, his eyes quickly adapted to the brightness around him.

Then came something sharp and shiny. Darkness fell around him for the last time. His song ended.

The water was cold against her skin. She had heard the song and had no choice but to respond to it. It spoke of romance and of finding one's true love. It promised pleasure beyond that which she had already known. It offered a chance to be reborn, a baptism into a new life.

Shedding what little she was wearing, she swam sang toward the song. Entranced by its melody, she failed to sense the danger around her. Taken suddenly, she was dragged Below. Sharp edges began their work.

The water turned red as darkness fell around her, the song changing to one of grim satisfaction. Then she heard it no more.

It was in a time before a knight known as Conor of Scotia became a hero, a time when he was simply a wandering sword-for-hire looking for adventure. He had just come from the Middle Kingdoms where he learned to be careful for what he wished – and of how he wished. Riding west then south, the knight soon came to the shores of the Great Sea.

Sainte-Paul was just another town on the edge of that sea. Conor had no special reason for stopping save that both he and his horse were tired. Tired of his journey, tired of his own cooking, tired of sleeping on hard ground with only his steed for company. He wanted hot food, a hotter bath, a soft bed and maybe even softer companionship. He hoped to find all four in the first tavern he saw.

Sainte-Paul was typical of the towns he had found in the south of Francia. An easy approach – no guards, no walls, nothing to keep anyone out. Much different from his own land, where every stranger was a possible enemy until proven otherwise.

Still, the town's trusting appearance was belied by the stares of its people. Some viewed him with curiosity. This Conor understood, guessing that it was not often that a man-at-arms rode through their streets on a battle charger. Others, though, glared at him with suspicion or even hatred and still others turned from him in fear.

For a moment Conor thought to remain on his horse and continue on to the next town. He might have, if he could have been sure of reaching it before dark. His reluctance to spend another night outdoors and the sudden appearance of an inn decided him. He would stay the night in Sainte-Paul.

Leaving his horse tied outside, Conor entered the inn. Ignoring the sudden silence that his appearance caused, he walked to the bar.

"Ale, please," he said in the language of Francia, one of the many he had had to learn as part of his training, "and a room with a bath. And have someone see to my horse."

The innkeeper hesitated but his reluctance faded when one of the knight's silver pieces landed on the bar's surface. All that was left was his surprise; surprise that someone from the barbaric North could not only speak a civilized tongue, but wanted to bathe.

"Yes, good knight, we have a room, one that was cleaned only two days ago and has not yet been slept in. And we can most certainly prepare you a bath before you retire. But as for ale, good sir, alas, we have only wine."

Conor smiled, for a minute he had forgotten where he was. "The wine of this country is worth the journey, landlord. A cup to start with if you please and food to go with it. Keep both coming until the bath water is good and hot."

The wine Conor was served was excellent and his meal of fish and fresh greens even better.

"Landlord," the knight asked as his cup was being filled for the third time, "this fish is, without any doubt, the best I have ever tasted."

"Thank you, sir, it is a ... local catch."

Conor would have inquired further but just then four armed men came through the door. Dressed in a similar fashion, they seemed to part of the town's Watch.

Trouble, Conor thought as three of the men walked toward him, the fourth remaining close to the door.

Loosening his sword in its scabbard, Conor thought again, Trouble. On studying them as they approached, he added, but nothing that can't be handled. He hoped that the landlord had not had time to take his horse to the stable.

"You will come with us," demanded the man in the middle.

Deliberately ignoring them, Conor took a last drink of wine and what would probably be his last bite of the excellent fish. Finally he looked up and said,

"No."

"That was not a request. You will come with us."

Without bothering to rise Conor said, "Gentlemen, I know all too well the probable fate of a stranger, a foreign stranger, when he surrenders himself to the Watch. I do not wish to suffer that fate."

With one swift move Conor overturned the table at which he was sitting, drawing his sword as he rose. A knife appeared in his left hand.

"I am Conor of Tuam, a knight of Scotia, son of Seamus, son of Liam, son of Conor. I am of the Fianna and trained with the Red Branch. Gentlemen, while I do not know how many men it would take to bring me down, the four of you are not enough. If, however, you think otherwise, I'll give you time to draw your weapons. The survivor can reimburse the landlord for the damages."

The man in charge has not made sergeant by taking chances or being stupid. Surmising that all the men of the Watch together might not be enough to defeat the man whose blade was dangerously close to his stomach he quickly came to a decision.

"Perhaps I misphrased my request, good knight. I had meant merely to ask your assistance in a matter most urgent. A man of your obvious training and experience would be invaluable in an investigation of ours."

Conor lowered but did not sheath his sword. "As your beautiful language is not my native tongue, perhaps it is I who misunderstood you, sir. Let it not be said that a knight of Scotia did not respond to a request for help. But ..."

"Yes?"

"But first, let's have some wine and more of that excellent fish. And then I think, a bath."

Conor was glad that he had eaten before seeing the body, or rather, half a body. It was the upper torso of a young woman.

"Where's the rest of her, Sergeant Philippe?"

Philippe shrugged. "Who can say? We found this much of her on the beach this very morning. As you were the only armed stranger in town you can see why we …"

The knight nodded. "Understandable. I may have made the same mistake. Who is she?"

Another shrug. "She has been in the water for some time. With the damage to her face, we may never know."

There are other ways of identifying a body, Conor thought as he looked at this one. Already he had seen one or two marks that someone … intimate with the poor woman might recognize.

"Anyone missing from your town, Sergeant?"

"My men have already checked, Sir Conor. No one. And I have sent word to the neighboring towns asking that same question."

"Very good. Now before heat and time begin their work on this poor unfortunate, may I suggest bringing in the single men of this village, and possibly those married ones who may at times forget their vows, to see if they might have known this woman."

"But how? As I have said, her face, it is … oh." Philippe shook his head. "It would not be right, to expose her like that."

"She is past caring, Philippe, and it was not right for her to die as she did."

"Of course, I will make the arrangements."

After the sergeant left, Conor began a closer examination of the body. Excluding what ravages the sea had wrought, she bore no wounds on either her front or back. Perhaps she was drowned then butchered, he hoped so, but the knight knew of only way to be sure of that and he needed what was left of her torso intact.

What tool was used, the knight wondered. Familiar with most types of edged weapons, Conor knew that no straight blade had been used. Judging from the damage, whatever had done the job was sharp but jagged. He thought maybe a chirurgeon's saw, but even that left smoother marks than what he found on the backbone.

"Sir Conor," came Sergeant Philippe's voice from the doorway, "I have brought some men and more are on their way."

"Good. Anyone refuse?"

"Not a one. Most are anxious to view the remains, they are … curious." This last was said with just a trace of disgust.

"They are human, Philippe." Draping a sheet over the area where the woman's lower body should have been he added, "Send them in."

"There's one thing, the priest is here. He wishes to be present."

"Tell the good father to pray for her soul, we'll tend her body. Now send in the men one at a time."

An hour went by, then two. Some of the men lingered, as to memorize this once in a lifetime sight. Others hurried past, barely glancing at the body. None showed any sign of recognition or guilt. Conor thought back to the Druids of his homeland who believed that in the presence of the killer a murdered body would arise and point. As much as he had argued with them, Conor wished one of those Druids were with him now.

Another dozen or so men had walked past when a youth entered the room. He was of that age that is between boy and man and just as the others like him had done, he walked past slowly and reverently, as if a great mystery was being revealed. Unlike the others, he reached out and gently touched the woman's arm.

"Philippe," the knight called out, "hold the line." Then to the youth, "What is your name, boy?"

"Etienne, Sir."

"You know her, don't you? You knew her, didn't you?"

Understanding the implication, the boy nodded. "Her name is, was Anne. She is from Sainte-Pierre, the next town over. We met one day. I had never … she was my first … I was her … her latest. She showed me what it was like to be a man and now she's …"

Seeing that the youth was close to tears, Conor pulled the sheet completely over the body. "I have to ask, Etienne, how do you know that it is she?"

"She has … two moles … here." He indicated her left breast. Conor nodded. He had seen them, known that a lover could not have failed to note them.

"Thank you. You may go, but speak nothing of this to anyone."

When the boy had gone, Conor called in the sergeant. "Philippe, come in, if you please."

When the officer appeared, the knight said, "Her name is Anne, the boy Etienne, well, you know how soon boys think they become men."

Philippe nodded. "One of my men has just returned from Sainte-Pierre. A woman by that name has not been seen for some days. It seems she was a very giving woman, one who shared her favors easily." He looked at the body. " Jealousy?"

"If so, jealousy mixed with madness, a dangerous combination."

"What is also dangerous, friend Conor, is a woman from one town found in ours. And a young man who knew her intimately if but briefly. There could be trouble."

"That kind of trouble can be handled. Now if you would, please bring in the priest to administer the last sacrament. If he objects, remind him of the Magdalene."

That evening, the boy Etienne stood on the shore where the woman's upper body was found and looked over the water. He had sinned, or so he believed. It had not seemed like a sin at the time, but now … he remembered the words of the priest from the pulpit, words about the sins of the flesh. He had not understood at the time but now he did. They had sinned, he had sinned and Anne had paid the price.

"She was the bigger sinner," said a small voice inside him. "She had been with many men, she led you into sin. It was not your fault, not your sin."

As young as he was, Etienne knew this to be a lie. Anne, poor sweet Anne, had not led him anywhere. He had gone willingly. It was their sin, not just hers but she alone had paid.

Then he heard it, a song that played to his heart. It sang of love found and lost, of joy and sorrow, of pain and redemption. Looking around, the boy could not find its source, then realized from where it came.

The song called to him and he had no choice but to answer. Without pausing to remove his clothes, Etienne walked into the sea to wash the stain from his soul.

At his table in the tavern Conor tried to think of what to do next. Sergeant Philippe's men had begun questioning the citizens of Sainte-Paul, hoping to find someone who had seen the woman Anne and, more importantly, anyone who may have been with her. Even knowing what trouble it might cause, he had also asked the Watch of Sainte-Pierre to inquire of its citizens about the movements of the victim and any strangers, outsiders or jealous lovers.

Not for the first time did the knight wonder what he was doing, why he had remained to help in this matter. He was just a man with a sword, not a hero or wizard of whom the bards sang. One of them would have spotted the killer right away and after a chase and maybe a beautiful maiden or two in peril, there would have been a great duel during which the villain would be vanquished and after which one of the maidens would have been most grateful.

But this was not one of those tales. There were no heroes. The victim, may her soul rest easy, was certainly no maiden and the villain was likely to be caught purely by chance. No, this was not one of those tales.

Thinking of tales caused Conor to remember something from earlier that morning. He was tending his horse when he saw the landlord with an enormous fishtail. He had wondered at the time if that was the "local catch" that the man turned into such a delicious meal. He had also wondered what had happened to the other half of the fish.

Half a fish and half a woman. Sitting at the tavern table Conor could not help put the two together. If the victim had not been indentified he might have thought … but no. The knight had seen many strange things in his life but women from the sea were still the stuff of legends and stories told to children.

Even as Conor put such fanciful thoughts out of his mind he heard a watchman call his name.

"Sir Conor, come at once. There's another one."

Led to the beach Conor saw two watchmen standing by a small figure. As the man who came to get him started toward the water, the knight held him back.

"Wait," he said. "Have you been down there?'

"No, Sir."

"Then let's not disturb things anymore than they need be. Wait here and keep the curious from coming down."

Taking a roundabout way to the body, Conor studied the sand, seeing only two sets of footprints. Nor had he seen anymore by the time he reached the water's edge.

Sergeant Philippe and one other stood over the body. Looking down, Conor saw that it was Etienne's. He had been killed in the same manner as had Anne. Choking down what he was feeling – horror, uselessness, a sense that he had somehow failed the boy – the knight asked,

"Has anyone been down here?"

Both men shook their heads.

"Yours, and now mine, are the only tracks." Looking out over the water, Conor added, "Whoever it was came from the sea."

An idle thought of the mer-people crossed his mind. The knight chased it away with,

"Who knew about the boy?"

"Only us," Philippe said.

"Anyone from Sainte-Pierre might have seen them together," the watchman said in anger. Then he ran off.

"I'll stay with the body, Philippe. You try to stop that hothead before it's …."

The news had spread. A crowd had gathered. Even now the watchman who had been with Conor and Philippe was talking to them, exhorting them, riling them up.

"… too late."

Some of the crowd remained. Others followed the watchman.

"They will be going toward Sainte-Pierre, to seek revenge for Etienne." The sergeant looked down at the body. "Just as I am sure that there are those in that town who blame us for the death of one of their own. There will be blood spilled today, Sir Conor."

"Enough blood has been spilled, Philippe. Remain here. I'll send someone to help you with the boy."

Riding ahead of the angry townspeople, Conor intercepted them just moments before they met a similar mob from Sainte-Pierre. The sight of the armed knight gave both groups pause.

Now this is something I can handle, Conor thought, at least I hope I can.

As he had told Sergeant Philippe, Conor did not how many men it might take to bring him down. But from the size of both mobs there looked to be enough. Still, they were just townsfolk and he a trained knight. And part of his training was how to avoid a messy fight.

"Who wants to die today?" Conor shouted loud enough for all to hear. When there were no replies except whispers and mumbling, he shouted again,

"Who wants to die today? Let him step forward and I will grant his wish."

Again there were no replies. No one stepped forward.

"Then return to your homes. Let the Watch handle this."

"But they killed Etienne," called the watchman who had incited the Sainte-Paul mob. Some of the people behind him murmured their agreement.

"Who did?" the knight asked. "Point them out and I will slay them for you."

The watchman grew silent. Conor turned to the crowd from Sainte-Pierre.

"And is there anyone you would have killed for the death of the woman Anne?"

There is one in every crowd. This one shouted back, "Someone has to pay."

"Someone will," the knight replied. "But not now, not today. Go home. Two deaths are enough. Do not seek to add more to this tragedy."

Their anger defused for now, the two mobs slowly dispersed. Conor waited for all to leave, the last to go being the watchman who had started it all. Giving the knight a sullen look, he too finally departed.

"That one will bear watching," Conor said to his horse. "But that is Philippe's problem. Mine is to make good on my pledge that two deaths are enough."

The torsos of both bodies had been found on the beach. Despite an exhaustive search of the homes and country sides of both towns, the remaining parts of neither victim were located. Nor had any fresh grave been found. It seemed to Conor that, for whatever reason, the killer had consigned the lower halves of the victims to the sea.

With that thought in mind, Conor set up a vigil on the beach. The night was cold, and as full as the moon was, it shed light but no heat. With only a blanket for warmth, the knight stood his lonely watch and looked out over the waters of the Great Sea.

A flash of silver. At first Conor thought he might have imagined it but then saw it again. A flash in the moonlight. Staring out over the water he both saw and heard it, a great tail rising out of then slapping the surface of the sea.

"Local catch," he quietly said to himself, marveling at the size of the fish.

Then he heard the music. It came from over the waves and wafted on to the shore. It sang to Conor of love and passion, promising to fulfill his most ardent desires. The song shifted and became one telling of the glories that could be achieved if only one sought them out. A third tune told of the treasures of the deep, waiting for one brave man to dive deep and claim them.

He was tempted, Conor was. A young man still, he had never found true love, and the song of passion fulfilled drew him toward the water's edge.

In his own country he had heard tales of brave heroes and great kings, and so was inspired to become a knight. And what knight does not want his own praises sung? Thoughts of glory drew him closer to the water.

And what man could not use treasure? If not for now, then to set aside for his later years when his body can go no more a roaming.

Without realizing it, Conor found himself at the water's edge. But for recent events he might have continued until he was under the sea, his armor dragging him to the bottom. But he had learned in the Middle Kingdoms that nothing comes without a price and that promises were no more solid than the air they on which they came.

His training saved him. Knights of Scotia are taught how to defend themselves against many kinds of danger, those that threaten the soul as well as the body. They are also taught arts other than those of battle and war.

"Close." Looking around, Conor saw a rocky outcropping jutting into the water. Carefully walking out on it, he let his voice drift over the sea. "Now let me sing you one."

Suspecting now that the legends were true, that the sirens of the sea were more than just a children's tale, Conor sang his own song.

His voice was not pretty. It would never successfully woo a fair maid unless she had already decided to be won. His was a warrior's voice, heard best in the mead hall after a hard won battle and far too much ale. Still he sang.

Conor sang of a woman whose joy in life was sharing that joy with others. He sang of a boy whose first step toward manhood had been his last. He sang of sadness – the sadness of loved ones, the ache that each death leaves in the hearts of those who remained.

His song was echoed and left an ache in his own heart. Never had he felt the pain and sorrow of death and loss as he had that night. He learned of lovers ripped from one another, and how cruel fate returned the bodies of those lost to the sea.

The song from the sea shifted and became one of justice sought and vengeance found. And on that song Conor suddenly knew all, knew that the legends were true, knew that more would be lured into the depths and why, knew what the local catch had been.

Even as his stomach churned with the thought of meals recently eaten, even acknowledging the rightness of the cause, he could not, would not allow any more innocents to die.

Conor sang of the deaths of those innocents and his intention to prevent more. His song was of a great fleet of fishing vessels sailing along the coast. He sang of nets and hooks and spears, of poisoned waters and Greek Fire. He sang of the black powder from Cathay that caused great destruction and how it could be made to work under water. Conor sang of the cruelty of Man and how it would be employed against the peoples of the sea.

Unless … His voice hoarse, his stomach threatening to disgorge all of what he had eaten in the past few days, Conor sang of peace. He sang of deaths on both sides and justice that he himself would mete out.

Silence.

Had his song been heard? Had it been heeded? Or must he give the warning that would mean war between the land and the sea?

In the moonlight he saw them, head and bodies of men and women. No, not quite. The eyes were not right. In the light of the moon they shone somewhat like a cat's. And they had not hair but tendrils. Their hands when raised were webbed. These were the Mer, no longer legend.

Two swam closer. Soon they too were up on the rocks, supported by their strong upper limbs. Conor could easily tell that one was male and the other female.

"Too many have died," came a voice like a song that was more in his head than his ears. Only by seeing her lips move could Conor tell that it was the mermaid who had spoke. He was about to agree, when the merman added,

"Too many of the People. Your kind have separated lover from lover, mother from child, brother from sister. Blood has been spilled. More blood must follow."

"Your blood will follow. Your sea will fill with it. You have heard my song. It was no idle boast. Mankind is a cruel race when we are threatened. When we war on what we fear it is not to the death but to extinction."

"We have no choice, we know no other way." The two were about to slip away when Conor shouted,

"Hold."

When they did he asked, "Yours is a warrior race?"

"It is," came the musical voice of the sea maiden.

"I too am a warrior. I offer a warrior's challenge. Let us fight, here, tonight, for the fate of all."

"And how may that be?" she asked. "You cannot enter our world and we," raising herself up, she flashed her long silver tail, "cannot stand in yours."

"We have spears," offered the merman. "Stand on these rocks, human. If you can survive our throws, we would count you as victor and stop our predation. If you cannot, you go Below and so does your knowledge of us."

"How many throws?"

"Ten of ours were lost," replied the maid, "so that many throws."

"You killed two of my people," countered Conor, "eight throws."

"Agreed." The male slipped back into the sea. The female mer, however, remained.

"You wear a strange shell, human. It must all be removed before the challenge can commence."

Conor nodded. "But just the armor, my lady of the sea. The rest stays on."

Her mouth formed a disappointed frown, one that seemed to Conor to be universal among females no matter what species. "Pity, I had hoped …" Then she smiled, "If you survive this challenge, I may perhaps offer you a more difficult one."

There was no mistaking the invitation, or maybe it was a ploy to distract him with other thoughts. Briefly wondering if and how such a challenge could be met, Conor gave a knightly bow and replied,

"Then my lady, you have given me another reason to win."

Another smile, another flash of her tail and she disappeared beneath the waves.

Divesting himself of all armor but his sword and buckler, Conor stood ready to meet the challenge. He wondered from where the first throw would come. Heads appeared above the surface. Diversions, he thought as he weighed his chances.

About even. The mer were used to throwing under water. Hitting a target on land might be more difficult. Or so he hoped.

He did not see the first spear coming. It flew over his head. The second splashed into the sea in front of the rocks.

Two gone, thought the knight even as he knew they were getting the range. Putting himself deeper into a warrior state of mind, he scanned the sea.

There, a head and an arm. He stopped that spear on his buckler. Turning quickly, he deflected another with his sword.

The fifth spear grazed his leg, a sixth came dangerously close to his head.

He sensed rather than heard the mer behind him. The male had climbed onto the rocks and was preparing to throw. Conor had little time to do else but drop flat as the spear passed over him.

A scream then cries of anguish filled his head. Had the last spear come he could not have blocked it. When he rose Conor saw why he still lived.

A merman was on the rocks. He had come close in order to use a short thrust to end the knight should the other spears fail. When Conor dropped, the seventh throw found him instead.

Letting go his sword, the knight rushed to him and drew him up on the rocks.

Conor would have saved the mer if he could. As it was, all he could do was hold him as songs of mourning and loss filled the night.

A male's voice entered his mind. "It is over. You are the victor."

"There is no victor here," Conor said as he handed the dead mer back to his own kind. "And it is not over."

When the sun rose the next morning there was no one at the inn save the landlord and Conor.

"You have arisen early, Sir Knight. Some of our local catch to break your fast?"

"I think not. I … have lost my taste for fish. Come, landlord, and sit beside me." Conor threw a silver piece on the table to tempt the man. When he was seated,

"I spoke with the Mer last night."

"The who, good sir?"

"The Mer, the People of the Sea. The source of your 'local catch.' Are you telling me you did not know?"

A lie almost came from the landlord's mouth. The look on the knight's face stopped it. A nod of his head established the landlord's guilt.

"Who else? Your wife?"

The landlord shook his head. Conor allowed him the lie.

"Who brings them to you?"

"There is this fisherman. By accident he found their spawning ground. He is skillful with his net. He brings us what he catches."

"He supplies only you?"

The landlord shrugged. "Who can say?"

"Tell me his name and when I find him, he will."

It was then that both men became aware of noises coming from out front.

"That would be the folk of both towns gathering. I had Philippe spread the word that I might have news of the murderer today. Good sir, you have a choice. I can march you outside and give you to them, those people who just yesterday were ready to slaughter each other because of these deaths. Or we can slip out the back."

Conor allowed the landlord a moment of hope before adding, "So I can give you to the Mer. I understand that they have ways of keeping a man from drowning, of allowing him just enough air to live on while his body feeds their young. Your choice."

"What of my wife?"

Conor looked at the front door. "That way and she at least gets to live."

Then to the back. "That way, I make no promises."

Together the two men walked out the front of the tavern. A quick hanging followed.

Conor paid one last visit to the rocks on the shore. In the moonlight he sang of justice done and then of a fishing ship, a location and a time. Together, he sang, they would end this.

Two days later, on a dock not too far from Sainte-Paul, Conor stood watching a fishing ship burn. Boarding the ship by force of arms, he had found the evidence of the crew's guilt – a dead mer cut in two. That's when he fired the ship, but not before giving its captain and his men a choice – they could face the flames or his sword, or take their chance in the water. He did not say what fate awaited those who chose the latter.

With hooks and gaffs, two decided to face his steel. They lay dying at his feet. Seeing their comrades fall, the other crewmen jumped overboard.

That's when the screaming started. It quickly stopped when the men were dragged under.

The captain was the last to die. Rejecting the flames, the sea and the knight's sword, the captain drew his own blade and ended his life. As the flames consumed the corpse, Conor reflected that there were hotter fires awaiting him.

And so it is ended, Conor thought as he walked down to the sea. He listened for a moment, expecting a song.

At first there was none. Then as he turned to leave a lone voice sang to him, telling him of a place and a time and a challenge yet to be met.

A Knight of Scotia, Conor thought, should not refuse a lady, nor should he refuse a challenge. Eager and curious, he sang back his acceptance.

THE PAIN OF BEING
C.J. Henderson

"I wonder what pleasures men can take in making beasts of themselves!"

"I wonder, madam, that you have not penetration enough to see the strong inducement to this excuse; for he that makes a beast of himself gets rid of the pain of being a man."
Samuel Johnson

"**O**h, Marv, I wish ... there's so ... oh God, this really looks like the end this time!"

"Sweetheart, as much as I hate to agree with an assessment so negative ..."

There was no doubt that producer/anchorman Marvin Richards' feelings were in complete unison with those of his executive assistant, Lora Dean. Richards was the driving power behind *Challenge of the Unknown*, the most successful reality show to ever hit television. On the one hand, technically it was basically only a news show. But oh, what news.

"I think you're right."

Challenge was a weekly look at what was going on in the wonderful world of the weird and strange. If there was a ghost on the loose, a UFO to be revealed, a werewolf, vampire or team of ice dancing, zither-playing zombies of which the nation needed to be informed, Richards and his crew were there to do the informing. Thursdays at 8:00. With hourly updates to all major stories available at their website.

"I, I just don't understand it, Marv ..." said the young woman, watching the circle of deadly things all about them drawing closer, "how does something like this happen?"

"Well, you know what I always say, sweetheart ..." answered the producer as the dripping creatures slowly closed in on them from every direction;

"People are stupid."

As the closest of the monstrosities reached toward the trembling couple, Richards' brain raced back to how their predicament had started. All the while, a part of his mind whispering that the fact they had been surrounded by a slow-moving school of sentient sea beasts might mean that he himself was not all that bright, either. In fact, looking into the various pairs of dead fish eyes closing with his, the rest of the anchorman's brain soured slightly as he could not found any way he could disagree with his self-assessment.

"Congratulations, Marvin. Looks like you and your best will be heading for New England."

"Really? And is there any particular reason I would be doing such a thing, Jeffrey?"

"A most wonderfully particular reason, my son. Something new and exciting, wild and provocative, indeed, possibly the greatest single infusion of WOW! this show has ever …"

"One word it for me, Jeff."

"Mermaids."

Richards actually allowed his head to swivel a touch so that he could make the barest eye contact with Jeffrey Milton, the network vice president leaning half his body into the producer's office at that moment. Tilting it just so, the anchorman squinted so as to cover his excitement. Then, his look one of proper neutrality, in a tone meant to convey disbelief rather than the unbridled hope which was actually surging through his system, he asked through the camouflage of a forced yawn;

"For real?"

"Real as we can tell. Fishermen off the coast of Massachusetts caught some kind of mermaid or merman or mer-whatever in their nets last night. Now, the thing did manage to get away, and their photographic evidence is for shit – cell phones at night on the ocean, oy – so, all they've got to show for their story is torn nets, but ..."

"But, it's a story ... yeah, I get it. Any diluting coverage yet?"

"Ummmmmmm ... it seems our local affiliate up there did a 'can-you-believe-this' spot."

"Oh ... did they?" Richards seized on Milton's dismissive tone, knowing he had found the weakness in his adversary's maneuverings. "And, tell me, how did that go?"

"Oh, you know," answered the vice president, knowing his weak attempt at subterfuge had already been uncovered, "It is possible they might have ruffled a few feathers with their depiction of ..."

"They made these fishermen look stupid, didn't they?"

"Some might interpret ..."

"Breeding resentment toward television folk in general ..."

"Such is possible ..."

"Resentment that I'd have to overcome if I went in there ..."

"A situation," responded Milton quickly, "that makes it easier for you to go in with an understanding attitude ..."

"Or putting us in the role of second-wave jackals come to make them look even more foolish ..."

"Giving you the chance to let the healing begin."

Richards stared at the vice-president for a moment, considering his next move. In truth he did need a bit of filler – their forthcoming episode was still about six minutes light. But, to jump on a story at the suggestion of a mere VP would mean a loss of face throughout the corporate hierarchy.

"Still," he thought, "we've never had anything like a mermaid before. Could be a fun story to do just for the opportunity of pissing off the Disney people. Again."

Finally unhooding his eyes a bit, signaling that he was willing to consider the idea – possibly – Richards turned his head on his neck as if trying to unkink a muscle, saying;

"Well, Jeff, I don't know ... packing a team up and shooting all the way up the coast ..."

"It's not that far ..."

"And, I do so hate damage control work ..."

"Come on, Marv, ol' boy ... we're taking a pounding in that marketplace. Do it for me, what do you say?"

Suddenly the producer found his gears turning. Milton never used an endearment like "ol' boy" unless he was on an angling expedition, casting about for something he not only needed, but which he was incapable of getting from anyone else. Smiling, allowing his lips to part just the right degree to signal he understood their unspoken subtext, Richards countered;

"Now, Jeff, I'd love to help you, but well, you know ... what kind of a spot are you going to be putting me in if I start running up the budget in mid-season? You know what the end of the hall is going to say if ..."

"Leave those guys to me. The affiliate really screwed the pooch on this one."

"Shouldn't have made these fishermen look stupid – right?"

"Fish people, goddamned fish people, wearing gold chains, no less. Oy, jump a judge," snapped the VP, forgetting himself for a moment, "what kind of backwoods knuckle dragger tells a story like that? How can you blame our people – I mean, who in the name of God can blame anyone for laughing at ..."

Then, Milton suddenly caught himself, realizing how insensitive his lapse into common sense – let along logic – might have sounded to anyone passing by. Gulping audibly, he hung his head, then finally threw the last of his cards on the table.

"Okay ... it's bad. Time for the audience reveal – the bastards are threatening a law suit. If you were to get up there and take them seriously, turn on the old Richards charm ... let them know that no one in the media would ever ..."

"Well, no one at our network ... right J.M.?"

"Absolutely, M.R."

The VP's smile of relief appeared so sincere Richards was willing to give at least two-to-one odds that it might be genuine. After a few more minutes of pretending to care about anything besides themselves, the two executives parted company – Milton to return to his office to check his Facebook page to see if he had made any new friends since that morning, and Richards to summon Dean to his office. As she entered his faux-modern domain several minutes later, he asked;

"What kept you?"

"I was down in Finance, getting our vouchers."

"What vouchers?"

"Hotel reservations, meal budget, travel expenses from here to Massachusetts and back, crew allotment ..."

"Boston," asked the producer. "I hope – yes?"

"We'll be flying in there, but then we'll need to take a rental up the coast to the village where our litigious net jockeys are located." When Richards looked at his assistant askance, she rolled her eyes while asking him;

"You do know I can hear everything that goes on in here – right?"

"Yes."

"And our forthcoming episode is still about six minutes light – right?"

"Yes."

"And you weren't really considering turning down a chance to irritate the Disney people. Right?"

"Never." As the anchorman grinned at Dean, she asked;

"So what's the problem, boss man?"

"Well," Richards admitted, "I guess I'm just not used to having someone around here that ..."

"Knows her job?"

"Hummmmm ..."

"Can anticipate your every need?"

"Well ..."

"Stuck around and put up with you, your ego, and your crazy shenanigans long enough to figure out what has to get done, when it has to get done, and then – Heaven help us, could it be true – goes ahead and does it?"

The anchorman touched a finger to his nose, nodding his head as he shouted;

"Bingo. Yes ... those things. All of them." The producer arched his eyebrows, then asked, "If I throw myself on your mercy can I get a smile out of you?"

Dean gave Richards a half-smile in spite of herself. As she transformed it into even less of a smile, however, creasing her brow for effect at the same time, the producer said;

"All right, yea verily, I get the idea. So, anyway, oh patron saint of dearly beloved television producers, when do we leave?"

"A call to Legal told me that Massachusetts Local 832 of the Trawlers, Fish Packers and Lobsterteers Union next meets on Monday. If we're going to do any damage control before the weekend allows every bar in town to become a breeding ground for anti-network resentment ..."

"Say no more," interrupted the anchorman, throwing his hands up in mock surrender. "I take we're leaving after lunch?"

"Grab your jacket. I ordered travel lunches. They should be delivered to the garage in ..."

The young woman glanced at her tablet, tapped it twice, then slid it into her side bag, announcing;

"Six minutes, Mr. Richards. Do try and move yourself along ... would you? I've already had your emergency travel bag sent downstairs ahead of us."

Force of habit making him glance to where his emergency kit should have been, he marveled over the fact Dean had been able to have it removed from his office without his noticing. Reminding himself that it for such reasons that he not only had hired the young woman in the first place, but why he so tirelessly worked to keep her in that position, he nodded politely, saying;

"Why certainly, my queen."

And, so saying, Marvin Richards pushed himself up out of his chair, grabbed his jacket as instructed, and then checked the contents of his shoulder bag, hoping he could make certain he had everything he needed in just a few seconds.

"After all," he said quietly, grinning to himself as he watched Dean's well-formed posterior sway ever-so-perfectly as she crossed the outer office to the elevator bank, "wouldn't want to not be in the garage in six minutes now, would we?"

"I'm sorry," answered the head clerk on duty at the front desk of the union hall for the Massachusetts Local 832 of the Brotherhood of Trawlers, Fish Packers and Lobsterteers, "but the fellahs have dropped the suit. Once the newspaper and radio people, the TV types and the what-nots from the computer and all, all of them just buzzin' around here, causin' trouble, laughin' and makin' fun of the crew ..."

"And now they're embarrassed," offered Dean in a sympathetic voice. "They'd probably just like all this attention to go away."

"Wouldn't you, young lady?"

"I guess that would matter," interrupted Richards, "on whether or not I'd really seen a mermaid."

"You callin' them boys liars?"

"How could I, sir," answered the anchorman. "I haven't met them, heard them tell their story, gotten to ask them questions, gotten to watch their reactions ... people and events have to be judged one at a time. And yes, my friend, yes indeed," Richards admitted;

"I do want a story. And I would not mind in the least if it were sensational – if it were packed with actual mermaids from one end to the other."

"But ..." offered the clerk, his eyes narrowing.

"But," agreed Richards, "what I really want is to make certain that the truth is revealed. That whichever story is the real one is the one that goes up on the screen."

The clerk crossed his arms across his chest. Not so much in a hostile manner, but in the fashion of one being off-putting, searching for some time to think.

"So, that thought in mind," asked the producer, looking to enlist the clerk's cooperation from another angle, "the boat that caught the mermaid was out of ... where, exactly?"

The head clerk of Hall 832 stared at Richards as if he were someone's mentally defective nephew. Shaking his head sadly, the thin, wrinkled man answered;

"Newburyport, young fellah. I told you before. They was on the waters roughly halfway between their own port and Ipswich. That's where they were when they caught whatever it was got this whole ruckus started.”

Consulting a large map of the coastline on the wall there in the front office of the Local, Dean found the two towns in question easily enough. Running her finger from the mid-point over to the coast, she asked;

“That would’ve put them right out from the town of ... Innsmouth. Anybody from Innsmouth ever catch anything like this?”

“No, way ... nosiree, bob.” Appearing on the verge of possibly chuckling at such an idea, the clerk added, “Not on your life, little lady. Couldn’t happen.”

“And why is that, sir,” asked Dean.

“Because, miss, ain’t nobody from Innsmouth could’ve caught no mermaids any time anyone in this room could’ve heared about, because there taint been no fishin’ vessels registered out of Innsmouth in over seventy years.”

“That would make it harder,” agreed Richards. Doing some of his own casting about, the producer asked, “But aren’t these towns all along the coast here primarily fishing towns?”

“Not Innsmouth. Was once. Not no more. Not in a long time.”

“What do they do there then,” asked Dean nonchalantly, using her passive, background-checking voice. “Manufacturing, maybe?”

“Don’t rightly know,” answered the clerk after a moment of thought. “Don’t much care, either, I reckon.” When the *Challenge* people merely stared at him, the older gentleman added;

“Folks what were brought up with good sense make it a habit to steer clear of Innsmouth. Even those without much sense, good or bad, tend to leave that place alone.”

“Why’s that,” asked Richards, hoping for even a tiny bit of mystery to help enliven the story he had come to cover. The clerk put an actual moment of thought into how he might actually respond, then answered;

“Can’t rightly say. Just always been that way. People in Innsmouth keep to themselves. Don’t send no goods out nowheres, don’t cater none to tourists. Used to have a hotel, used to have a bus went out there ... don’t think they do anymore.”

The trio chatted for a few minutes longer, but it had become evident to Richards that the Massachusetts Local 832 of the Brotherhood of Trawlers, Fish Packers and Lobsterteers did not have much more to offer them. Heading back to the mid-size sedan they had rented at the airport, Dean asked;

“So, where to next?”

“I don’t know, rightly. What do you think? If you were the producer ...”

"You mean in name – finally. Because we do know who does most all the work around here."

"Oh, 'sharper than a serpent's tooth,'" responded Richards with a chuckle. "Yes, ignoring your swift sense of betrayal, if you were calling the shots, and your head was on the budget line ... where would you point us next?"

"To the fishermen the union seems comfortable in keeping off camera," she answered without hesitation. "We already know the suit's a bust. Not much sympathy for people going to court over being made to look stupid because they ran around saying crazy things."

"You think these guys are crazy?"

"After what we've seen," answered Dean, her tone startled and a touch dismissive. "It certainly is possible. But, please, you know as well as I do it's a lot easier to believe in damned things once you've seen a few of them up close."

"Fine," said the producer. Guidingly, he added, "So they believe. But why do we want them in particular?"

"Because people are laughing at them and making their lives miserable. Because they've already gotten defensive over that fact."

"Meaning ..."

"Meaning they are the only people around here that are going to be willing to help us ... mainly by getting back out on the water and – if possible – snagging us a real live mermaid."

"And even if we don't find ourselves a mermaid," responded Richards, nodding, "we'll have plenty of footage of them trying."

"Which makes it win, win," offered Dean, smiling.

"Yes, it certainly does," agreed the producer, saying, "I have trained you well. We make a great team."

"We make a great team because I trained you well," responded Dean. Tilting her head with a "that's that" angle, the young woman turned and headed for the door. Watching her walk away, Richards thought;

"Well, I guess that tells me."

And then followed his assistant to the door, finding himself half in an inordinately good mood and half wondering just what they might actually find in the waters off the coast. Richards had noticed that so far no real descriptions of the New English mermaids had been offered. The media had been plastering the airwaves and Internet with every public domain image of woman with fish tails in existence.

But Marvin Richards had learned that things came in all shapes and sizes beyond the imaginations of screenwriters. A reporter from California whose path had crossed with his several times had told him about men and women more fish than human – things which in no way, shape or form had anything along the order of talking crustaceans or the ability to sing show tunes underwater to their credit.

What the west coast journalist had told him about was a world of creatures resembling not so much Superman's sometime girlfriend of Lori Lemaris than they did the Creature of the Black Lagoon. Still, as he watched Dean disappear through the doorway, he found himself suddenly worrying about her beyond the annoyance of working out insurance forms for workman's comp issues. Sighing as he reminded himself that following him into the nonsense of the beyond was her job, he hoped;

"Ahhh, who knows ... maybe the guys on the boat were all just drunk." Taking a deep breath, he speculated, "sure, an entire drunken crew. Oh yes, that has to be it."

And, finally completely depressed, Marv Richards headed outside for their rental car, and whatever brand of insanity they were walking into that time.

🜂

"So, no one on board was drinking?"

The captain of *Three-Legged Mary* frowned at Dean's question, not overly placated by her assurance that it had to be asked "for the record." Captain Stupp was all a television crew could ask for in a New Englander seaman. Burly, thick-shouldered, white-haired, but with a beard shot through with thick black streaks, he was as photogenic as any could wish for.

"A couple of beers got emptied, but that's got nothing to do with what happened."

"No one's trying to say it did, captain."

"Yeah, right," snarled Stupp. Turning toward Richards, the older man snapped, "you people, you're all the same. All you want is your story. You don't care anything about us. This is all just some joke to you ..."

"No," interrupted the producer. "That's where you're wrong."

Stupp narrowed his eyes, but did not respond. In a world of phones that acted as video recorders, where the government hung cameras on every available pole, most people had begun to modify their behavior accordingly over the years, and the captain was no different. With the anchorman of *Challenge of the Unknown* sitting across from him, he was not about to blow up and give the producer footage that might be exploited. Not after doing so for the local news team. Bad enough, he thought, that everyone in town and the surrounding area was snickering about him and his crew. The captain had no desire to making nation-wide laughing stocks out of them. Instinctively understanding that such might be the case, Richards continued, saying;

"And I'll explain why you're wrong. Am I here for a story? Yes, of course I am. But, the question you need to ask yourself is, what kind of story am I after." As Stupp maintained his stoic silence, the producer offered;

"You see, the thing about television is, you have to know what those coming at you really want. Those guys that interviewed you before, they didn't care what kind of story they got out of you. Local news team," Richards said the last three words with a disdainful sneer calculated to connect with Stupp, "they don't care what they shovel up ... they're just trying to fill air space and sell commercial time ..."

"And you're not," asked the captain.

"Certainly we need to fill our show," admitted Dean, "and sell enough ads to pay for it all. But, I believe the operative word in Mr. Richards' statement was 'just.'"

"Lora's correct," cut in the anchorman, enjoying double-teaming Stupp. "They can afford to be sloppy. We can't. We're national. But more than that, we've got a mandate – to find the weird and the supernatural, the unexplained and the unbelievable. Now, you tell me, captain, have you ever watched Challenge?" Once Stupp admitted he had caught the show once or twice, Richards followed up, asking;

"All right, since you've seen us in action, you tell me, sir, do you ever remember a time where we made fun of anyone for believing in ... well ... in anything? Anything at all?"

"Can't rightly say I can," admitted the captain.

"That's correct. We couldn't afford to. Someone sees something they can't explain. They know the cops and everyone else are going to try and downplay whatever it is they say they saw. Bigfoot, the ghost of their dead grandma, bad-ass fairies – whatever – everyone wants to believe in something, but most are afraid to say so. We need people to trust that we won't mock them, because we need for them to let us know when their dead grandma comes to visit so we can have our cameras there."

The captain considered Richards' words for a moment. He stared at the anchorman for a few seconds, then finally signaled the bartender that he would like to get another round for the table. As the counterman nodded, Stupp said;

"This next round, it's on you."

"And why is that?"

"Because, Mr. TV Man," answered the captain, indicating himself and his crew at the next table with a wave of his hand, "it's going to take us at least another round before we up and take you out on the *Three-Legged Mary*, searchin' for mermaids."

"Two rounds," shouted one of the mates, while another tossed out;

"Yeah, mermaids ... or whatever that damn thing was."

"Another two rounds it is," answered Richards. Turning to Dean, he gave her a slight roll of the eyes, letting her know that, yes, he had heard what the second seaman had said, and yes again, he would ask about it — after they were all safely out on the water.

And then Marv Richards pulled out his wallet, sliding his credit card and two twenties to the waitress who brought over their next round. He let her know that he would be picking up the tab for both tables, that the cash was her tip because, well, screw the government, and that he would like her to have the kitchen wrap a couple of sandwiches for each of them to take off with them into the night. The woman nodded politely, giving the producer a solid, forty dollar smile before she disappeared to do his bidding.

As Richards watched her walk away, he thought for possibly the ten thousandth time that no one walked away quite as nicely as his lovely assistant did. And then, after allowing himself that one moment of frivolity, he got back to the more immediate task of making certain the captain and crew of the *Three-Legged Mary* soaked up enough courage to head out into the night in search of another mermaid, or as the one of them had offered;

"Yeah, mermaids ... or whatever that damn thing was."

At slightly after midnight, Richards, Stupp and the rest had been out on the water for over an hour. Realizing all too well the symbolic power of the witching hour, the anchorman finally brought up the question that had been on the tip of his tongue since Jeff Milton had first mentioned mermaids to him in the first place. Which was, of course, exactly what did this particular mermaid look like. The mate who had requested a second round offered;

"Let me get on the record that none of us never said nothing about mermaids. All right?"

"Fine by me."

"This was no half-woman, half-fish thing with pouty lips and Vidal Sassoon hair ..."

"Didn't have no hair at all," offered another.

"Gentlemen," asked Dean quietly, making it obvious she was going to film the answer, "what did it look like?"

"Yeah, fellahs," added Richards. "I mean, what brought us out here was that we heard whatever it was you caught, it ripped its way out of your nets, and then escaped. Frankly, I don't care if it was just a giant crocodile ... on our show giant crocodiles are news, and the guys that wrestle them are cool. So, tell us ... what was this thing?"

Stupp and his crew took a moment, one which the *Challenge* people pretended not to notice. They had expected hesitation on the part of their hosts. All available footage of the initial news report had been studied carefully during the trip to New England, e-mailed to the producer by his production staff. Richards had not missed the fact that it had been the local newsmen that had first used the term "mermaid," and that the seamen had gone silent shortly thereafter, never actually describing what they had caught in detail.

The producer knew instinctively what had happened. The news team might have worked for a local station, but they were outsiders. Not community members. None of them had grown up locally. They were, like most people in television, transplants from somewhere else, rank and filers hopefully working their way up to a network position somewhere. Only the best realized early on in their careers that they had to wear a veneer of their locale if they ever hoped to make the big time. Indeed, the producer was thinking warmly of his days as a weatherman in Texas when one of the crew finally said;

"Okay ... number one ... this thing, we don't know if it was male or female. Just that it was human ... ah, human-shaped. You know ... legs, arms, head ... like where we have them."

"So humanoid," said Richards, "but not possessing any identifying sexual characteristics. No genitalia, obvious female breasts, nipples, even...?"

"No, sir," answered another. "Yeah, when it got out of the net, it walked like a man, but what it was ..."

"Green, that's what it was," piped in the first mate. "Gray-green all over. It didn't seem to have no trouble breathin' outta the water, even though it had gills--"

"Gills and a nose," countered the first. Then, just as quickly, he amended his statement, adding, "ummm, not a nose, but like slits, where a nose should be ... like nostrils, kinda, without the nose."

After that everyone, including Stupp, was contributing details. The thing had been of average human height, with prodigious, bulging eyes which never closed. It had hands and feet, but instead of fingers or toes it had possessed claws attached to one another by thick webbing. All agreed to the gray-green coloring suggested by the first mate, though several added the fact the creature had possessed a white belly. The thing's skin had been mostly slippery to the touch, except along its ridged back which was covered with scales.

"Quite the beastie we're describing here," said Dean in an approving voice. Still filming, she asked;

"And, wasn't there something about this thing wearing jewelry? Gold jewelry?"

The crew went silent once more, nervously looking one to another, until finally one of them offered;

"Oh hell, in for a penny ... yeah. The thing had a gold chain around its neck. Not like girls wear, but heavy-like, thick links. You know, like a real chain, not a decoration."

"Oh, this is just all too nifty," agreed Richards. "I can't wait to see one of these things."

"What about more than one?"

As all heads turned, they saw the first mate pointing over the *Mary*'s port side, his face showing nothing that resembling happiness. At Stupp's order, the ship's search light was aimed in the general direction indicated by the first mate's index finger. And, as everyone else rushed to the side, they saw what he had seen, some eight humanoid figures moving through the water, not much more than their ridged backs breaking the surface.

"Oh man," said one of the crew, "that's a whole lotta Squidly Diddlies comin' this way."

"This what you were expecting, Richards?"

"Expecting ..." answered the producer, the communal feeling on deck rapidly becoming one of trepidation, "You never really 'expect' anything so much in this business as hope for ..."

"Jenkins," shouted Stupp, his instincts not liking anything about what was happening, "Get to the engines and get us the royal hell out of here."

"Now, captain ..."

"Shut it, Mr. TV Man," snapped Stupp. "There's something ten kinds of wrong here, and ..."

The captain's retort was cut short as a horrible scratching noise made its way up over the starboard side of the *Mary*. Seconds later, even as the vessel had begun to move, the sound was identified as that of claws, claws enabling their owners to scale the sides of the trawler. The crew grabbed up anything that might be used as a weapon, but to no avail. The creatures proved to be incredibly swift and equally strong. As his men tried to hold the monsters off, Stupp grabbed hold of Dean and Richards by their elbows and began dragging them toward the back of the vessel.

"The *Mary*'s only got one dingy, and you two are gettin' in it and gettin' out of here."

"But, captain," protested Dean, "what about …"

"Shut it," snapped Stupp. "We was fool enough to come out here, back to the same spot, we're gettin' what we deserve. At least if you two survive, people'll know we weren't crazy."

As the sound of blows and screams tore through the night air, the captain's passengers did as they were told, Richards whispering;

"Don't argue. We can keep shooting from the dingy."

Such was not to be, however. Even standing on their tiny boat's central bench, the anchorman could not get a clear shot of the goings-on aboard ship. Worse, the sounds of struggle began to rapidly diminish, indicating that it would not be long before the *Challenge* staff members would have nothing to distract the invading creatures from themselves.

"Marv," said Dean, "I know the show must go on, but …"

"Say no more," answered Richards, getting down off the bench, heading for the motor at the rear of the dingy. "It may well be time to take a brief commercial message."

And then, just as the producer had finished speaking, his hands on the dingy's outboard motor, the sounds of something breaking the ocean's surface – splashes making approximately the amount of noise one would expect from a large humanoid form entering the water from a height of, say, the deck of the *Mary* – were heard some eight times.

"Oh my God … Marvin …"

"Yeah," the anchorman answered, his hands desperately searching for the motor's starter, "I know …"

"All those men, the captain … they, they …"

Dean's words were cut off as a small explosion sounded, followed by a burst of fire which began to rapidly spread across the *Three-Legged Mary*'s deck. At the same time, Richards' fingers found the starter button. As the engine came to life the producer took hold of the tiller, turning it at an angle so as to head the two of them back to shore. As he piloted the small vessel, Richards took note that his assistant had her camera trained on the scene behind them, filming the burning trawler. He nodded with approval.

That's my girl, he thought, knowing that "camera operator" had never been part of her job description. While one half of his brain computed the problems they might have using her footage – Dean not being a member of the correct union – the rest of it wondered at the attack.

The popularity of *Challenge* did not rest so much on the strange and horrible things it revealed to its audience week after week, but the context within which these things were revealed. Richards had often been acknowledged as a master storyteller, and thus, even while in full blown retreat he found himself consumed with the question, what was the story in which he had become involved that time? The real story? The whole story?

"Oh crap," he muttered as they neared the shore, "I got a bad idea I know what this was all about."

And then, he felt his spirits faltered as he scanned the shoreline ahead of them. Dean, dutifully filming the blazing *Mary* behind them, as well as the dark shapes pursuing them through the water, could not see what the anchorman could – not at first. When he began slowing their speed, however, she turned to question him, only to take in what he had.

"Oh ..."

The one word was all she could manage as her eyes scanned the beach, taking in the multitude of forms waiting for them. She did not question Richards' not veering off. Even the slightest of glances revealed that they were surrounded. That they were being herded to the shore. That their remaining time on Earth looked to be extremely limited.

Neither spoke. Partially it was fright, basic human terror over the fact that the end seemed near. Moreover, though, their silence revolved around the fact that neither of them wanted to speak first. As their dingy made contact with the rough shore, a thick voice before the pair growled;

"Out."

Not knowing what else to do, Richards and his assistant did as they were commanded. The producer clambered over the dingy's side first, offering his hand to his assistant once he was on the beach. True to her calling, she handed him the camera and then climbed over the side without assistance. Richards found himself bursting with pride that at even such a time Dean's concern was for the show over their own lives.

"Well," he thought, staring at the menacing shapes all about them, "we might not survive this, but we're going out like newsmen."

The pair were forced inland by the growing crowd of amphibians, more than a few wielding tridents, pikes and swords. As they reached a central clearing, a place obviously used by the locals for beach parties, the two found themselves utterly surrounded by the growing crowd of horrors. As they drew closer, Dean whispered;

"Oh, Marv, I wish ... there's so ... oh God, this really looks like the end this time!"

"Sweetheart, as much as I hate to agree with an assessment so negative ... I think you're right."

"I, I just don't understand it, Marv ...," said the young woman, watching the circle of deadly things all about them drawing closer, "how does something like this happen?"

"Well, you know what I always say, sweetheart ..." answered the producer as the dripping creatures slowly closed in on them from every direction, knowing exactly what his assistant meant. Finally seeing the missing puzzle piece to the story in his mind's eye, he said;

"People are stupid."

Then, picking one of the creatures to represent them all, he stared at the approaching monster and asked it;

"Aren't they?"

The horror stared at Richards, stopping its forward motion at the same time. As it did, all those around it did so as well. And, while all the assembled nightmares stared at him, Richards asked;

"The fishermen, the men from that ship," the anchorman pointed to the still blazing vessel out on the ocean, "they didn't just accidentally capture one of you ... they stole from him. Yes?"

"Yesssss," answered many of the creatures with one voice.

"They stole his gold ... didn't they?"

"Yesssss," came the gurgling response once more, after which, the one Richards had noted earlier as somewhat of an authority figure stepped forward and said;

"Once ... all of us ... like you. Weak, pale. Gold a gift from God ... our God. Allowed us to become as we are ... strong. Immortal. To steal our gold ... greatest of sins."

"All right," answered Richards, searching desperately for a way out of their situation. "That's fair. But ... you do know ... we didn't have anything to do with that. Right? You know that – right?"

"Doesn't matter," answered the creature. "Offense made. All concerned must die. God must be honored."

Dean stared up into Richards' eyes, searching for even the slightest degree of hope. Out of all the emotions she found there, however, optimism was not one of them. As she clutched him all the tighter, the producer told her softly;

"Sorry I got you into all this, sweetheart."

"Oh Marv, it's all right. I knew what I was doing. Good jobs are hard to come by these days." As she smiled at him, she added, "And, it was a good job."

Always able to judge an audience, Richards knew their time had run out. Knowing he had but seconds left, he let the camera fall from his hands, finally dropping all of his shields and hugging Dean back as he told her;

"Lora, just so you know ... I do love you."

"Oh, oh Marv ... you have to know I love you, too."

And then, after their years of denying their feelings and working to protect themselves from simple human emotion, the two closed their eyes and kissed. Richards hugged his assistant with all the strength he had, realizing that if he had to die, he could not think of a better place to do so. He had loved her for ages for *too* long – wanted her, needed her. A part of him felt foolish for having waited so long. Most of his mind, however, was lost to thought, able only to concentrate on the moment – the one they both had almost denied for too long.

Ignoring the world around them, all reality except each other forgotten, the pair embraced, their hunger for one another an overwhelming thing. Their kiss went on second after second, the sweetness of it blinding them to all else. Then, as their passion passed the two minute mark, the producer opened his eyes. He stared into Dean's also open eyes for the briefest of moments, then turned his head to look at those surrounding them, as one of them growled;

"This sucks."

"I told you," spat another. "Immortal sea creatures ... honoring Father Dagon and Mother Hydra ... for all eternity. This bites."

"Harry's right," came another voice. "We gave up humanity for this? Who wants to live forever?"

"Not me," came a new voice. "I want what those two have ..."

As Richards and Dean stared, utterly amazed at the sudden turn of events, the creature added;

"I want Love!"

And, that said, all of the monstrosities began to argue vehemently with one another. Listening as best they could, the *Challenge* team quickly pieced together that more than a century earlier, a local captain who had traveled to the south seas and back had returned with a chest of gold and a new religion, one which everyone in their town of Innsmouth had embraced. They had indeed grown stronger, swifter, as well as immortal. At the time, sacrificing their humanity with all its pains and infirmities – as well as its briefness – had seemed like a good deal.

"I hate this," screamed one of the creatures. "I want to feel again. I don't care ... I don't care anymore." Then, grabbing the glistening chain about its own neck, the thing ripped it free, golden links spilling to the sand as it screeched;

"I want love, too. I need it."

And then, before anything more could be said, several others of the scaly horrors tore off their own necklaces and threw them to the ground. Still clutching one another, Richards and Dean watched as the beach became littered with gold, and the monsters which had been threatening their lives a moment earlier all marched off into the black water before them.

"I think ... I think they're all gone."

Looking about, the producer craned his neck in one direction as his assistant looked in the other. Meeting back in the middle, the pair suddenly began to giggle. Then, caught up in a wave of crippling laughter, the two fell to the ground, overwhelmed with sudden relief. Finally, sitting up, the pair looked at each other, wondering exactly what came next for them. Picking up one particularly round golden ringlet, Richards held it out before himself toward Dean, saying;

"Sweetheart, I'd love to make a real last act gesture here and propose ... I mean, this thing looks like it would fit your finger, and I do want to marry you, but ..."

"But," answered Dean, taking the ringlet from Richards, "you're thinking it might not be best to start even a brief, human life together with the cursed gold of a vengeful god."

"Yeah ..." agreed the anchorman. Still amazed over the fact they were still alive, he looked into Dean's shining eyes, considering himself – as so many men have done so in similar moments since the beginning of time – to be the luckiest fellow in the world, as he said;

"But still ... you are going to marry me?"

"Sure," she answered, taking the upper hand offered to her as every woman has since the first one was offered, "if you play your cards right."

Richards smiled. Dean smiled back. And then, kneeling in the sand, the woman flicked the cursed gold off into the darkness as her man pulled her close, hugging her again. Kissing her once more. Knowing that he was, like so many before him, the luckiest man in the world.

Eventually they would stank up once more, sometime after the sunrise – brush themselves off and head up over the rise to see if they could spot any signs of civilization. It was not lost on Dean that Richards led the way, taking charge of their future, while leaving their camera filled with its unbelievable, one-of-a-kind footage on the beach behind them.

It was also not lost on the producer, later on when he finally noticed, that his bride-to-be had silently scooped up the camera he had forgotten, taking care of him – of them – quietly sliding into the role of the ever-so-essential woman standing behind her successful man. Keeping him from being the boob he would be otherwise.

As they trudged through the shore grass and weeds separating them from the roadway they had spotted in the distance, Richards took one final peek at the camera in Dean's hand, and then swept her into his arms once more, telling her;

"Baby, you're the greatest."

And, as in all great television stories, they lived happily ever after.

TINIAN SONG
Robert E. Waters

Jack David Dupont sat comfortably in the rear of the Rodman 38, the small yet powerful yacht he had rented for the weekend. A little deep sea fishing would do his eighty-year-old soul some good. "Money is no object," he had said to the man on Guam from whom he had rented the boat, and then proceeded to forget to buy the requisite gear one needed to do the actual fishing. But no matter. The kind of hooking he planned to do did not require bait.

"I don't understand why we're going out so far, Mr. Dupont," said Tito, the young Japanese boy who stood at the helm, ensuring that the ship plowed steadily through the turbulent waves. "There's nothing out here except bad chop and Ama divers."

And the Indianapolis. "What the hell is an Ama diver?"

The boy chuckled. "Women divers, Mr. Dupont. Japanese women. My grandfather used to tell me tales of hearing them when he was a boy. They would dive for shellfish, and their young bodies were perfect for the depths and cold of the deep sea. When they emerged, they would reinvigorate their lungs by breathing deeply, and the moans and wails that that activity created would echo across the waves like sad, terrible songs. In time, some of these divers became sirens and mermaids... so the stories go. Do you believe in mermaids, Mr. Dupont?"

Yes.

"No," Jack said, leaving his chair and moving carefully up the ladder to the helm. His old, creaky knees found it difficult to navigate the short distance, and his agitated mind wavered as the boat sloshed through the surf. "That's silly nonsense, Tito. You're like your father. I don't pay you to tell me tall tales. I pay you to steer the boat."

Tito nodded and chuckled again. "Yes, Mr. Dupont."

Tito was a good boy, and like his father and grandfather who had served the Dupont family for years, he enjoyed agitating. "We're out here to do some fishing, and that's what we're going to do."

Before them, the blue emptiness of the South Pacific opened up like a warm bath, water and sky fighting along the horizon like two great warrior nations. Jack closed his eyes and breathed in the salty air, remembering the time when he was a sailor in the United States Navy. He remembered the time well. It was a great time, a wonderful, exciting time. A time of honor and dignity. A time of fire, fear, and death.

"What kind of fish are you hoping to catch, Mr. Dupont?" Tito asked.

Jack looked at the young boy. Tito was no idiot; he knew there was no fishing gear on board. Jack smiled. "A big one."

He turned toward the horizon, closed his eyes once again, and remembered back to the day when a big fish had caught him.

July 30, 1945, somewhere between Guam and Leyte, South Pacific

Lieutenant Jack David Dupont slammed into the bulkhead, dropping his coffee cup and enduring a splash of hot liquid across his neck. He winced, but the pain was quickly washed away as his ship, the *USS Indianapolis*, a Portland-class cruiser, listed violently from the strike of a Japanese torpedo on its starboard bow. One or two strikes? Jack could not tell, but one massive explosion followed another, as officers and men scrambled for safety. Lieutenant Dupont collected himself quickly and began saving lives.

"Abandon ship!" he screamed over the deafening alert sirens. "Abandon ship!"

It was an order that the captain should be giving, he thought, especially since he, Dupont, had been billeted to the *Indianapolis* just two days ago on Guam. Where was the captain, he wondered. Probably in his quarters or on the bridge. It did not matter. Jack was the senior officer on the scene, and he was responsible for the welfare of the crew.

Through the billowing smoke and rising seawater, he helped wounded, scared men to their feet and guided them through the corridor that led to the deck. "Keep moving, keep moving!" One, five, ten men shuffled past him, up the ladder and out. Again, the helpless, doomed *Indianapolis* listed and settled by the head. Jack waited until the last of the men were out. He took an anxious step forward then stopped. Behind him, through the blinding smoke and searing heat of fire, he heard a voice. A whimper of pain and fear.

He rubbed his eyes clear and waded back through toward the voice. The water was up to his waist now; within minutes, it could be above his head. It was impossible to tell how the ship would react from one moment to the next against such terrible damage, and the sea would not humbly still itself to allow all the men to escape. Some men were already dead, Jack knew. It was his charge to see that those numbers remained low.

He found the boy who belonged to the voice, twenty feet back and around a corner, holding desperately to a bit of ripped hull. It gave the boy little protection against the water that spilled through a gash near his head; if the pressure had been any greater, the lad would have been ripped away and lost forever.

Jack fought his way through the rising debris and grabbed the boy's shoulder. "What's your name, son?"

"Ensign Michaels, sir," the boy said. "I'm sorry, sir. I, I can't move. I—"

Jack pulled Michaels away from the hull and held him close. "Don't worry, Ensign. I'll get you out."

Together, they worked back down the corridor. The ship had turned such that they could not walk steadily; one foot was on the floor, the other against the wall. Twenty feet felt like a hundred, as the boy's weight, aggravated by the ship as it turned slowly and settled starboard, forced Jack to bend his knees. He strained to keep them above the waterline.

As the water reached his neck, Jack found the ladder, and they worked upward. Jack pushed up with his weakening arms, letting the terrified boy press his weight into his shoulders. The water rose above Jack's nose. He held his breath. When the boy was out, he turned and grabbed Jack's arms and yanked him free.

As Jack cleared the exit, the ship rolled completely onto its side. Jack grabbed Michaels again to keep the force of the roll from taking them both down. He pushed with his legs, swimming frog-like while holding the boy with one arm and paddling with the other. A terrible moan and hiss of air exploded around them as the ship's stern jutted into the sky, held there for a moment, then began to fall.

One minute later, the *Indianapolis* disappeared into the waves.

She was gone, and Jack held the shocked boy close. Around the wake of the plunging ship, clumps of men held desperately to each other and to scattered debris. How many were left? It was impossible to tell. What mattered now was that he and the boy were safe, for the moment anyway.

A lifejacket floated by. Jack grabbed it and began fitting it onto Ensign Michaels.

"Are we going to die, sir?"

Jack shook his head. Surely a distress signal had been sent out before she sank; surely so, and all Jack had to do was to keep himself and the boy alive for a few hours. Just a few hours.

"No, Ensign," he said, putting the last strap of the lifejacket in place. "You're not going to die. I'll keep you safe. I promise."

Jack wiped away a tear and tucked the pistol into his belt. The memory of that torpedo blast weighed heavily on his mind. He felt weak, nauseous. He wanted to sleep, to take one of his infamous four hour naps that his third wife used to scold him about. But there was no time for that now. The sun was setting and they were almost in position.

All his life, he had resented the Navy's refusal to billet him to the *Indianapolis* prior to July 30. He had asked for a commission far before that and was more than qualified. But the ship had been tasked with a top secret mission, and no crew assignments were going to be approved until afterwards. It was only much later, after the *Indianapolis* sank, that he learned of what that mission was about.

The *Indianapolis* and its crew had been assigned to deliver important parts and equipment to Tinian Island for the nuclear bomb, the one they called Little Boy, the one that would be dropped on Hiroshima. The mission had been successful and had occurred prior to Jack's reassignment. So when people came up to him and asked him if he had been part of the *Indianapolis* crew, he could say yes, but there was no honor in that admission. It would have been nice to be able to say that he had been part of something important, something real and tangible. He had missed that chance by a few days. He had indeed been part of something historical, something that had never happened to the US Navy prior to or since that fateful July day, but he took no pride in that fact. For 58 years, he had lived with the memory and the guilt.

He climbed to the deck. The warm air of the South Pacific was comforting to his old skin. He breathed deeply, listening to the ocean waves slap against the hull. He looked port then starboard. Nothing but water and wide open horizon, with the setting sun casting a deep red shadow against the sky. A blood red sky. He nodded. *This is the place.*

"Kill the engine!"

Jack waited until the ship settled in the waves, then climbed up to Tito who stood there waiting. "Any weather coming our way?" he asked.

Tito shook his head. "No, sir. Nothing. You're very lucky about that. Being so far out, if we get stuck here, we'll …"

"We're right where we need to be, Tito." Jack covered the gun at his waist with his hand. He closed his eyes. "Can you hear that, Tito? Can you hear it?"

"Hear what, sir?"

"That voice. That beautiful voice."

It was the same one he had heard years ago, in this very spot. Jack pointed to the horizon. "Over there. It's coming from there."

"I hear nothing, sir." Tito turned to look where Jack pointed and as he did so, Jack pulled the pistol from his waist and drove the butt against the boy's head, knocking him cold.

Jack grabbed the boy before he fell and laid him carefully on the deck. He patted Tito's head gently and whispered, "I'm sorry, Tito. You're a good boy, but you would have tried to stop me from doing what I have to do."

He laid the pistol beside the boy and stood up. The voice was stronger now, the song close and insistent, calling to him, inviting him.

"I'm coming," he said, placing his hands on the railing and climbing up. He wavered there in place on weak feet, the arthritis in his joints screaming against a pain that he had felt for years. "I'm coming," he said, crouching down to gain his balance. "This time, I will do what I should have done back then."

And with all his strength, Jack David Dupont leapt into the ocean.

August 1, 1945

He howled like a dog, and with a broken paddle, smacked away a whitetip that grazed his leg. Through the dark waves, Jack could hear other screams of pain, sorrow, and desperation. Men, delirious with hypothermia and dehydration, were killing themselves by drowning or letting the sharks drag them away. On that first night amidst the detritus of the *Indianapolis*, he could hear pistol shots from men desperate enough to think that shooting into the choppy surf could actually strike a shark and drive it away, and maybe some had gotten lucky. But the blood that those bullet wounds created would simply bring more and more to feast upon those who screamed into the night sky, crying for their mothers, their girlfriends, or damning God for allowing such a terrible thing to happen. Jack swung his paddle again and missed his target; his arms were so weak that he could barely move them anymore.

Where is our rescue? It was a thought that had gone through his mind more than once, but no answer came. No one had come. The skies had been clear, the horizon empty. They had been forsaken, confined to die slowly on the pitiful remains of what he could grab as it floated by. On that first day, he and Ensign Michaels had been lucky to find a few bottles of clear water, a can of sardines, and a few mushy saltine packets that he let the young boy chew on while he tore a lifejacket off a dead sailor and fitted it to himself. The first eight hours were the easiest.

Then night came, and the killing began, slowly at first. Whitetips, a few makos, and at one point Jack had even seen the fin of a tiger shark through the glistening moon-light. An attack was accentuated by a quick, piercing scream by the victim, then a pregnant silence as those around the victim paused, then panicked, trying desperately not to be the next. They had been lucky again to find protection among a pile of broken tables and chair cushions, and Jack had even helped Michaels up onto the remains of a table to lie down and rest for a few hours. But then a group of survivors drifted by and attacked, taking the table and pushing the young Ensign into the water. Jack had tried to pull rank, had ordered them to stop, but in this killing field, rank and status were meaningless. One of the sailors had even punched Jack in the mouth. Later in the day, a sailor clutching another seemingly sleeping one, drifted by. When Jack tried to engage the man in conversation, he turned to reveal that he had eaten through the face of the other and was licking the blood off his fingers with a deranged smile across his face, like some werewolf or vampire in a Bela Lugosi film. Jack turned away from the disgusting scene and vomited into the waves.

"Please don't let me die," Michaels said. "Please don't let me die."

Jack was so tired of hearing the young man's voice, pleading with his Lieutenant to protect him. That was all Jack had done since going into the sea. He had given the boy the sardines; he had given the boy the last of his water; he had allowed the boy to eat the crackers. And now here they were, adrift alone again, while Jack screamed, howled, and beat the water with a broken paddle, driving away sharks that poked and prodded their way around them with glassy, lifeless eyes and rows of razor-sharp teeth.

Sharks circled and Jack swung the paddle. *I can't go on, I can't...*

Then he heard her voice, like a hand running across the strings of a harp, light and pleasant. Jack turned and looked through the debris floating around them, looking for a sailor that, in his delirium, was singing or whistling or both. But there was no one near, and yet the voice seemed to come out of the darkness like a light, faint at first, then stronger, and stronger, and stronger, until it was all around them like a fog. A cloud of music.

"Can you hear that?" he said, pulling Michaels into his arms. "Can you hear that music?"

The ensign shook his head. "What music? I don't hear any ..."

"That music. That voice."

Then up from beneath them, a shimmering light began to glow. The sharks circled, and the light came up and broke the surface. Jack closed his eyes from the splash of salt water, and when he opened them, she was there, floating before them, her dark, wet, radiant hair glued to her shoulders, her pale breasts accentuating dark nipples that stood rigid and taut in the cool water. Jack reached up and rubbed his eyes clear. *Now I'm seeing things*, he thought. *This is not real.*

"I am real," she said, "and I have come to save you."

Her voice was not American. She spoke English, but her accent was broken, more Oriental. Through the faint moonlight, Jack now saw that this woman, this creature before them, was Japanese, her eyes small and slanted, her cheekbones high and sharp. At his stare, she giggled like a little girl, and up from behind her flapped a tail, slick and broad like that of a dolphin. Flecks of red-and-green scales sparkled across the length of the tail as she swam around them, undulating like an eel and singing the most beautiful, wholesome song Jack had ever heard. Under those wistful notes, his mind grew peaceful, his heart stilled.

"I'm here to save you," she said again, flicking her tail and darting around them, "but only one. There are too many sharks, and I have only the strength to save one of you. Choose. You… or the boy."

Ensign Michaels' eyes lit up as he looked at Jack. Boyish, innocent eyes, pleading for protection. Jack knew which decision was the right one. *I am his superior officer. It is my responsibility to…*

But Michaels' face began to change, to twist and contort, until at last the face of the enemy emerged, the slanted eyes of a Jap and his snarling, buck-toothed mouth, cackling as he drove his bayonet into the soft belly of an American GI. This was not a scared little boy anymore. This was the enemy.

Jack pushed him away. "Me. Save me."

The mermaid's soft arms folded around Jack and she pulled him away. Suddenly, Ensign Michaels' face reappeared, and he screamed, "No! Lieutenant Dupont! Please! Don't swim away. Don't leave me here. Please!"

From the safety of the mermaid's embrace, Jack watched in terror as the whitetips swarmed and began ripping the boy apart.

A day later, Lieutenant Jack David Dupont was pulled to safety from the wreckage of the *USS Indianapolis*, delirious and humming the blissful notes of the mermaid's song.

Jack hit the water and did not try to swim. He drifted down, down, until the light above grew faint. Instinctively, he held his breath. He knew that he should open his mouth and breathe deeply, but that nagging desire for life still clung to him. *I should have just ended it then*, he thought. *I should have been the one to die.*

He forced his mouth open and took a deep breath. Salt water gushed into his lungs, the pain of it searing through his body like a fire. His chest heaved; he scratched at his throat. He breathed again, and this time the pain was not so bad. He closed his eyes, floated down and waited for the end.

He felt warm skin against his throat, the tenderness of fingers as they wrapped around his thin neck and squeezed. He opened his eyes, and she was there, the mermaid, staring back at him, her face mere inches from his. She was the same as before; he would never forget her face, her body. Her eyes were dark, her cheeks pale, but radiant with a bright glow that shimmered across her skin like a warm light. She had not aged a day.

Suddenly he was gulping water like air. He could breathe again.

"Why have you come back?" she asked. He could hear her voice as if they were sitting across the table from each other. "Why?"

"I'm doing what I should have done a long time ago."

"Why?"

"I should have been the one to die. I should have saved Michaels."

"You made a choice."

"You tricked me. You changed his face, confused me into thinking he was the enemy."

She shook her head, her supple hair waving slowly in the water. "I merely allowed you to see what you wanted to see, what your mind needed to see to make the decision that you made."

"Why did you come at all? Why not let us both die?"

She paused for a moment, then said, "Because you were so brave. I watched for two days, and I saw how wonderful you were, how you gave the boy drink and food, sacrificing your own comfort, your own health, for him. While others around you lost their minds, lost their sense of right and wrong, you kept your head, stayed calm. You were worthy of my attention."

"Why not just save him, then? Why force me to make the choice? Why not give him the choice?"

She laughed, and little air bubbles escaped her mouth. "That would have been no choice at all. In his state, he would have picked himself, with no regret. No. The real choice lay with you. It is always with the hero of stories that the real decisions lie, for the hero is the one with the power to go left or right. You chose to go left."

Jack shook his head. "I made the wrong choice."

The mermaid nodded. "Perhaps. But, you made a human choice, and now you are trying to make another. But this one will not bring your young Michaels back, and it may very well see the death of another young man."

"What are you talking about?"

The mermaid motioned up towards the yacht. "That young boy on the boat. Are you willing to sacrifice him to right a decision you made 58 years ago?"

Jack scoffed. "Tito will be okay. He'll wake up and drive the boat back to safety."

The mermaid smiled and pulled her hand away from his throat. "Really?"

Water gushed back into his mouth, and Jack struggled to breathe again. Above him, something hit the water, disrupting the calm stillness of his depth. He clamped his mouth shut and looked up at flailing legs and arms of a shape that he knew very well.

Tito!

The boy could swim a little. Under better circumstances, he'd be fine. But this water was unlike common pool or lake water. This was the ocean: mad, angry, unforgiving. With the strike to his head, he'd be weak and groggy. And the blood…

The blood!

Images of that fateful day came flooding back to him as he swam upwards towards Tito. Images of sharks. Their sleek, smooth bodies cutting through the surf, silent, deadly. The blood would attract sharks. He had to get the boy out of the water… now.

Tito seemed to be trying to swim down, but he didn't have the strength to move well. Jack had little strength himself, his old muscles straining to do the right thing, his lungs burning for lack of air. But he kept moving, straining against the darkness until he could feel Tito's arms.

The boy was mad, crazed with fear and pain. He yanked and tugged at Jack, grabbing his shoulders, trying to get his arm around the old man's waist. Jack tried to push him away. *Go back to the ship.* He mouthed the words, but could not hear them, the flood of salt water drowning them out. *Go back. Leave me to die.*

They broke the surface. Jack gasped for air. Life and energy flowed back into him. Every muscle, every bone ached. Tito would not let him go. He clung to his boss like *Velcro*, like Michaels had done years ago.

"Get out of the water!" Jack screamed the words at Tito. "That is an order."

"I'm taking you with me!"

"No, you don't understand. I have to die. I have to make things right, I …"

Jack stopped and watched the shadows pass beneath the water. One, then two, then many. Scores of them. They circled, their fins jutting above the water, then disappearing as others took their place. Around and around they circled, and Jack and Tito floated further and further away from the boat.

Tito screamed and punched the water, but Jack knew that would do no good.

"Where are you?"

"I'm right here," Tito said.

"No, not you. I meant her… her!"

Tito looked at him like he was mad. *Perhaps I am*, Jack thought, as he clapped his hands together to scare away a whitetip trying to nuzzle its way in between them. "Where are you? Where are you?"

"I'm right here."

He turned, and she was there, head and shoulders above the water, bobbing up and down, the strength of her tail keeping her afloat. She smiled, her teeth brilliant and sharp in the waning light. Her hair now red, her skin golden brown. "I'm here, and it's like old times."

"Don't do this again," said Jack, looking deeply into her eyes.

"Do what?" Tito asked.

"Don't you see her?"

Tito shook his head. "I see no one but you. Come on, let's swim. Let's get to the boat before we both die."

"Don't do this again."

"It should be an easy choice this time, no?" She curled her tail around him like a warm blanket. "So make your choice, Lieutenant. You or him?"

Jack opened his mouth to say what he had wanted to say for years. He turned to Tito and looked at the young man, but his face changed, like Michaels had. Twisted, dark, angular, slanted eyes, teeth crooked and foul. Tito laughed, and Jack heard and felt the sharp sting of two mighty torpedoes strike the *Indianapolis*, saw the Jap floating in the water before him drive his bayonet into Marine after Marine after Marine, cackling like a madman. Jack shook his head, blinked his eyes. He wanted to say the right thing, to do the right thing for once. But he couldn't; the face before him was the enemy, the one who had sunk the *Indianapolis*, the one who had attacked Pearl Harbor and had killed so many of Jack's friends and colleagues. He did not deserve to live. He didn't…

"No!" Jack said, turning on the mermaid. "No! The war is over. It's over!" He flung his arm at her, trying to knock her over. But she moved too quickly for him, disappearing below the water.

The sharks remained. Tito was trying to fight them off as they closed in. Jack grabbed the boy and started swimming. "Come on! We'll do this together."

They swam together, holding on to one another, kicking and punching and fighting off the sharks that swirled around them. Some tried to come in and nip at their feet and legs. Jack could feel their rigid, slimy bodies against his skin. He kicked and swam and screamed and did the best he could to keep himself and Tito alive. The young boy matched his movements, despite his weakness and the bloody whelp on the back of his head.

They reached the yacht, and Jack could not move, his old body giving out, his lung aching. It was Tito who pulled him aboard and laid him safely upon the deck.

As he lay there, the world seemed different to Jack now, smaller, closer, less dangerous, less uncertain. The guilt that he had felt for decades seemed washed away. He had been given the choice again. He had not made the decision that he thought he would make this time. He made another decision. He had stared into the face of the enemy and had decided to save them both. Why couldn't he have made that decision years ago when faced with the same illusion? Perhaps it had been too soon for such a choice. Perhaps in war, there can be only two routes to take. Right or wrong, up or down, or as the mermaid had said, left or right.

But Jack didn't need to be saved anymore, nor did he need the counsel of an illusion. Was she an illusion? Did she really exist, or was she always, like the twisted enemy face he had placed upon Michaels and Tito, a mirage?

Did it really matter?

Jack let Tito help him sit up. He craned his neck to the wind. "Can you hear that, Tito? Can you hear her song?"

Tito turned to listen. "No, sir. I don't hear anything."

Jack smiled. "Neither do I."

UPON WAVES, WIND, AND TIDE
James Chambers

"**Y**ou begged me to show you," Ebb said.

"I know," Naia said. "But should we really be watching something so personal?"

The two crouched on a low hill above the beach. At the water's edge, frothy surf glowed in the waning moonlight as it coiled itself around the feet of the old man they had trailed from the woods. The wind kicked up, and the man wiped spray from his brow. When Ebb was a boy, they might have had their pick of who to follow on any night, but these days there were far fewer people in the city. He and Naia had staked out the paths to the beach for four days before anyone came, and they had not been surprised to see Caron Tucker appear. Nor would it surprise anyone in the city to find the old widower gone tomorrow. Many had thought it only a matter of time. Bent by age and a lifetime of hard days, Mr. Tucker looked like most who gave themselves back to the water – spent, broken, and lost.

"Oh, don't get squeamish on me," Ebb said.

"I'm not squeamish," Naia said. "It's only – I've never seen anyone give themselves back to the water. Aren't we intruding? He might not want us watching."

"You're bringing this up now?" Ebb said. "He doesn't know we're here. The water will take him or it won't just the same. But if you want to leave, we'll leave."

"I want to see them." Naia frowned. "I want to see the mermaids."

"Then we stay. But you'll probably see nothing."

"I know." Naia placed her hand over Ebb's, entwining her fingers with his, and shifted closer until their bodies brushed together. "But maybe I will. And you'll see. You always do, and if I stay close to you…"

"Maybe." Ebb shrugged. He did not want to raise his hopes that Naia – or anyone else – might ever see the things he saw. "If the mermaids take him. If the others don't come."

"What do the others look like?"

Naia had asked him that before; Ebb gave her the same answer as always – silence. Although it pleased him to describe the beauty and grace of the mermaids, he would give her no idea what the others were like.

A loud *plunk* came from the darkness beyond the breakers. Ebb and Naia scanned the black surface of the sea. Mr. Tucker paced faster along the shifting waterline, his plodding feet scattering languid sprays of water, his eyes cast toward the dense expanse of night that hung over the shore. Out of sight, something heavy splashed, like a big fish jumping. Mr. Tucker froze in place. Naia squeezed Ebb's hand. Together they watched the shifting wave crests brighten and vanish in the moonlight.

"Are they coming?"

"I don't know," Ebb said.

They listened awhile, but heard no more unusual sounds. Mr. Tucker resumed pacing. Naia sighed and let go of Ebb's hand. She took an object from one of her pockets and handed it to him.

"I made this for you," she said. "To say thank you. I was saving it for later, but I want to see how it looks on you now."

Ebb uncoiled a loop of braided sea grass, which Naia had fashioned into a strand for him to wear around his neck. A small, perfect twinned nautilus shell dangled from it, fastened by a silver link. The working of the braid was fine and tight, and the silver link was shaped with a twist that made it resemble a pair of conjoined dewdrops, an echo of the double shell. It matched a bracelet around Naia's wrist, which had a silver dewdrop clasp, and Ebb thought it was the most beautiful piece she had ever made. He slipped the strand over his head and let the shell fall against his chest.

"Where did you get the nautilus?" Ebb said. "You know how hard it is to find a twin that's not broken?"

"Tell me about it," Naia said. "I've had that one since I was little."

"What? Oh, no, I can't accept it."

Ebb began to slip the necklace off, but Naia stopped him.

"I want you to have it," she said.

She pulled him to her and kissed him.

It was not their first kiss, but it was their most intense yet, and it caught Ebb unprepared. Until that moment, he would not have guessed he could feel any closer to Naia than he already did. She was his best friend since childhood; of all the friends he had ever known only Naia had never been frightened of him. He let the necklace drop to his skin and stroked Naia's hair. In that instant, it seemed to Ebb that all of existence was defined in the heat radiating from Naia's body, in the sweet smell of her skin and hair, in the softness of her lips, and the faint salt flavor of the air forever spiced by the sea. Then the crash of something loud hitting the water broke the spell. Ebb and Naia pulled apart and scanned the sea. Two more loud splashes came. Mr. Tucker knelt in the surf and cried out the summoning words.

"Here I am!" he called. "In the water life began, in the water life survives. I give myself back to the water! I give myself back! Let my life be renewed!"

Naia gasped at the anguish in Mr. Tucker's thick, uneven voice, and Ebb admired her for her compassion. Even though it was discouraging to watch people give themselves back to the water, Ebb had often done so in secret, and he found the words too familiar to move him.

In answer to Mr. Tucker's plea, a series of wild splashes came from the far side of the breakers.

"They're here," Ebb said.

"Where?" Naia said.

"Out there." Ebb pointed. "Swimming in."

"But it's getting so dark. Is a storm rolling in?"

Naia squinted at the churning surf dotted with flickers of shadow that refused to resolve into anything recognizable. There was no doubt, though, that Mr. Tucker saw something in the sea. That was clear enough from how he backed away from the water, his hands thrust out in front of him, his face drawn and colorless with terror.

"It's like darkness is leaking into my eyes," Naia said. "I can't even see the moon now."

"It's not them, anyway." Ebb was disappointed. "It's… the others."

"But where? I don't see them."

Naia crawled right up against Ebb and trained her eyes in the same direction as his.

"I can't even see Mr. Tucker, now. It's like… like I've gone blind." Naia rubbed her eyes and looked all around her. "No, wait. I can see you, Ebb, and the hill, and the trail behind us. It's only… only the beach that's… blacked out?"

"That's how it goes," Ebb said. "They won't let you see."

"But they let you," Naia whispered. "Why *not* me?"

The sounds of violent thrashing came from the water – followed by screams. Whatever had come for Mr. Tucker was driving him out of his mind with fear. Ebb was relieved that only Mr. Tucker had come tonight. The days when people gave themselves back to the water by the dozens, when the chorus of their voices rose in screams of terror and cries of joy, still echoed in his childhood memories. Mr. Tucker's long last cry faded away; soon after, the splashing died out.

Ebb relaxed.

"The darkness is gone now. The moonlight's coming back," Naia said. "Has Mr. Tucker gone back to the water?"

"Yes," Ebb said.

"I see him now," Naia said.

Caron Tucker's remains stood at the edge of the surf, his body comprised now only of sand that would be worn down and carried away by the waves, the wind, and the tide.

"I'm sorry you didn't see them," Ebb said. "Maybe… it's better you didn't. It was the others. When I saw it was Mr. Tucker, I thought they might come."

"Why?" Naia asked.

"Because Mr. Tucker was a monster," Ebb said. "Sometimes the others come for the monsters."

"Oh," Naia said.

The sound of Naia's disappointment scraped at Ebb's isolation, sweeping away the intimacy he had felt earlier. He stood and brushed himself free of sand. Being alone was nothing new; when it came to this, he had always been alone – and might always be. In all other ways he was lucky to have Naia. He smiled, extended his hand, and helped her to her feet.

"Do you want to go see his sand?" he asked.

Naia shook her head. "Everyone has seen what gets left behind. Let the tide take it."

"Then we should go before the sun comes up," Ebb said.

"Do we report Mr. Tucker?" Naia asked.

"Are you serious? We're not even supposed to be out here. You want people to know you're sneaking around in the middle of the night – *with me*? They'll think you've gone off the deep end too. Anyway, there's nothing to be done for Mr. Tucker. No one will miss him tonight. Let him be found in the morning like everyone else."

Ebb led the way to the woods that had once been part of a park at the heart of the city. Naia held his hand, uncomfortable in the dark.

It still amazed Ebb that she believed in him enough to have come this far, to the beach in the dead of night in search of sharing a truth it seemed only Ebb would ever see. Nothing he tried seemed capable of helping Naia – or anyone else – to see the things he saw. He wished he knew how to make it happen if only to reassure himself that what he saw was real. His life would be so much easier if someone else confirmed it, especially if it were Naia, but he would not wish on her all that he had suffered. Besides, after tonight, he was almost certain his gift of sight could never be shared.

A branch cracked in the woods. Ebb stopped and gestured Naia to stay quiet.

The brush ahead of them rustled.

Footsteps crunched fallen leaves and sand.

"Could it be someone else returning to the water?" Naia whispered.

"Maybe. I don't know," Ebb said.

From the sound of it, several people were approaching, but Ebb could not say how many because the footsteps came from multiple directions. He did not want to be discovered in the dark with no way to protect Naia. He pulled her around, thinking to run back to the beach, to head for the water, but then a hard, heavy weight struck the side of his neck. The pain shocked him, and the stone knocked him off balance. He lost hold of Naia's hand and fell. Naia screamed against a riot of crashing as people stormed through the brush, and then the first of many fists pummeled into Ebb's back. More followed, striking his sides, his head, driving him against the ground. A flurry of fists and feet sliced the shadows, each one jabbing or kicking Ebb, igniting flares of pain throughout his body. The beating was fast and brutal, and Ebb tasted blood in the back of his mouth. His ears rang after several punches to his head, and Naia's voice sounded muted and faraway, screaming for his attackers to *stop, to go away and leave him alone* – but they ignored her.

Ebb knew why.

A shrill, commanding voice urged them on.

The voice of Mayor Pearl.

Naia's mother.

One of the attackers kicked Ebb in the chest, his foot cracking apart the twinned nautilus shell.

Naia screamed again. Ebb glimpsed her trying to pull his attackers away, only to be yanked clear by her mother. Naia's cries rose and fell like the noise of waves crashing, receding, crashing....

Ebb grasped their rhythm and used it to blot out the pain.

Like diving underwater.

Cut off from sound and light.

Away from anyone else.

Enclosed.

Safe.

If only the sea was closer...

He could escape there.

No one could ever catch him in the water…

…but the water is so far away…

A fist connected with the back of his head, driving his face to the ground. Dirt and sand filled his mouth. He spit it out and waited for his punishment to be over. It lasted until he thought he could no longer bear it – and when it ended, he lay on the ground, gasping for air. He assessed his condition and sensed that, despite the jumble of throbbing pains throughout his body, nothing seemed broken, no major injuries sustained, although he felt as if all the wind had been knocked out of him. It was a brutal playground beating, and Ebb was familiar enough with those.

"Take him to the beach," Mayor Pearl said.

"No!" Naia said. "Why are you doing this? He didn't hurt anyone!"

Ebb rolled onto his side to see Naia, her mother, and the boys who had beaten him, three of Naia's four brothers: Trak, Donal, and Marts. Ebb was too weak, his thoughts too fractured to even attempt to filter his vision. As he looked at them, he saw how they appeared in the invisible world, and what he saw terrified him. They were all monsters – except Naia, whose beauty was so radiant she seemed translucent and brimming with moonlight. Ebb used her light to distract him from his fear. The sight of her was more than enough for that; and he had learned as a boy how to keep his terror from controlling him – a necessary skill for a child surrounded by monsters.

Ebb pushed himself up onto his hands and knees. Marts put his foot on Ebb's back and drove him back down.

"He's tainted, Naia," Mayor Pearl said. "He's rotten. He's foul. His mind is broken. His madness is a poison that will spread if I don't purge it now. It was one thing to dismiss the things Ebb says he sees when he was a child, but now – he's almost a grown man! The councilors and the people have been asking me to do something about him for years. Ebb frightens people, Naia. He upsets things. He makes people doubt they should return to the sea when their time comes and that puts all our survival at risk. For what? Delusions? Fairy tales of mermaids and monsters and an invisible world that only he can see? What he says he sees isn't real, but the danger it creates *is*. Did you think I didn't know you were out here running around with him? It makes me ashamed you can't see it for yourself, that you're out here in the night doing – I don't even know *what* you're doing."

"That's not how it is. What if …," Naia said.

"Stop it, Naia!" Mayor Pearl shouted.

"… what if it's true?" Naia said. "What if we simply can't see the world how Ebb does? His gift is real. He's a good person. Don't hurt him like this.

We should make people see …"

"Naia, enough." Mayor Pearl's voice softened. "I know you don't want this for Ebb. You were friends before his madness. I knew him then too, and he was a fine boy. Never knowing his mother, losing his father so young – he's had a hard life. We all wanted to protect him. We loved him. But… we can't anymore. Not when he clings to heresy. Not when he's misleading you and warping your thoughts. He'll ruin everything. It pains me that it's come to this. When you're older and you've gained some experience, you'll see – there's nothing else I can do!"

"But… what if he's right?" Naia said.

"Even if he is, I can't let him be." Mayor Pearl looked to her sons. "I said, *'Take him to the beach.'*"

Hands gripped Ebb. The movement stirred his pains, and he groaned. His feet dragged in the sand as Mayor Pearl's sons carried him along the path. Ebb avoided looking at their faces for too long; each was monstrous and vile, riddled with fear, hate, doubt, and cowardice, warped so far there was almost nothing human left. They looked like…

…but he didn't like to think about that.

The worst was Mayor Pearl; her face was like that of a broken porcelain doll with dead, expressionless eyes set amidst a multitude of fine, angry cracks. She was bitter, unchangeable, and swollen with fear. The world was not how she or the others who lived in the city thought it was. It was not the world they had known before the Flood Times. Yet they refused to see how much its very nature had been altered. Only Ebb saw the truth, with his gift that had come from the sea. It had come to him in darkness forty feet down on a stormy day when his father's fishing skiff capsized and plunged them overboard. He should have drowned that day like his father did, like Naia's, like so many other fathers – but he was too strong a swimmer, even as a child. He washed up on shore, spared, left orphaned, alone, and frightened. He knew the fear Mayor Pearl and the others felt because it was the same fear he had felt when he first realized his gift: fear of living in a world very different from what they understood or wished it to be.

That was not enough, though, for Ebb to forgive or pity them.

They were monsters even if their fear had made them so.

When they reached the beach, the boys dropped Ebb on the sand and then went to see Mr. Tucker's remains. Mayor Pearl joined them by the sand figure.

She lowered her head and spoke the traditional words: "May the waters bless our brother who has gone back to the sea. May his life be renewed and return to us."

Fat chance of that, Ebb thought. He had ideas about what happened to those who gave themselves back to the water, and it was not returning to the city. There were fewer babies born in the city every year, fewer people to tend it. Fewer people, period.

Nothing lasts forever.

The breaking dawn lightened the sea and the sky by the second.

Mayor Pearl walked to the water's edge, searching for something.

A few minutes passed before a motor sound grated against the gentle noise of the surf. It came from the west. A small powerboat appeared, cutting past the needles and bones of the few ruined buildings left standing tall enough to rise above the surface. Piloting it was the Mayor's oldest son, Redley. When the boat drew closer to shore and Ebb saw the anchor in the back, he knew what they intended for him. Naia realized it too, and she screamed.

Mayor Pearl grabbed her daughter's arm and yanked her up short. "Stop that! Don't you understand? The more he goes on about monsters, mermaids, and the others, the more frightened people become? Life's hard enough without worrying that something in the sea ... *will come for them* ... that if they give themselves back to the water something horrible might take them and they'll never be renewed. There's only the sea out there, and the sea is the source of all life. The sea returns to us the lives we give it. I can't let him take that away from us. We need the sea to survive, Naia, *all of us.* Even if it means Ebb won't."

"You're cruel!" Naia bolted from her mother. She ran to Ebb, knelt in the sand beside him, and raised the jagged remnants of the twinned nautilus shell on her fingers. "Let's give ourselves back to the water. Right now. Together. Let them take us, and we'll never be apart."

Ebb shook his head. He gasped to speak. "I'm the strongest swimmer... in the entire city. I'll last a long time. I'll... find a way to free myself."

"No," Naia said. "No. Say the words with me. Stay with me."

"They need you, Naia," Ebb said. "They need someone... who'll remember the truth."

"No, Ebb, no," Naia said.

"I'll always be with you." Ebb slipped the necklace off and hung it around Naia's neck. "You'll... never forget me."

Trak and Donal dragged Naia off and forced her to sit near her mother.

The powerboat cut through the shallows until it grated against the beach. Redley jumped out and dragged the boat onshore. The four brothers lifted Ebb and threw him onto the small craft. Then Mart clamped a shackle around one of Ebb's ankles; it was linked to a long chain fastened to the anchor. When they were done, Redley and Marts shoved the boat into the water until it floated. Then they jumped in and gunned the motor. The craft sped straight out from the shore, skipping over low waves, and leaving a wake painted pink by the rising sun.

The boat traveled farther and farther from shore, but Ebb felt no fear of the water.

He knew the sea here as if it was his home. He knew its currents and its secrets and what hid in the sand and seaweed below its surface. He knew the maze of fallen buildings and flooded streets, the forgotten wrecks of ships, cars, and buses overgrown with anemones and coral and teeming with schools of green and silver fish. No one could swim as far or hold his breath as long or pull as big a catch in his net as Ebb.

I'm the best swimmer who's ever lived in the city.

But it was not enough to buy him any more tolerance.

If he had kept the things he saw to himself, if he had ended his friendship with Naia before they fell in love...

...maybe then Mayor Pearl would have let him be.

There was more in her condemnation of him than fear that he would endanger the city's survival. That was plain in the fact that she was making Naia watch his execution.

The boat stopped more than a half a mile out, where the deep water began.

Redley cut the motor and let them drift.

Ebb stared at Naia's brothers, only a few years older than he was. When he looked at them without his sight, they looked young, handsome, and innocent. *Lies and masks.* If he had never seen behind them, they might have been friends. They might have swam, and sailed, and fished together. Instead, both had bullied and beaten up on Ebb all through school. For as long as he had known them, they had been monsters.

Redley and Marts said nothing as they lifted the anchor and tossed it over the side of the boat. It crashed the water with a wide splash and plunged out of sight.

Ebb scrambled to his feet. The chain trailed away beneath the surface, a silver shimmer drilling down into the dark. As the last of it rattled over the side, Ebb inhaled as deeply as he could, and then dove overboard before he could be yanked into the water. The coolness of the sea embraced him. It was murky and quiet beneath the surface. He readied himself to be pulled into the depths, but the chain went slack, and he found himself swimming toward the dim light of dawn above him. His face reached air. He gasped and struggled to rise, but the chain drew tight. The anchor was locked far below him. Treading water, he kept himself a few inches above the surface. Enough to breathe, enough to see the shore – where the accumulation of deadwood and debris that marked the high-tide line told him his reprieve would not last for long. Naia knelt in the surf, one hand stretched out to him, the other pressed to her mouth. Her mother stood beside her, and even at such a distance, Ebb perceived her ugliness.

Redley started the outboard and steered the boat to shore. When it arrived, the two boys dragged it onto the beach. Then they sat with the others in the sand by Mr. Tucker's effigy and waited.

An hour passed.

The rising sun warmed Ebb's face, and he felt the deepening twinges of muscle fatigue as he treaded water against the weight of the chain.

No one on shore had moved. Ebb knew Naia would not leave while he was in sight, but he wished her mother would take her away. He hated Mayor Pearl more for what she was doing to Naia than to him. He wanted to sink and be done with it to end Naia's suffering, but he found that as long as Mayor Pearl was there, he could not give up. Her presence invoked his defiance, and he took strength from that. He had lived most of his life in defiance; he would not surrender now. They had made him an outcast, beaten him, spurned him, and it had only ever hardened his resolve to give them the truth.

Only Naia had never feared him.

Never hated him.

Had... *believed in him.*

"Naia," Ebb said.

Water splashed over his lips.

The tide was rising.

He dove under and struggled to free himself from the chain, but it was impossible.

His air ran out, and he returned to the surface.

More time passed, and the waters crept over his face, washed into his mouth.

It was early afternoon when he looked upon Naia for the last time.

When Ebb went under, it was like the day he fell overboard and blacked out near the bottom. That day he had woken safe and sound on the shore...

Maybe...

For a time there was the quiet gloom of the sea.

Then all became darkness.

Naia let the waters rush over her.

She had not moved or cried. The tide had brought the waves to her chest but despair paralyzed her. The broken nautilus shell bobbed in front of her, tethered by dried sea grass that was coming unbraided as the water soaked it. After awhile – after Ebb did not resurface – the grass strand broke. The shell drifted away on the current. Naia watched it go.

Mayor Pearl kept her children on the beach until twilight. The receding tide took chunks of Mr. Tucker's remains with it until enough of his legs were gone that the rest of him fell over into the water and dispersed in the currents. Seeing him fall, Naia realized the beach was a burial ground, the sand the ashes of all those who had given themselves back to the water. Ebb would be denied even this.

At dusk, Mayor Pearl sent Redley and Marts to recover Ebb's body. They dredged around by lantern light with a pole and a gaffe, and Marts even dived in with a waterproof flashlight, but they returned with an empty boat.

"You're sure you looked in the right place?" Mayor Pearl said.

"One hundred percent," Redley said. "The weight of the chain sunk him to the bottom, that's all."

"Better that way," Mayor Pearl said. "It will be as if he never lived."

"You should have let him give himself back to the sea," Naia said.

"No. It's a travesty when someone so young goes back to the sea," Mayor Pearl said.

"*This* was a travesty, mother," Naia said. "This… was…"

Her words trailed off. Outrage drove her to rise from her place in the sand, which she had not left all day, and she slapped her mother.

Mayor Pearl recoiled.

Redley laughed.

Naia ran.

She crashed the surf, pushing in up to her waist, and then she screamed: "I'm here! Come for me! Take me! In the water life began, in the water life survives – I give myself back to the water! I give myself back! Let my life be renewed!"

Donal and Trak came splashing after Naia and dragged her back to the shore.

"What have you done?" Mayor Pearl shouted. "You have to get away from here, away from the water!"

"No," Naia said. "I'm going with Ebb."

She dug her feet into the wet sand and fought. Her brothers tried to grab her again. She dodged them, threw herself into the waves, and tried to swim but the water was too shallow. Her brothers surrounded her and pulled her out of the sea. Naia felt helpless – as if everything inside her was breaking to pieces and only Ebb could help her hold it together, but Ebb…

…Ebb was gone…

"Why?" Mayor Pearl said. "Why would you do that over a boy who lost his mind?"

"Because what Ebb saw was real." Her skin wet and slick, Naia slipped free from her brothers' hands then ran through the surf again, dodging them. "And I want to see for myself. I want to believe! I don't want to be a monster."

"Monsters…," Mayor Pearl said. "The only monsters are fools. Now, let's go before the water takes you!"

"I want to be with Ebb," Naia said.

"Naia, stop!"

Naia's brothers dashed around, trying to grab her. She evaded them, working her way farther from the beach. Out in the sea, something splashed and churned, but Naia was too distracted by avoiding her brothers to see what it was. It sounded as loud as a storm squall, but the sky was clear and the wind calm. Naia slipped to her hands and knees. Water splashed her face. She was soaked from head to toe, her shirt and shorts pasted to her body. She struggled to rise, but she was so tired and her body felt so heavy. Her brothers were only inches away from her, and then with shocking suddenness they became confused. Trak and Donal stumbled past her and were almost knocked down by waves. Redley and Marts stopped dead and gaped around them. Even Naia's mother seemed affected. The surf lapped at her legs as she inched along it, hands reaching, calling Naia's name as if …

… *she can't see me,* Naia thought.

The darkness had come to them, but for Naia the beach brightened and the water seemed electrified with fragments of starlight, the sea alive and vibrant with motion. Graceful forms sliced the dark surface. Dozens, swimming toward shore. Their faces rising and falling among the wave crests – the most beautiful faces Naia had ever seen.

"Ebb… I believe…," she said.

Her mother's voice came from the beach: "Naia? Where are you? Naia! Where did you go? Come back to me before it's too late!"

Naia ignored her. She could not look away from the water.

The mermaids were gathering. They were even more beautiful than Ebb had described them. More than she could count were coming together beyond the breakers, each stunning and luminous in the night, their perfect upper bodies riding powerful scaled fins that pushed them through the water. They watched Naia as if waiting for her to do something. Behind them, other shapes cut and jumped in the water. Dark shapes. Naia glimpsed gleaming black skin and scales, razor-edged fins, barbed claws, and shimmering eyes that reflected the stars – *the others*.

One of the mermaids – a woman with golden hair, green eyes, and pale, perfect skin – swam forward. "You have offered yourself to the water, but you don't really wish to return."

"I…," Naia said. "I miss Ebb."

"Who are you talking to?" Mayor Pearl said.

"She speaks to me, Pearl. I am Rogue," the mermaid said. "I am Ebb's mother, and you are the woman who tried to kill my son."

"No, no, that can't be. Ebb's mother died when he was born," Mayor Pearl said. "It's a trick. Who are you? Leave us alone!"

"You're so stubborn, Pearl," Rogue said. "You refuse to see so much, and worse you deny it to others."

"Is… Ebb *alive*?" Naia asked.

"Yes," Rogue told her.

"Don't believe her, Naia. She's a liar like Ebb was," Mayor Pearl said. "Ebb's dead. He has to be."

"You're an ungrateful fool," Rogue said. "This world belongs to the waters now, and we rule the waters. You owe your existence to me. Every time your city seemed sheltered from the worst of the storms, every bountiful catch your fishers brought home, every illness that seemed to be cured by the sea breeze – that all came from my people. All we took in return were the lives of those who gave them to us. Ebb's father was one of you. He could not free himself from my song – but he never feared me. I sent our son to live with him because I hoped he would help you understand. You refused to hear what he said. You showed him only fear and violence."

A figure swam past the mermaids and stood in the shallows: Ebb.

He walked onto the shore and handed Naia the broken nautilus necklace.

"I snatched it out of the current," he said.

Naia embraced him and pressed her face against his neck and shoulder. "Ebb, I'm sorry I said the words. I was so angry, and I …"

"Shh, it's okay," Ebb said.

"Is this what you've always been?" Naia asked. "One of them?"

"Part of me, yes. But I never knew it until now," Ebb said.

"Oh, Ebb. I thought you were dead."

"Hey, at least you finally got to see them, didn't you?"

Naia looked surprised. Then she smiled. Seeing the mermaids filled her with joy, but when she looked at her brothers and her mother, the core of her being twisted with horror.

They were monsters.

"Is this what you've always seen?" she asked Ebb.

"Yes."

"I'm so sorry."

"I'd rather see the world for what it is than be like them," Ebb said.

"Can you come back?"

"There's never any going back," Ebb said. "You can come with me, though. We can be together, but there's a price."

"What price?" Naia asked.

Ebb did not answer. He only waited while the dark figures lingering behind the mermaids moved past them and climbed onto the shore. The others were everything ugly in the sea. Shark eyes, and squid beaks, and the shells and tails of horseshoe crabs. Fins like those of a manta ray, fingertips like blowfish spines, and hard, jagged scales spotted with rot. They thrashed the water as they came and revealed themselves to Mayor Pearl and her sons. Their screams froze Naia's heart. She tried to think of her family as monsters, as the things she had seen, but she could not – at least not entirely. Only Ebb's grip on her arm kept her from running to help them.

"It has to be this way," Ebb said. "They'll go back to the water. They'll become like the others, but at least their lives will have been renewed."

Naia wanted to bury her face against Ebb's chest, but she could not stop watching.

Water flowed out of her mother and her brothers. It spiraled in streams through the air to join the sea, where a black whirlpool swallowed it. Where the others touched her brothers and her mother, dryness spread through their bodies, changing them to sand, spreading outward from each contact until soon only sand was left. Satisfied, the others slipped back into the sea. The mermaids lingered awhile longer and then went after them.

Rogue was the last to disappear beneath the surface, but Naia sensed her still nearby.

Naia studied the five statues of sand. They looked like her mother and brothers as she remembered them from before tonight – from before she shared Ebb's sight.

Ebb clasped Naia's hand and wound the fraying strands of the nautilus necklace around their fingers. "You wanted to see," he said.

"Yes," Naia said.

"Let me show you," Ebb said.

Naia followed him down the beach, through the waves, and into the water.

BIOGRAPHIES

DANIELLE ACKLEY-MCPHAIL - Award-winning author Danielle Ackley-McPhail has worked both sides of the publishing industry for over seventeen years. Her works include the urban fantasies, Yesterday's Dreams, Tomorrow's Memories, Today's Promise, and The Halfling's Court, and the writers guide, The Literary Handyman. She edits the Bad-Ass Faeries anthologies and Dragon's Lure, and has contributed to numerous other anthologies. She is a member of the New Jersey Authors Network and Broad Universe, a writer's organization focusing on promoting the works of women authors in the speculative genres. She can be found on LiveJournal (damcphail, lit_handyman), Facebook (Danielle Ackley-McPhail), and Twitter (DMcPhail). Learn more at www.sidhenadaire.com.

MICHAEL A. BLACK is the author of 17 books and over 100 short stories and articles. He has a BA in English from Northern Illinois University and a MFA in Fiction Writing from Columbia College Chicago. He was a police officer in the south suburbs of Chicago for over thirty years and worked in various capacities in police work including patrol supervisor, SWAT team leader, investigations, and tactical operations. His Ron Shade series, featuring the Chicago-based kickboxing private eye, has won several awards, as has his police procedural series featuring Frank Leal and Olivia Hart. He has also written two novels with television star Richard Belzer of Law & Order SUV. His hobbies include the martial arts, running, and weight lifting. His most current novel is Sacrificial Offerings.

JAMES CHAMBERS' tales of horror, crime, fantasy, and science fiction have been published in numerous anthologies and magazines. In 2011 Dark Regions Press published his collection of four Lovecraftian-inspired novellas, *The Engines of Sacrifice*. Publisher's Weekly described it as "chillingly evocative." Most recently, Dark Quest Books has published his zombie novellas, *The Dead Bear Witness* and *Tears of Blood*, the first two volumes in the Corpse Fauna novella series. Chambers is also the author of the short story collections *Resurrection House*, published in 2009 by Dark Regions Press, and The *Midnight Hour: Saint Lawn Hill and Other Tales* with illustrator Jason Whitley. His stories have appeared in the award-winning anthology series Bad-Ass Faeries and Defending the Future, and he has also written numerous comic books including *Leonard Nimoy's Primortals*, the critically acclaimed *"The Revenant"* in Shadow House, and *The Midnight Hour*. He is online at: www.jameschambersonline.com.

JOHN L. FRENCH – Having worked over thirty years for the Baltimore Police Department as a crime scene investigator John L. French has witnessed more than his share of what horrors one person can inflict on another. Working with patrol officers and detectives, John has been involved in putting many of these people behind bars for very long sentences. In 1992 John began writing crime fiction, basing his stories on his experiences on the streets of what some have called one of the most dangerous cities in the country. His books include The Devil of Harbor City, Past Sins, Here There Be Monsters and Paradise Denied. He is the editor of Bad Cop, No Donut which features tales of police behaving badly and To Hell in a Fast Car: On the Road to Death and Disaster

C. J. HENDERSON is the creator of at least a dozen different series, including supernatural investigator Piers Knight, the team of Blakely and Boles, PI Jack Hagee, and of course the wacky cast of *Challenge of the Unknown* (soon to appear in their own collection). He has written some seventy books hundreds of short stories, thousands of non-fiction pieces as well as the hilariously disturbing children's book Baby's First Mythos. After you read his story here, he invites you over to www.cjhenderson.com to comment on his work and to read some more.

NEAL LEVIN is a game designer, author, and publisher. His work in game design includes credits with: Ambient Games, Bastion Press, Dark Quest Games, EN Publishing, Mystic Eye Games and Top Fashion Games. He is a member of the Garden State Horror Writers, EPIC, HWA, and SFWA. As a publisher he is the Acquisitions Editor for Dark Quest Books, and former Editor-in-Chief for ADF Publications. As a short story author he has work in anthologies from many publishers, but most suggest he shouldn't hold his breath waiting on a response. Luckily as a Mer he doesn't have the problem.

C. ELLETT LOGAN spent the first half of her life in the Deep South, an experience that informs her settings and troubles her characters, Southern-Gothic-style. A member of Sisters in Crime and Mystery Writers of America, her short stories are published (or will be published) in the following anthologies: To Hell in a Fast Car, Chesapeake Crimes, and Mermaid 13.

Book one of her Quagmire Murders series, Miasma, is complete. Her website is www.celogan.com.

ROY MAURITSEN It was bound to happen, with pictures being worth what they are in words, that a successful creative artist would eventually entertain the idea of writing a novel. Roy's interests were somewhat atypical as a child. Aside from art and science, there were books and movies--science fiction and fantasy themed--and also role-playing games like Dungeons & Dragons, and a love of fairy tales that started at an early age with a dusty, 1941 hardcover edition of Alice's Adventures in Wonderland. Exploring every creative avenue available to him, Roy took every art class he could in school, and also any writing class, especially creative writing. Roy has received several awards in recognition of his artwork. But for this artist-turned-writer, the saying "a picture is worth a thousand words" wasn't enough this time. There was a story to be told, and it demanded to be written. That novel is Shards Of The Glass Slipper, published in March of 2012. This fairy tale epic fantasy adventure is also the inspiration for Shards, a concept album that Roy collaborated on and the fourth studio release by the band Gene Pool Zombie. Roy has also somehow managed to have a successful career as a digital artist and graphic designer, and also designing book covers and TV commercials. When he's not trying to figure out how that happened, he enjoys photography, volleyball, SCUBA diving, and traveling. But most of the time, he works on 3D artwork, writing short stories for upcoming anthologies, and working on the follow up to Shards of the Glass Slipper. Roy lives on Long Island, New York, with his wife, Caren, and their dog, a Newfoundland mix named Coda.

TERRI OSBORNE has far too many things on her plate, but she wouldn't have it any other way. Her literary life is spent wandering the annals of time, venturing as far back as the First Century CE with Doctor Who, and as far into the future as the 24th Century with Star Trek. At The Waterline continues her original Realms Next Door universe, where mermaids, ancient djinn, dark fae, vampires, werewolves, and little grey aliens live and work alongside humanity. She is a regular contributor to syfy.com, and is the owner of Loose Canon, an alternate history publishing venture.

DARREN W. PEARCE lives in the West Midlands, UK with his wife Gill, his three cats, Malcolm, Rosie and Midnight. Darren has a long-term dream to write a Doctor Who novel at some point in his life and has been devoted to that series since he saw the re-runs of Hartnell's era on the BBC. In 2008 with the help of Gill he put the first ever webcomic online for the Chronicles of Wyrden, a comic based in the setting that is intended for many of his novels and short stories. He is currently writing the Doctor Who rpg supplements.

KT PINTO – Awarded 2012's Best Author on Staten Island – KT Pinto writes about vampyres, mutants, witches, merfolk, werebeasts, deities, courtesans, criminals, and pop stars... sometimes all in the same story. For more information, go to http://www.ktpinto.com.

HILDY SILVERMAN is the publisher of Space and Time, a 45-year-old magazine featuring fantasy, horror, and science fiction. She is also the author of several works of short fiction, including "Damned Inspiration" (2009, Bad-Ass Fairies, Ackley-McPhail, ed.), "The Vampire Escalator of the Passaic Promenade" (2010, New Blood, Thomas, ed.), "The Darren" (2009, Witch Way to the Mall? Friesner, ed.), and "Sappy Meals" (2010, Fangs for the Mammaries, Friesner, ed.). She also contributed an essay on the history of genre magazines to Sense of Wonder: A Century of Science Fiction (2011, Leigh Grossman, et al, ed). Hildy is the co-president of the Garden State Speculative Fiction Writers and in the "real" world, she is a Senior Writer at LexisNexis.

PATRICK THOMAS – With over a million words in print, PATRICK THOMAS keeps busy writing the popular fantasy humor series Murphy's Lore as well as its After Hours spin-offs. His Mystic Investigators series has grown to include the Bullets & Brimstone and From the Shadows both with John L. French and Once More Upon a Time and the upcoming Partners In Crime both with Diane Raetz. Patrick's syndicated humorous advice column "Dear Cthulhu" has been collected in Have a Dark Day and Good Advice For Bad People. Laurence Fishburne's production company Cinema Gypsy Productions has taken a film and television option on Patrick Thomas' urban fantasy Fairy with a Gun. His website is www.patthomas.net.

ROBERT E. WATERS – Since 1994, Robert E Waters has worked in the computer and board gaming industry as technical writer, editor, designer, and producer. A member of the Science Fiction and Fantasy Writers of America, his first professional fiction sale came in 2003 with the story "The Assassin's Retirement Party," Weird Tales, Issue #332. Since then he has sold stories to Nth Degree, Nth Zine, Padwolf Publishing, Mundania Press, Marietta Publishing, and Dark Quest Books. His most recent stories were published in the Grantville Gazette, Baen Books' online magazine dedicated to stories set in their best-selling 1632/Ring of Fire Alternate History series. Between the years of 1998 – 2006, he also served as an assistant editor to Weird Tales. Robert currently lives in Baltimore, Maryland, with his wife Beth, their son Jason, and their cat Buzz. Robert's website is www.roberternestwaters.com.

APOCALYPSE 13
CREATURES OF LEGEND...
YOUR TIME IS UP!
DEFCON 1
...WARNING...
TACTICAL
MISSILE LAUNCH
INSTRUCTION MANUAL
FEATURING 13 DOOMSDAY STORIES BY:
JOHN FRENCH, ROY MAURITSEN, DIANE RAETZ, PATRICK THOMAS
ROBERT WATERS AND MANY MORE!
Upcoming release from
PADWOLF
PUBLISHING
visit padwolf.com

IT'S A CRIME TO MISS THESE GREAT STORIES!

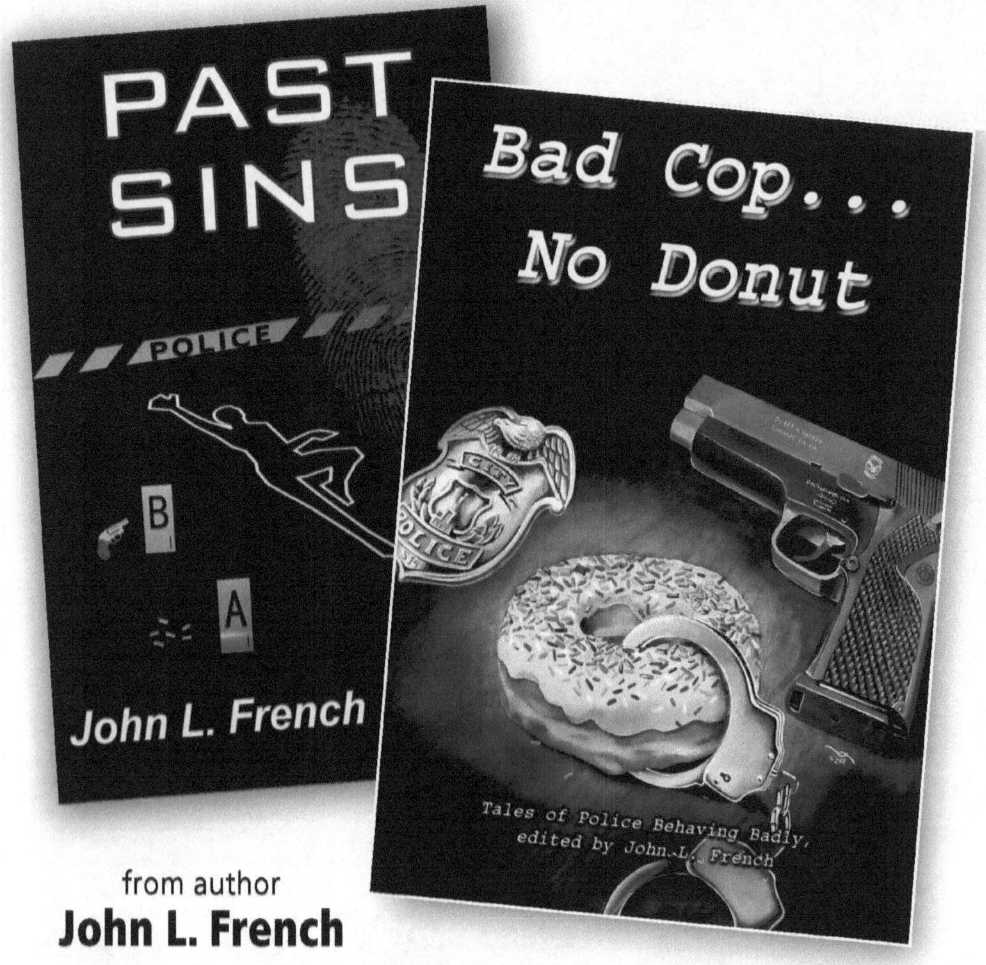

from author
John L. French

TRY SOMETHING *NEW!*

(Don't worry, she won't bite...much)

PADWOLF

PUBLISHING

v i s i t   p a d w o l f . c o m

www.ingramcontent.com/pod-product-compliance
Lightning Source LLC
Chambersburg PA
CBHW031235210726
48287CB00003B/784